Eye on you – The Whipping Post

By Joe Hamilton

A Gabriel Ross Mystery – Book 8

A Primer

This is the 8th book in the *Eye on You* mystery series. For newbies, The Eye on You Detective Agency was formed in 1979 by Gabriel Ross and his silent partner Ben O'Shea, a Biloxi Police Detective. Jacqueline Cooper was the agency's first significant client (*Eye on You – Right Place, Wrong Time*), and as luck would have it, she became Jacqueline Ross at the end of the first book.

Over the years, the agency has grown in business, reputation, and employees. The initial office was relocated to a bigger space in Gulfport, and Rachel Henderson was hired as a receptionist/associate. Arnie Sims joined as a part-time associate.

Book One   *Eye on You - Right Place Wrong Time*
            (formerly titled *Murder in Biloxi*)

Book Two   *Eye on You - Rock Me like a Hurricane*

Book Three   *Eye on You – Mississippi Queen*

Book Four   *Eye on You – Gimme 3 Steps*

Book Five   *Eye on You – House of the Rising Son*

Book Six   *Eye on You – Born on the Bayou*

Book Seven   *Eye on You – Knights in White Satin*

Book Eight   *Eye on You – The Whipping Post*

This story is a work of fiction. Any resemblance to actual people is a pile of hooey. I hope you enjoy the story. If you do, let me know. Some readers might think this book's title is based on the Allman Brothers' song "Whipping Post." While I love the song, they'd be wrong. The title is The Whipping Post, with a "The."

ISBN   978-0-9939999-8-7

Table of Contents

Cast of Characters

Rachel Henderson	Manager/Receptionist/Secretary/Associate for the Eye on You Detective Agency
Don Kittyburg	AKA Don Kooper; Rachel's off again-on-again boyfriend
Gabriel Ross	Half-owner along with Ben O'Shea, of the Agency
Jacqueline Ross	Gabriel's wife
Benjamin Ross	Gabriel and Jacqueline's two-year-old son
Mayor John Baxter	Former Biloxi Mayor, now a permanent resident at the Mississippi State Penitentiary
Deputy Weber	Harrison County Deputy Sheriff
Travis Franklin	A teenager Gabriel befriended in the first book
John Dietz	Former President of the Biloxi Chamber of Commerce
Glenna Sparrow	The client
Larry Sechfinger	Baxter's lawyer
Madge Baxter	Baxter's wife
Wolf	AKA Earl Gruber, a very fine person

Wendy	Bartender
Penn Maddox	An interesting person
Bradley Nash	Penn's boyfriend
Nia Tines	High school friend of Penn's
Reche Tines	Nia's older brother
Jethro Coyle	A friend of Don's
Penelope Maddox	Penn's grandmother
Travis Franklin	16-year-old friend of Gabriel's
Connie Franklin	Travis' mother
Adele	Dietz's personal executive assistant
Sheriff Harker	Sheriff in Mobile County AL
Sheriff Giddins	Sheriff in Hinds County, MS
Robert Harrigan	Warden at Talladega Federal Penitentiary
Carl Sears	Works at Glenna's *Amoco* station
Wolf	Leader of the Aryan Brotherhood
Klink	Treasurer of the AB
Schultz	Tattooist for the AB
Burkholder	Member of the AB
Hochstetter	Member of the AB
Robby Bintwater	AKA Charlie Manson – cellmate
Samantha Fitzgerald	Lawyer for Low, Ball and Lynch

Prologue

March 2nd, 1985
Gulfport, Mississippi

Gabriel

A phone call early Saturday morning usually means bad news. Judging by the darkness, it was early. Too early. I looked over at the alarm clock and saw that it was only 5:15. I swallowed my anxiety and grabbed the phone to silence the rings.

"Meet me at the medical examiner's office in fifteen minutes. You have to see this," said the voice.

"Whoever this is … can you call back in a couple of …" A crack of thunder interrupted me mid-sentence. I heard a gust of wind blowing against the house, followed by what sounded like a firehose hitting the window. A perfect morning to stay hunkered under blankets.

"It's Weber. I'm ordering you to get your skinny white ass up and come with me to see Abrams at the ME's office."

I looked over at my wife, Jacqueline, who was making little groaning noises. Our two-year-old son Benjamin must have had a nightmare and was snuggled in beside her. "I don't work for you, Deputy Weber," I whispered, trying not to wake my sleeping angels.

"It's important, Gabriel."

"What's going on? It's barely five o'clock. Abrams won't be there this early."

"The storm killed the power," shouted Weber over another crack of thunder. "Check your watch. It's almost 7. He'll meet us there."

"And what am I going to see?"

"Gabriel, it's someone…well, you'll want to see this."

***

I'd first met "Ole Creepy," better known as Chester Abrams, about a year ago. The man was tall and slim with a prominent hooked nose. He had a balding crown of gray hair and a matching scraggly beard. At that time, a deputy sheriff had discovered a body in a steamer trunk floating in the bayou. I'd arrived just as Abrams was examining the scene. I'd recognized the body right away - an older woman named Edna LeGrand. She'd been folded up like a baby stroller and stuffed into the trunk. The smell was overpowering, and the flies had been everywhere, including in Abrams' beard. I'd quickly thrown up my lunch, causing Ole Creepy to snicker.

Abrams had held the medical examiner position for as long as I've lived in Biloxi. I was told you didn't need medical training for the job because it was an elected position, like dog catcher. To that end, he had everything he needed – a recognizable name. Chester's uncle, Wallace Abrams, had served as the Congressman for the 4th District for over twenty years. Also, because Mississippi sorted candidates alphabetically on the ballot, Abrams was always the first name voters would see. At least until someone named Aardvark decided to run.

The ME's building was located on the pawnshop side of town. The building itself was ancient and had a leaky roof. The constant drip of rain into metal buckets punctuated the silence. Fluorescent lights hummed and lit up the room, giving it an eerie glow. Weber and I stood on either side of the metal gurney. The room was cold, and I was soaked to the bone. A smell of disinfectant tinged with just a hint of rotting corpse lay in the air. The body, according to Weber, was what I needed to see. Abrams stood by the head of the gurney holding a clipboard, taking his sweet time - apparently doing some last-minute calculations. It took an enormous effort to resist ripping the sheet off the corpse. I looked over at Weber. He gave me a shrug and a stupid grin. Finally, I couldn't take it anymore. "Is someone going to tell me what's going on?"

"A couple of kids out fishing near Bayou Bernard found this yesterday," explained Weber. "The body was caught up in the roots of a cypress tree."

"From what I can tell," added Abrams, "It's been in the water for some time."

"How long would you say?" Weber asked.

"Tough to say. I'd guess anywhere from a week to maybe two, on the outside maybe three."

The guy had no clue.

"A body's decomposition in the bayou," continued Abrams, "is impacted by the temperature of the water, the current, the physical environment, among other things." Abrams looked at me. "Weren't you there when we recovered the steamer trunk with the body of the old lady?" I nodded, and he started chuckling to himself. "You might remember me saying the trunk acted like a coffin and kept the body relatively intact. Different thing here."

Abrams pulled the sheet back, causing my heart to skip a beat. The black man was naked and looked to be around six feet tall with a slight build. His face was all puffed out like someone had gone crazy with Botox. "There's significant post-modem animal predation."

"What does that mean?" I asked, relieved to take my eyes away from the body.

"Fish, snakes, turtles." I'd always thought turtles were good guys. "Judging by the missing left foot, I'd say gator."

"Can you confirm the man drowned?" I asked, trying hard not to throw up.

"He had bayou water in his lungs. So, with one small proviso, I'm going to label this as death by misadventure."

"You're going to say it was accidental?"

"He went swimming, and the current got him. A diagnosis of drowning is based more on the circumstances of death rather than on any tests. The rule I've always gone by is if a body is found in the water with no bullet holes in him, then he drowned."

The man was a genius and should run for dogcatcher. Surely people don't go skinny dipping in the middle of February. "You said you had one proviso?"

Abrams gestured to Weber, and the two of them lifted the corpse onto his front. Several raised welts were visible across his back. "Judging from these marks, I'd say this man was recently whipped."

Part 1

Chapter 1

February 25th, 1985
United States District Court
Hattiesburg, Mississippi

Mayor Baxter

"The accused will stand for the jury's verdict."

As I stood, the foreman spoke – "not guilty on all counts." Pandemonium broke out in the courtroom. I gave a whoop of joy from the defendant's table. Everyone turned to look at me. Judge Ramirez banged his gavel three times.

"Order, order in the court. Perhaps the defendant misheard. The jury has found you guilty on all counts."

"Ah, fuck!" I said as the judge's words landed. *How could this be? There must be some mistake.* There was a buzz of whispers as the spectators reacted. I looked at the judge - his lips were flapping, making sounds but not words. He was talking to the jury. He then turned and looked down at me, giving me a stern look. "Mr. Baxter, the jury has found you guilty of embezzlement, bribery, extortion, racketeering, money laundering." He stopped and took a deep breath before continuing, "fraud, tax evasion and breach of trust. These are very serious crimes, for which the sentence is," he paused again as he added up the years in his head, "twenty years. I will have you back in my courtroom in a couple of weeks for sentencing. In the meantime, I order you to be held at a Federal Correctional Institute pending sentencing."

"Ah, that's too bad. Well, you win some, you lose some," my Jewish lawyer said in his sing-song voice. He opened his attaché case and started gathering his papers.

I was dumbfounded. This wasn't supposed to happen. "Is that all you can say? After all the money I paid you, Sexfinger?"

"Once again, it's pronounced just as it's written - Sechfinger. Of course, we'll appeal. No one is more shocked about this than me. The judge made some serious errors."

"You're fired!"

"Suit yourself," Sechfinger said, walking out quickly.

I took a look around before my eyes came to rest on the judge. He appeared to be eating a burrito. He looked back at me and shrugged his shoulders as if to say you should have taken the deal. I'd been offered a much-reduced sentence if I agreed to testify against Frank Reznikov. Frank, the murdering, scheming creep who had his dirty fingers in almost all illegal businesses on the Gulf coast. Frank was currently awaiting trial in Louisiana himself for murder and racketeering. His chances of being acquitted were improving daily since his hired killer and potential witness for the prosecution had mysteriously stabbed himself to death in the showers at Angola State Pen. Of course, I'd considered the offer. I'd have been a fool to dismiss it. On the first day of the trial, a massive car bomb had exploded outside the courthouse shattering the windows. I'd gotten the message.

***

I was hustled out of the courtroom to the prison bus. A swarm of reporters stuck their microphones in my face, asking for a comment. "It's a sham. I'm the victim here. Biggly. A bunch of left-wing types and their friends in the fake news media are trying to discredit the good work of my administration. Their accusations are a pack of lies. This is a dark day for democracy. Just look at the development happening along the Gulf Coast. I'm the only one who could have done that."

"How do you think you'll adjust to life in prison?" asked a man I recognized from the *Herald*.

"I won't be there long enough to enjoy their hospitality. On that note, I, John Baxter, will be going on a hunger strike to protest the inhumanity of this verdict."

***

Once on the bus, I was joined by fourteen other orange jumpsuit-wearing convicts for a five-hour bus ride to Talladega, Alabama.

"Why are they sending us so far?" I asked the Charles Manson lookalike sitting in front of me.

"To fuck with you," he said, turning around. All he needed was a swastika carved into his forehead. "It's federal. They can send you wherever they want."

"Waste of time. I'll no sooner get there, and they'll have to release me." There was a time I'd mused about being able to walk down Beach Blvd and shoot someone, and my ratings wouldn't drop. Manson turned away and looked out the window. "Seriously, I'm not…you know a …" I said, unsure of what to call myself.

"A convict?" said a heavy-set balding man sitting across the aisle from me. He looked like Al Capone. All of a sudden, Capone stood up and, with his arms outstretched, asked, "Who here is a con-vict?"

There was a chorus of hoots and hollers of "not me," along with a lot of hysterical laughing. Finally, the bus driver told everyone to pipe down.

"I'm the Mayor of Biloxi. I'm being railroaded," I protested.

The bus erupted in laughter again before Capone said, "Well, well, let's all salute the Mayor of Buh-luhk-see."

I let the laughter die down and occupied myself by looking out the window. I could see my reflection. I'd aged ten years in the past year. My skin no longer had a rich golden glow from hours in the tanning booth. My hair, long a symbol of youth and vitality, was cut as short as the fuzz on a tennis ball. After about five minutes, I leaned forward to speak to Manson. "What did you do?"

"Sold some pot. Got me thirty years."

"Thirty years? What's that with probation?"

"Ain't no probation. This here is Federal."

"Seems stiff."

Capone then leaned over and touched my shoulder, speaking loudly. "Not as stiff as my dick's gonna be when I'm taking a shower with the Mayor of Buh-luhk-see!"

The bus erupted in laughter.

Chapter 2

Gabriel

As my business partner, Ben O'Shea liked to say – she was a couple of miles away from Prettyville. She, being the forty-something woman with frizzy dark hair, sprinkled with white streaks, perched in my office. She was skinny as a rail and continually fidgeting, reminding me of a bird. Or was that because her name was Sparrow? Glenna Sparrow. Based on the wrinkles around her hairy lip, I took her for a smoker so, I offered her a Benson and Hedges from a pack I keep in my desk. I don't smoke myself, but sometimes it puts people at ease. She took one, saying she'd been trying to quit. When I gave her a light, her hands shook like a virgin on her wedding night. Maybe she was just nervous meeting the famous Private Detective Gabriel Ross.

"You know these things stunt your growth. Is that what happened to you?"

I laughed and shook my head. I love little person jokes. At just over five feet tall, I've heard them all. She sat back and looked at me through a cloud of smoke. I guessed that her navy-blue and white striped pantsuit was expensive.

She wore a wide brim red straw hat, which matched her blood-red lipstick. "Can I get you a coffee, Mrs. Sparrow?"

"No, I'm fine. You may call me Glenna."

"Alright, Glenna, what brings you in?" I pulled out a note-pad from my desk. Now that the Agency was computerized, Rachel, my associate, was on my case to improve my handwriting.

"A deputy sheriff named Weber suggested I meet with you to discuss my husband. You're aware of my husband, Dirk Sparrow?" Her tone suggested only an idiot wouldn't be.

The name sounded vaguely familiar. "I've been away for a few months. I might have missed something." I made a note to call Weber.

"He disappeared five weeks ago. It's been in the *Herald*. The police are telling me that there's nothing more they can do."

"That's a long time to be missing. This must be very upsetting for your family."

"I've been telling them Daddy's on a business trip, but I can't keep that up. They're starting to ask questions."

"Does Deputy Weber have any theories about what might have happened?"

"Between you and me, I've seen tree stumps in the bayou with a higher IQ. He told me a story about a rutting bloodhound he used to have that would take off for weeks only to return later on his own."

Typical Weber. "This must be very difficult for you." Once again, I waited for a reaction. There wasn't one. "Tell me about your husband."

"He just turned fifty. He's starting to get those love handles that men get. I'm trying to get him to exercise more." Then as if she'd run out of things to say, she added, "He runs an Amoco station."

He's been missing five weeks, and the first thing she can think of is his love handles? "Is he under any emotional stress?" When interviewing prospective clients, it's always important to be tactful, so I twirled my finger by my temple.

"Are you asking if he's nuts?"

"Suicidal?"

"No. He runs a successful business." The ash on her cigarette was over an inch long. I edged the ashtray closer.

"What can you tell me about the day he disappeared?"

"January 14th - five weeks ago today. He went off to work and never came home."

"When did you notify the police?"

"The following morning, when I noticed his bed hadn't been slept in."

"You sleep in separate beds?"

"He claims I snore. His preference."

"How's your marriage?"

"It's fine, perfect," she said, a little too quickly.

I waited a couple of moments to see if she would elaborate, but she sat there smoking her cigarette. I felt like asking her if she knew how to blow a smoke ring. I've been married twice, and in my limited experience, there was no such thing as a perfect marriage. My first marriage had ended when I'd discovered my wife had a thing going with the mechanic that repaired our Ford Pinto. If you know anything about cars, you know they saw a lot of each other. "Are his suitcases missing? What about his passport?"

"His suitcase is in the closet. I never thought to look for his passport."

"Ever since 1972, you need a passport to travel to another country. What about other family he might have gone to visit?"

"He has a brother somewhere in Colorado, but they haven't spoken in years. Other than that, it's just the kids and me."

"Friends?" I moved the ashtray closer again. The ash was now over an inch and a half and starting to curl. She ignored me.

"Some. The Rotary Club. I've checked with everyone in our Rolodex, and no one has any idea where he is."

"Just to confirm, you want us to find out what happened to your husband?"

"Can you do that?"

I ducked the question. "What do you think might have happened to him?"

She shrugged her shoulders as if I'd asked her if she liked broccoli. She handed me a check for $1000 already made out to the *Eye on You Detective Agency*. "For your retainer."

Our creditors need to be paid, and finding missing persons is what we do. There was no logical reason to turn down the case, yet a little voice at the back of my mind, the one that warns me about falling pianos and other bad things, was squawking like a cockatoo. The check was drawn on her single account at the *People's Bank* in Biloxi.

"Is this your first marriage?" I asked, relieved when she finally used the ashtray.

"Of course. In July, it'll be our twentieth anniversary. We were going to go to Hawaii."

I picked up the past tense. Was she suggesting that dead men wouldn't want to go to Hawaii, or had she lost hope of finding him? If so, why give me a grand? "Hawaii? Nice." I watched her closely but saw no emotion. I revised my opinion. Rather than bird-like, Glenna Sparrow was a cold fish. "So, you're wealthy? Could this have been a kidnapping?"

"Weber asked the same thing. It's been five weeks. Wouldn't there have been a ransom demand by now?" Her tone suggested that she was talking to a five-year-old. "But in answer to your question, my mother has money."

"Alright, Glenna," I said, putting the check in my drawer. "Did Dirk have an account at the People's bank?"

"I'm not sure."

She'd been married for almost twenty years and didn't know where her husband did his banking? I've been married six years, and my wife, Jacqueline, knows precisely how many coins I have in my pocket. "Can you think of anyone who might want to hurt your husband?" She looked at me and cocked her head. "Did he have a temper? Did he recently have an argument with someone?"

She paused for a moment as if to say something, then looked at her watch. "Nothing comes to mind."

"Do you have a recent photo of your husband?"

"No."

Of course not - I could have predicted that one. I made a note to ask Weber if he thought the wife was a psycho. "I'd like to stop by the house and get one, maybe look around, talk to neighbors, that type of thing. Will you be home all day?"

"I'm having my nails done at 10 AM. I should be home after." I didn't want to interfere with her busy schedule and said I'd be there around noon.

"I asked you if you could find him?" she repeated.

"I'm confident we can find out what happened to him. It might take a while. After five weeks, Mrs. Sparrow, you need to prepare yourself in case there's bad news." I don't know why I said that. Maybe it was because I didn't like Glenna Sparrow. "Are you sure there isn't anything else, Mrs. Sparrow? Sometimes the smallest detail may on the surface seem unimportant but can make a difference." We locked eyes for what seemed like a long time. She was good at staring, but I was better.

"There's one thing. I don't know what it means." She snuffed out the cigarette in the ashtray. "It's probably nothing. If I tell you about it, I'll need another cigarette."

Chapter 3

Mayor Baxter

I tried to swallow my anger, but the more I thought about that judge, the more my rage grew. He'd been laughing at me. Sitting up there all judgy with that smug look on his Mexican face. I didn't belong in prison. I was the Mayor of Biloxi.

It was the Jew's fault. I'd wanted to use Reznikov's lawyer but was blocked by the prosecutor, who argued it would be a conflict of interest. Thinking back now, Sexfinger had lobbied hard for me to take my chances with the jury. I can still remember his words, 'Don't be a mashugana. All you need is just one man. Just one man with a seed, a tiny seed of doubt, and this will be behind you.' He'd shrugged his shoulders and said, "Or take the deal, and you'll be dead before lunch."

I wondered what kind of reaction my conviction was getting in Biloxi. I had many influential friends who were likely outraged. I imagined mass protests, rioting, and an angry mob storming city hall on my behalf.

Al Capone was snoring - a deep snore followed by a whistling noise. I couldn't understand how the man could sleep. He was about to lose his soul. Taking his liberty wasn't enough. Sexfinger said most of what I owned would likely be seized to pay for court costs. This made me think about Madge. She hadn't even attended the trial. When the judge pronounced the verdict, I saw other women in the gallery weeping for me. Being mayor of the fastest-growing city in America came with its pressures. When you're an important man, women are always throwing themselves at you. They'd let you do just about anything. I guess they can't help themselves. It wasn't as if Madge hadn't strayed. She was carrying on something with her bank manager until he mysteriously hung himself in a closet.

I was about to drift off to sleep when I looked over at Al Capone, who was sleeping with his head facing towards me. The man was a pig and a blowhard. The comment about the showers had been disturbing. As if reading my mind, Capone's right eye flashed open, and he winked. "I like how that orange jumpsuit matches your hair."

Chapter 4

February 25th, 1985
Gulfport, Mississippi

Gabriel

"About a week before Dirk disappeared," continued Glenna, "I'd returned from visiting Mother. She's not well and lives alone in Meridian. I had told Dirk to stay home and look after the business and the kids. The night I got back, we were reading when he told me about something that happened earlier in the week. A bunch of guys from the garage had gone to a bar to celebrate someone's engagement."

She stopped the story for a moment to take a drag from her cigarette. "There was some kind of disturbance at one of the other tables. A woman was arguing with a man. When it started to get physical, Dirk jumped in to break it up. In the process of scaring the other guy off, the woman's drink spilled, and Dirk, of course, offered to buy the woman another. She told him that the man had been obsessed with her and that she was frightened, so Dirk invited her to join his group. No one was hurt, and he drove the woman home."

"Drove her home?" I repeated.

"That's what he said. He didn't elaborate. He told me that he'd put the incident out of his mind until this woman called our house later in the week and spoke to our seven-year-old son Jeremy. When Dirk came in from the yard and found our son on the phone, he spoke to her."

At this point, Glenna Sparrow paused the story and let out a sigh. "According to my husband, she called to invite him over for a drink to say thank you for coming to her aid. After declining her offer, Dirk told the woman that his wife was away and he was looking after the kids. She said something about next time before he hung up."

I waited a few moments for the climax. Finally, I asked, "Anything else?" She shook her head, and I recapped. "So, your husband told you about an encounter and a subsequent thank you call. Do you think there's something more to this?"

"I thought this man from the bar might be worth a look. Maybe he wanted to get even with Dirk."

"Did you tell Deputy Weber about this?"

"Deputy Weber thinks all men are like his dog, remember?"

Chapter 5

Gabriel

Rachel arrived at the Agency and looked bewildered when she walked into my office. "Weren't you supposed to have a meeting with Mrs. Sparrow?"

"The Sparrow has flown."

Rachel plopped herself down in a chair. "How did it go?"

I handed her the check. "Her husband's missing."

"I knew that. It's been in the papers."

"A little heads-up next time."

"I was curious about your take and didn't want to spoil it."

Maybe because I had just spent time with an ugly woman, but Rachel was looking exceptionally beautiful. She had her lustrous dark hair up in a bun and wore a form-fitting dress that showed off her traffic-stopping figure. "Well, spill it, Mr. Detective. Why did she insist on such an early appointment?"

"Early bird gets the worm."

"I get it. Because her last name is Sparrow, you're going to trot out every bird saying you know."

"No, she's a little too fish-like for a sparrow," I said, looking down at my notepad, where I'd drawn a picture of a fish.

Rachel looked at her watch. "You spent a whole thirty minutes with her, and that's it? A picture of a fish?" Rachel's business card said Private Investigator-Associate-Receptionist and Office Manager. It didn't say, former love interest. But that's another story.

"She's cold. Don't most married couples have joint accounts?"

"That's what's bothering you? She doesn't have a joint account?" Rachel looked at the check. "I can tell you that if my relationship with Kittyburg ever gets off the ground, I'd never in a million years have a joint account with him." Rachel had an on-again,-off-again relationship with an agent from the Mississippi Bureau of Investigation who played fast and loose with the truth.

"It's not just that. She's too composed for someone whose husband is missing. You remember how Jacqueline reacted last spring when I went missing for three days. She was ready to demand the Governor call out the National Guard."

"You have to admit that your wife might be a little… emotional."

I conceded that my half Chinese, half French-Canadian wife could be a handful. When Jacqueline and I had argued about her no longer wanting to be buried alive or having her husband kidnapped, she and I had escaped on an extended vacation. It had been an opportunity to work on our marriage. We're still working on it. To Jacqueline's credit, she hadn't threatened to run me over when I'd said I was going to work that morning.

"Mrs. Sparrow might just be aloof."

"She's crazy as a loon. But no point jumping to a conclusion. She said Deputy Weber recommended us."

"That's nice. He's in my good books after he saved my life." With Weber's help, Rachel and Don Kittyburg had been able to lessen the loss of life in foiling a recent domestic terrorist plot.

"I'm going to call Weber and get his take. On another matter, have you made up your mind about the office?"

Rachel had stepped in and taken over the business during my absence. "I have. These past few months have taught me a great deal about myself. I've decided that I'm just not ready to run the Agency. Don't get me wrong. I love working here, but I'd like to go back to being just an investigator... associate... and receptionist."

"Maybe you should keep the business card for now and think it over. You've been through a lot lately. People threatening you, boyfriends you can't trust, a millionaire psychopath who won't take a paternity test, I could go on.

You've done an awesome job. But you don't have to take it from me. I got a call from Mrs. Hopkins talking about how wonderful you've been finding her son's real birth mother. Then, Smith, the lawyer, said you single-handedly won his paternity case."

Rachel smiled at the compliment and said she'd think about it.

***

It took a few tries, but I finally connected with Weber. "It's Gabriel. Thanks for sending Mrs. Sparrow over."

"Don't mention it. You guys do good work. Rachel, she runs things there, right? She was something on that domestic terrorism case. I know it's hard to believe, but she even taught me a few things."

"Can we talk about Dirk Sparrow?" I asked, cutting him off.

"I have a stack of unsolveds on my desk, and they're not all small potatoes either. Ever since Hiller Park, we get a bomb threat every day. I don't have time to waste chasing missing husbands."

"So is your gut telling you Dirk left on his own?"

"I had this bloodhound once…"

I cut him off again. "She told me your dog story."

"You've met the woman. She'd be enough to make any man head for the hills. My guess is he's shacked up with some babe. Maybe some island in the Caribbean. Probably Aruba, it has the nicest beaches. Beautiful palm trees, crystal clear water, gentle breezes…I was thinking of taking a little holiday once things slow down."

"Why would he leave his business, leave his home, leave his kids?"

"Well, in fairness, you just caught the case. Let me save you a bit of time. The Amoco station is in her name. The house, likewise. Good point about the kids, though. Assuming they're even his."

"What does that mean? Did you find out she was cheating on him?

"The kids don't look a thing like him. But all that is for you to find out. I interviewed the mechanics he supposedly manages, and they knew bupkiss. I talked to his neighbors, and they saw bupkiss. I spoke to a couple of people from the Rotary Club, and they heard bupkiss. I even went so far as to go to his bank. He hasn't used his account or his credit cards since he disappeared."

"Anything else?"

"If you want my advice, the lady is stinking rich. If you poke around for a month or two, you'll score a good payday.

By that time, he'll be tired of screwing his floozy, and he'll be back on his own."

***

Rachel flopped in the chair in my office again. "Well, how did that go?"

I shared Weber's dog theory and that Dirk Sparrow was lying on a beach somewhere with a floozy. That brought about an eye roll. "Weber was very complimentary about you."

"I said he was in my good books. I still think if brains were dynamite, he couldn't blow his nose."

"Listen, I meant to ask you about Kittyburg. Are you two together?"

"It's complicated. He's up in Jackson and wants me to move up there. I'd be closer to my folks, but my brother just moved to Mobile, so for once, I'd like to be near him. Don said he was promised a promotion, but after everything that happened, he's not sure they're going to give it to him."

"I don't understand. I heard you guys were heroes and saved a bunch of lives."

"We did. But one hundred and sixty-eight people still died. People are protesting in the street. The Governor said someone has to pay. The DA felt we didn't have enough evidence to charge anyone. So, the focus is on the MBI's investigation."

"Do you think he did anything wrong, Rachel?"

"No, not at all. I think Don's a hero. But this seems to be more about politics than about whether he did anything wrong." After a moment, she asked, "Since we're sharing, can I ask you a question?"

"Sure, go ahead."

"You told me the time away with Jacqueline was good and that you talked and worked some things out."

I nodded, thinking about the best way to explain a complicated situation that I didn't fully understand myself. "She knows I love the Agency. She knows it's gotten into my blood. I don't think I'd be happy doing some office job. From my end," I recited from memory. "She wants us to be happy and to have a big, healthy family. That means she has to feel safe and know that I'll come home alive."

"So, you didn't actually work anything out?"

"Nope. We more or less settled on a test for six months. If I can't make it work, she's agreed to consider other employment opportunities for me."

Chapter 6

February 25th, 1985
MBI Field Office
Jackson, Mississippi

Don

I was ushered into the boardroom by a woman, too old and cranky to be anywhere but a nursing home. "Ah, donuts. I haven't had breakfast," I said enthusiastically, spying a plate of pastries on the table.

She gave me a threatening stare and snapped at me like a Doberman. "Hands-off, they're for a Director's meeting later this morning."

I looked at my watch and realized I was early. I was anxious about the board of inquiry. It would likely determine the fate of my career. Rachel had called earlier that morning to say good luck and to tell me not to get rattled. Her words were still in my mind. *"You saved lives. You did what you could. Those deaths are not on you. No matter what happens today, remember you'll always be a hero to me."* I told myself to calm down and paced around the boardroom table. I looked down at the parking lot six floors below - a bunch of faceless, suit-wearing bureaucrats, who likely had never risked their lives, never saved a life, never fought for their country, got out of their cars with their fucking attaché cases, and made their way to the building.

I looked over at the plate of pastries. Looking around and not seeing the old woman, I stuffed a powdered jelly-filled donut into my mouth. My mouth was still full as the boardroom door opened, and Joyce Coogan walked in. She was the Director of Special Operations. A few years ago, at a Company Christmas party, I'd had a bit too much to drink and had made a pass at her, not realizing her fiancée was sitting at the same table. Ever since then, things have been awkward. Following her in were two tall men wearing matching dark suits and carrying attaché cases.

"Good morning Agent Kooper," Coogan said, choosing to use my real name. She walked to the head of the table and pointed to her mouth. "You've got a bit of icing sugar... Let's all have a seat. I have another meeting scheduled here in twenty minutes." She pointed at the donuts. "That's why there are donuts."

I finally swallowed the donut and wiped my hands on my pants. "Where's Fred?" I had hoped my immediate boss would be there and would have my back.

"Fred's no longer with the Agency. He accepted a position with building maintenance."

"Shouldn't he be here? I was in communication directly with him throughout this whole mess."

"So you're acknowledging that your investigation was a mess." Coogan sat down and pointed to a chair. "Have a seat, Kooper." In front of her was a tape recorder. She pressed the record button and spoke up. "This is a board inquiry into the conduct of agent Don Kooper. This is Director Joyce Coogan. Also in the room are Agents Cross and Smiley and, of course, the aforementioned Don Kooper, AKA Don Kittyburg."

"Before we get started," I stood up and spoke directly to the tape recorder, "I didn't mean to say the investigation was a mess, just that the outcome was...messy."

"Are you saying that 168 people dying is messy?" said one of the suits.

"Don't put words in my mouth, Cross," I snapped, sitting down.

"I'm Smiley; he's Cross."

I looked back and forth at them - confused. Cross had a perpetual sarcastic grin, while Smiley looked angry and about to lunge across the table at me.

"Was Special Agent in Charge Carol George made aware of your lack of progress?" asked Coogan.

"Fred Moller was my boss. I assumed he would brief her."

"You assumed?" Cross smirked.

"Next question." I shook my head and turned to Coogan. "If he was here, you could just ask him."

"The decision to deploy the police forces downtown when the bombs were at Hiller park was yours, was it not?" Smiley glared at me.

"That was what I was led to believe."

"Or, misled to believe?" added Cross, raising his right eyebrow. "What led you to think the bombs were going to go off downtown?"

"The militia group leader was talking about the demonstration that was planned, and he had drawn a map with buildings and cars. Some of the cars had an "X" drawn through them." When no one said anything, I quickly added, "That suggested they might be locations of car bombs."

"That's it?" Cross had a mocking smile. "Did anyone ever specifically say the bombs would explode downtown?"

"When they were talking about the demonstration, they'd make this gesture with their hands. You know, like something blowing up." Cross and Smiley shared a knowing look. "It sounds like you guys think I murdered those people."

"How do you explain the personal items found in the house in Gautier, where the bombs were made?" Smiley asked, his face reddening and the cords in his neck growing rigid.

"And why were only your fingerprints found at that house?" tag-teamed Cross.

"This is all in my written report," I said, taking a deep breath. "Jackson Lange admitted he'd been in my apartment. He took some of my things so he could frame me. As for the fingerprints, they must have wiped down what they touched."

"Right," said Cross. "You were set up. I forgot."

Coogan leaned forward and stopped recording. Speaking as much to Cross and Smiley, she said, "Enough of this. Agent Kooper, no one here is trying to suggest you set out to murder anyone. This inquiry is about whether you took the necessary steps during this assignment to protect the public and apprehend those responsible. Let's get to the heart of the matter. We have 168 people dead and no one to hold accountable. You have given us absolutely no evidence, no wiretaps, no documentation, no corroboration. My personal view is that you accepted this assignment with some reluctance. In so doing, you allowed yourself to believe what these people were saying."

"Have you spoken to Fender?" I asked, referring to one of the bombers who had agreed to help the police find the remaining bombs.

"As a matter of fact, we did," said Smiley. "He admits to helping you place the bombs in the park. He told us you were a very angry young man, and all of this was your idea."

"I bet you've never worked undercover, have you?" I helped build the bombs. I didn't have much choice. I needed to gain their trust so that I could warn people." Turning to Coogan, "Come on, I was the one who sounded the alarm about the bombs. Why would I have done that?"

"It wasn't just Fender," continued Smiley. "We picked up everyone from that militia group of yours. They all had the same story. They participated in a lawful demonstration downtown to exercise their second amendment rights. No one said anything about bombs. A couple of them said that you were the only one talking about bombs and that you made yourself out to be an explosives expert."

There was silence as Cross and Smiley looked over at Coogan.

I reached over and took another donut.

Chapter 7

February 25th, 1985
Gulfport, Mississippi

Gabriel

The wind had kicked up as I turned onto Hillcrest Road, a quiet residential neighborhood with a mixture of two-story and bungalow homes. I got there early and planned to do a little snooping by checking in with the neighbors. The Sparrows lived in a Cape Cod-style home on a cul-de-sac bordering a forest. I felt a twinge of sadness for the Sparrow's kids as I looked at the Star Wars swing set in the side yard. It must be hard to have your father go missing. I sat there thinking about how much my son Benjamin had enjoyed our time up north. We'd filled our days with sledding, skating, and throwing snowballs at his mother.

I parked my VW Bug at the curb and noticed the car was starting to rust around the fenders. Both Jacqueline and Rachel were pushing me to trade the vehicle in. While investigating a paint shop/ stolen car ring last spring, Rachel had arranged to have the Bug painted pink, thinking it would propel me to action. It did just the opposite. I stubbornly put up with notes left under my wipers about maxi-pads that I later learned had been left by Jacqueline and Rachel.

The name on the property next to Sparrow was Cozens. A middle-aged woman wearing a peach-colored housecoat answered my knock. "Good morning Ma'am, my name's Gabriel Ross. I'm a private investigator looking into the disappearance of your neighbor, Dirk Sparrow." I handed her one of my business cards.

"Yes?" she replied, holding the housecoat closed against the wind with her hand.

"If you would be more comfortable, we can talk inside."

She considered this for a long moment and then reluctantly opened the door to let me in, "Excuse the mess. I'm a little behind on my cleaning."

She offered me coffee, which I politely declined. Once settled in her living room, I explained that Glenna Sparrow had hired me to look into her husband's disappearance.

"I already told a deputy that I didn't know them. Other than to wave and be neighborly."

"And where would you see them?"

"I see the kids playing in the yard. I see her sometimes at the grocery store. They don't go to my church, otherwise, I might be able to tell you more." She paused for a moment before adding, "I don't think they're Christian."

"Tell me, Mrs. Cozens, what makes you think that?"

"Just a feeling." I noticed a framed photo of a man on the end table wearing an air force uniform. When she saw me looking at it, "That's my Bert. He's a Captain over at Keesler Air Base."

"He's very distinguished in the uniform. Have you heard any rumors about the Sparrows?"

"I don't truck much with gossip, but with everything in the paper, their name came up a few times at my bridge club. And, of course, at the sewing club. Then there's the reading circle, oh and the Church Bake sale." She paused for a moment as if she was debating saying something else. I decided to wait her out.

Sure enough, a few moments later, she said she had a story. "When they first moved in, that'd be about five years ago, Bert and I went over to introduce ourselves and welcome them to the neighborhood. I even brought over a chicken pot pie I picked up at the Piggly Wiggly. She wouldn't even take it. Imagine that? She said they were vegans. Well, I didn't know what that meant until later when Mabel, from the bridge club, explained a vegan just doesn't eat meat. So, there we were, standing on the step with our chicken pot pie, and I didn't think she was even going to let us in. Mr. Sparrow finally came out and invited us into their living room. They were still unpacking, but there were all kinds of African statues and masks. You know, kind of voodoo-like," she said, making scary hand gestures. "One of the statues had a boy with a gigantic, …, Oh, I don't want to say. Let me just say it was quite rude."

I nodded, "Is that the reason you don't socialize with them?"

"No, to each their own, I like to say. We just found…" she stopped as if trying to find the right word. "You know the expression, 'She was all over Dirk like a duck on a June bug?' Bert said she was hard to take. She was continually talking down to her husband and ordering him around. Bert told me later that he wouldn't want to socialize with her for fear she might rub off on me."

I thanked Mrs. Cozens and felt like saying that I didn't like Glenna Sparrow much either.

Chapter 8

February 25th, 1985
Talladega Federal Correctional Institute
Talladega, Alabama

Mayor Baxter

It was after dinner by the time the bus drove through the gates of Talladega Federal Penitentiary, and I was already regretting my comment about a hunger strike. We were marched into processing and then to the showers before being assigned to cells. I was happy to hear that I wouldn't be sharing my cell with Al Capone and his stiffy. Having spent the last three months at the Harrison County Detention Centre awaiting trial, I was prepared for the eight-foot by the six-foot concrete box. It had two bunks and a metal toilet at one end. The only window in the cell was small and built into the door, looking out over the hallway.

A large, ape-like man sat on the other bunk, reading a comic book.

"Hi, my name's John Baxter. You might have heard of me." I held out my hand, which hung in the air as the ape didn't bother looking up. "I guess this is my bunk." I put my prison clothes and blanket on the other bed. "Can you tell me about the routine for tomorrow?"

"Fuck off, Fatso."

I thought that was funny coming from a guy who had to weigh two hundred and fifty pounds. He was wearing a red jumper unbuttoned and pulled down to his waist, revealing a hairy chest and man-boobs, which would be the envy of most women. "I guess I'll just lie down here and take a nap. Hey, I noticed that your jumpsuit's red - mine's orange. Is that because I'm new?"

"I said, shut the fuck up."

***

A guard came by, swinging a nightstick. "Lights out at 8 PM." I jumped up and approached the guard, reading his name off his uniform, "Hello Mr. Koenig, my name is Mayor John Baxter. Is the kitchen still open? I missed dinner." The man gave me a tired look and said no. "Could I get an early wake-up call then?"

"Wake up for everyone is 6:30, and breakfast starts at 7:15."

"Mr. Koenig," I lowered my voice and nodded to my cellmate. "Why does he get a red jumpsuit?"

"Orange is for medium security convicts who present a medium risk. Red is for high-risk offenders." The guard looked over at the ape, adding, "He beat the crap out of his last cellmate."

As Koenig turned to leave, I whispered, "Any chance of getting another roommate? I'm not even supposed to be here. I was supposed to be sent to a minimum-security facility. I'm not in the same league as," I mouthed, "that guy."

Koenig smiled. "You'd best make friends. From what I hear, you're going to get a long sentence."

I lay down on the cot again. I was tired, hungry, frightened, and felt like crying. As Mayor, I'd sat through a boring presentation from Amnesty International. They'd had a bee in their bonnet about the number of rapes happening at the Biloxi jail. They'd claimed there were more than 100,000 prison rapes each year in America. I'd dismissed them, saying coddling prisoners was just another example of how the left was trying to ruin the prison system.

***

I must have dozed for a few minutes. When I woke, there were two large men, one with a swastika tattoo, standing over me.

Chapter 9

February 25th, 1985
Gulfport, Mississippi

Gabriel

As I was saying goodbye to Mrs. Cozens, a red Mercedes pulled into the Sparrow's driveway. I walked over and said, "Hello."

"Can you believe that?" Sparrow gestured to my car. "I have half a mind to call the police and have that piece of crap towed away. I think it's lowering my property value just by being there."

I ignored her comment. "Have you got a few minutes to talk?"

She continued to mutter under her breath as she led me into the house. Judging by the shopping bags, she had bought herself some more goofy hats. She dropped the bags beside the couch and motioned for me to sit down. There were three black ebony masks on the wall. On the mantle over the fireplace was a foot-high statue. It was likely what had offended Mrs. Cozens. The figure was of a young boy sporting a twelve-inch boner.

"Are your kids at home?"

"Probably in their rooms."

"I'd like to meet them." My eyes scanned the living room, looking for family photos and finding none.

She went to the staircase and called out, "Jeremy, Michael, come down here at once." The boys bounded down the stairs like a runaway train. "Boys, this is Mr. Gabriel Ross. He wanted to meet you."

"Good morning," I said, giving them a broad smile. They both had dark hair and light skin like their mother. I asked the taller of the two if he had spoken to the woman on the phone a month or so ago. There was a moment of silence before Mrs. Sparrow said, "Jeremy, answer Mr. Ross' question."

"Yes."

"Can you tell me what she said?"

"She said her name was Penn and that she was a friend of my father's," Jeremy said uncertainly before looking at his mother.

"Go on," Mrs. Sparrow ordered.

"I told her he was outside cooking on the BBQ. Mother wasn't home, and Father doesn't like to be interrupted, so I told her he couldn't come to the phone. She asked if I was Jeremy and whether it was okay to talk to me. I said sure, and then she asked if I was as handsome as my father. I said I didn't know. She said she knew I was because she'd seen me. She said she bet that all the girls in grade two must be chasing me around the schoolyard. She went on for a while, asking me dumb stuff like my favorite subject, whether I liked my teacher, whether I liked sports, if I had a dog, that kind of stuff."

"Did she speak to your brother?"

"Just me. Mikey wouldn't have known what to say." He turned and flashed his brother a self-important look.

"Was there anything else that you remember?"

"I asked her if we were related, you know, like an aunt. She said no, but I could call her Aunt Penn and that we were going to do a lot of fun stuff together."

"How old did she seem?"

"I don't know. Not as old as," he nodded his head towards his mother.

"Jeremy!" Mrs. Sparrow called out.

"How long was the call?" I interrupted.

"I don't know."

"It was a long time," Michael spoke for the first time. "I know because you missed most of *Gilligan's Island*."

***

Once the boys left, Mrs. Sparrow gave me a tour of the house. Typical two-story, everything orderly and neat, including the boy's room. I found a black and white polaroid of a man standing in front of the Amoco station on Jeremy's dresser.

"My husband. You can have that if you want."

When I'd first heard the name Dirk Sparrow, my mind had conjured up a man's man. A dark-haired Sylvester Stallone-like man. Now looking at the picture, I wouldn't have said Dirk was rugged. He had a slight build and a mischievous grin with short, closely-cropped black hair. He was an attractive man. Certainly, more attractive than his wife. Most noticeable was that Dirk was black. I now knew what Weber meant when he said the boys didn't look like their Father.

"Here's his passport. It was in his dresser." So much for Weber's Aruba theory.

Once we returned to the living room, I said, "My wife works for an art gallery in Ocean Springs. You have some fascinating pieces," I lied, pointing to the kid with the huge schlong. I made a mental note to ask Jacqueline how valuable this crap was.

"That's a fertility God. I spent some time working overseas for an import/export company. As a perk, they let me have a few pieces."

"Is it supposed to improve your sex life?"

"Supposed to. I can lend it to you if you need some help." She took it off the mantle and pointed it at me. "This is the Greek God Priapus. He was cursed with having a permanent erection. You'll be happy to know that back in ancient times, small penises were considered to be attractive. Men with small cocks were considered rational, intellectual, and authoritative, while those with larger ones were seen as foolish and lustful."

I was pretty sure I had just been insulted. Her comment was below the belt.

***

I was still smarting as we stood on the step, saying our goodbyes. I turned and asked her for the location of the Amoco station.

"It's 4008 Popps Ferry Road. You could talk to Carl. He's been pretty much running the station since Dirk disappeared."

"Is it true the gas station, as well as this house, are just in your name?"

"Why is that important?"

"At this point, I don't know what's important, just asking questions."

"Well, yes, Dirk didn't have money, so my mother lent us some. One of the conditions was that everything be kept in my name only."

"Did you have life insurance on Dirk? To protect your interest in the business?"

She narrowed her eyes, then looked away. "Again, this has nothing to do with why I hired you, but yes, I took out an insurance policy on him. And before you ask, it is for $250,000, roughly the value of the business." While I was contemplating my next question, she closed the front door.

I walked down the driveway and considered what little I'd learned that morning. Mrs. Cozens and her husband thought Glenna Sparrow was a weirdo and a bully. Sparrow used to work for an import/export company, and she had an issue with the size of my penis. Probably the most valuable part of the visit had been the discussion with Jeremy. It sounded like this Penn woman might have been more familiar with the family than I was led to believe.

As I neared the VW, I looked back at the house and saw Glenna Sparrow watching me from the kitchen window. Rather than get in the car, I went across the street to talk to another neighbor.

Chapter 10

Mayor Baxter

"You Baxter?"

I nodded and raised myself on my elbows. One of the men standing over me looked over at my ape cell mate and told him to mind his own business. The ape shrugged his shoulders as if to say, 'Be my guest.'

The man with the swastika tattooed on his arm said his name was Wolf. "We have some questions."

I nodded, ready to seig heil if that's what they wanted.

"We're your welcoming committee.," Wolf flexed his muscles. The other guy licked his lips, staring menacingly at me. "Are you a fag?"

"What? No, of course not. Are you looking for a fag?"

Wolf ignored the question. "You a kiddy diddler?"

"You mean a person who has sex with kids?" I was shocked that someone would dare ask the Mayor of Biloxi such a question. Wolf gave me an angry look until I shook my head. "No, no, of course not."

"Are you a snitch?" My eyes went back and forth between the two men. Truth be told, I was regretting not taking the deal. "A rat?" Wolf added.

"No, no, I'm a standup guy. I would never...." I said nervously.

"Then tomorrow at chow, you'll sit with us. We're the Aryan Brotherhood."

Chapter 11

Gabriel

My conversations with the other neighbors revealed little else that was relevant. Across the street, Mrs. Pinder said she had a hate on for Glenna ever since she had called the police about her poodle. Once, because she was barking, and a second time because she allegedly took a dump on the Sparrow's lawn. The neighbor two doors down had been surprised to hear that Dirk was the old lady's husband. She thought the man to be too young and too black.

When I thought it was clear, I snuck back to my VW and drove off to find the Amoco station.

***

Pulling up to the pumps, I heard the little bell ring. The price for regular was a ridiculous $1.19 a gallon. When I first drove down to Biloxi in 1979, the price was a mere 52 cents. Oil embargoes, OPEC, and Middle East conflicts had all gone into boosting the price. There was a tap on my window as I turned off the ignition. I expected to see a sheik in a white turban, but no, it was just a freckled-face, red-headed kid staring back at me.

"Welcome to Amoco. Fill it up with premium for you, mister?"

"Regular's fine." I handed him a sawbuck and asked him to wash the windows. As the kid started to pump the gas, I asked, "Is Dirk Sparrow working today?"

"Not right now - vacation. I heard someplace warm like Aruba." I was waiting for him to tell me the dog story when I spotted a man wearing coveralls working on a car in one of the bays. I gestured towards the man, "Carl?"

"Yes, sir, Mr. Sears is in charge while Mr. Sparrow is away."

I got out of the car and thanked the kid. As I approached Carl, he turned and smiled. "How's the bug running?"

"Fine. Great car."

"Kind of an unusual color," he grinned. I figured the white man was in his forties. He had longish dark hair combed back in a mullet along with a wicked pair of pork chop sideburns.

"Yeah, it wasn't my choice. Sometimes you have to go along with things just to get along." This prompted Carl to raise an eyebrow and to wipe his hands on a greasy rag.

"The kid tells me Dirk Sparrow's on vacation."

"You a friend of Dirk's?"

"No, my name's Gabriel Ross. I'm a private detective. Glenna Sparrow hired me to look into his disappearance."

Carl nodded and wiped the sweat off his forehead, leaving a greasy smudge. "I tell the boys to say that if anyone asks. But pretty much everyone knows the truth on account of the stories in the *Herald*."

"Is Dirk a good boss?"

Carl shrugged, "I guess as bosses go. He's more or less one of the guys."

"What kind of things does he do here?"

"He's in his office on the phone or doing payroll. When we get busy, he helps out. Sometimes he gets us coffee, maybe sandwiches. There's a deli down the street. Yeah, come to think of it …he's a pretty good boss."

I pulled out my notepad and flipped through some pages. "Were you at that celebration a while back?" I was struggling to read my writing. I showed him the notebook and asked him if he could make it out.

"Something about a bar and someone getting married. You must be referring to when we went to Shaggy's on Beach. One of the guys was getting engaged."

"Can you tell me what happened?"

"You know, some deputy already came by and asked a bunch of questions. He was a bit of an ass trying to impress me with how much he knew about cars. I didn't tell him much, but seeing how you're working for Mrs. Sparrow," his voice dropped a couple of notches as if someone might be listening. "You referring to the guy?"

"Yeah, can you tell me anything about him?"

"White guy, dark hair, kind of long like mine. Maybe 6 foot two, wore an Ole Miss hoodie. I thought he was going to kill Dirk from the size of him, so I was ready to jump in. The guy looked like he might have pumped a little iron."

"What about the girl?"

"Penn, I guess that's short for Penelope. The last name might have been Maddox, but don't quote me - it could have been Madison or something like that. She was pretty enough. White, mid to late twenties, very slim, kind of athletic. Average height. Blonde with a ponytail."

"Tell me what happened."

"She was sitting with the guy a few tables away when we got there. They were having a problem. Voices got raised. That's when I first noticed her. The guy stood up and slapped her a good one. It was kind of a thwack sound. You could hear it over the music. Then Dirk went over. There was a bit of a scuffle, I think the guy might have been drunk, but that's no excuse for hitting a girl—anyway, more shouting and then some shoving. The whole thing might have lasted a few minutes. The guy backed right down and left. The girl lost her drink in the scuffle, so Dirk bought her another. Because she was frightened, Dirk invited her to join our table. That's pretty much it. I think he might have driven her home."

"Did Dirk talk the next day? Maybe say something about the ride home?"

"Like did they ...."

"Yeah, maybe she wanted to show her appreciation."

"He said he just drove her home. I'd be surprised if there were something. He's kind of a straight arrow, and you know he has Mrs. Sparrow."

I wanted to ask him if he'd ever met Glenna Sparrow. "Did she say much when she was at your table?"

"Not much. I got the impression she hadn't been seeing the guy that hit her for very long because someone asked her where he worked, and she said she didn't know. Oh, she said his name...Brad or Bradley, I don't remember the last name."

I scribbled that in my notebook. "This was a Tuesday night. Was the place crowded?"

"Maybe a dozen."

"Did she say anything else at the table? Like where she worked?"

"Some kind of club. To tell you the truth, I'd had a few. You should talk to Mitch or Kenny; they might remember something else."

"Mitch and Kenny work here?"

"Yeah, they come on at 4 PM."

"Okay, I'll circle back. Here's a question for you. Did Dirk happen to show pictures of his family to her?'

"They were sitting beside each other, but I didn't see anything like that."

"What can you tell me about the day Dirk disappeared?"

"It was a Monday. He was already here working in the office when I got here. He said he needed me to check out his car because the brakes were kind of spongy. That's his car over there." Carl was pointing to a rusty 1970 Chevrolet Belair. It looked like it had seen better days.

"Mind if I take a look?"

Carl went into the office and came back with a key ring. The key was on a piece of string with a paper tag with Dirk neatly written on it. "I haven't had time to look at it. Anyway, around lunchtime, he said he was meeting someone and got in a cab."

"Do you remember the cab company?"

"No, but it might have been yellow."

Practically every taxi company on the coast had yellow cabs. I walked over to the Belair and checked it out. Unlike Glenna's red Mercedes, it was showing its age. Most new cars were now equipped with bucket seats - this one still had a black leather bench. I looked through the glove compartment and found an owner's manual but no travel brochures for Aruba. The ashtray was clean and looked like it hadn't been used for a while. I got down on my knees and looked under the seats and found nothing, not even a couple of coins.

The trunk held a spare and a jack and nothing else. I took a look at the back seat and marveled at how wide it was compared to the VW. On impulse, I opened the back door and got in. As I enjoyed the feel of the leather seat, the freckle-faced kid knocked on the window.

"Hey, Mister, do you mind moving your car? It's blocking the pumps." As I was getting out, I opened the small ashtray in the door and found a cigarette butt. I noticed it had pink lipstick.

"I'm leaving Carl," I called out to the man. "Thanks for the information. The man walked over to me as I stood by the bug.

He extended a greasy hand saying, "Can't see how I was much help."

I shook his hand and said, "Dirk's car looks to have been recently cleaned."

"Dirk was kind of fussy that way."

"Say did this girl, the one from Shaggies, smoke?"

He thought for a moment. "Yeah. I believe she did."

I gave Carl a business card, "If anything else occurs to you about Dirk, give me a shout."

He looked at the card, and said "Now that we're talking…I remember something else about the girl. She was sipping one of those fancy drinks." His face broke into a broad smile. "The name stuck in my mind. It was called a slippery nipple."

Chapter 12

February 25th, 1985
Gulfport, Mississippi

Gabriel

Taking my cue from Carl, I stopped at the deli and picked up sandwiches. I got Rachel an avocado, sprout, and cashew sandwich and roast beef and horseradish on a sesame seed bun for me. When I put her lunch in front of her, my boss-score went through the roof. As we ate our sandwiches in the office, I brought her up to date with what I'd learned.

When I finished, she said, "Something's bugging you, I can tell."

"Glenna Sparrow. She's a queer bird."

"Here we go again," she said, rolling her eyes.

"The way she slammed the door in my face when I asked about the insurance makes me feel there's something she's holding back."

"Maybe she thought you were inferring something."

"That she made him disappear to collect on the $250,000? According to Weber, she's loaded."

"So, what do you think she's holding back?"

"I don't know."

"Would you ever run away to be with another woman?"

"No, but I'm not married to Glenna Sparrow. According to her son Jeremy, the woman on the phone said she'd seen him. She said she knew he was as handsome as his father. According to Carl, Dirk didn't show the girl any photographs at the bar. So how would she know that?"

"Maybe Dirk showed her the photos on the way home? You know, I'm not going to sleep with you, but here's a picture of the wife and kids."

"Maybe. Or maybe the husband saw the woman again later that week and neglected to tell his wife that part of the story."

"Maybe," Rachel said, doing something sexy with a dill pickle.

"There's something else." I pulled the photo of Dirk in front of the garage and put it in front of her. "Notice anything?"

She stared at the picture for a moment before saying, "Not really, he's black, and she's white. He's got a nice smile. He looks happy."

"There are few things that don't add up. One, his kids are fair-skinned with dark hair."

"I saw a picture of Glenna Sparrow in the *Herald*. She's ghostly white with dark hair."

"I'll give you that, but from the picture, he's a lot better looking than her. In my experience, good-looking people tend to stick together."

"That's not a thing."

"Yes, it is. Think back to high school. Didn't you hang out with the other hot girls?"

"No," she scoffed.

"Come on, how many butt ugly boyfriends have you had?"

"Present company excluded?"

I almost choked on my roast beef sandwich. "Ow, ow … that hurts."

"You know, I'm just teasing. You're very dishy."

"That wasn't even the worst insult of the day."

"What was worse?"

"Sparrow said something. I can't repeat it while we're eating."

"Well, your theory's bullshit. I went out with that old professor you said reminded you of Kermit, the frog."

"I said his voice was like Kermit's. But listen, there's something else. Carl said the guy who was hassling the girl was big and muscular as if he worked out. Take another look at this picture and tell me this guy could intimidate someone like that."

"Maybe the guy was big, but a chicken. Maybe he was too drunk to fight. Maybe Dirk told him his hands were lethal weapons." She pantomimed someone delivering a Karate chop. "I don't know."

"You have to admit that there's something hinky about all this."

She nodded as you would to someone who wasn't all there. "Thanks for the sandwich. What's your next move, Sherlock?"

"Find this Bradley guy."

Chapter 13

Gabriel

It was a short drive over to Shaggy's. The patio, which opened onto the beach, would have been packed during the tourist season. Today near the end of February, it was deserted. I went over to the bar where a man with a ponytail was making what appeared to be margaritas. "I'll have one of those."

"Coming right up, my friend." I took a seat at the bar and watched as he rolled the top of the tall glass in salt and then poured a mix over a couple of ice cubes. He topped it off with a green umbrella.

"Thank you…must be offseason," I commented, looking around and seeing only two other people.

"Yeah, this is the after lunch, before dinner lull. Stick around. If you're looking for fun, the after-work crowd likes to party."

I put one of my business cards in front of him. "I was hoping you could give me some information about something that happened about six weeks ago."

"Yeah, what might that be?" His face grew stern, which meant he had a low opinion of cops, detectives, and anyone with a question.

I pulled out my notebook again and tried to decipher my notes. "Tuesday, January 8th. There was a bit of a fight between a woman and her boyfriend. Were you working that night?"

"I work most nights, but you're going to have to do better than that. This is a bar. People drink too much and get into arguments all the time."

"There were a bunch of mechanics here, and they broke up the fight." I took a sip of the margarita - it went down smooth. The bartender shrugged his shoulders. "I think the woman's name was Penn," I added. "Maybe Maddox or Madison. Mid to late twenties, pretty with an athletic build. She's a blonde."

The man scratched his head and said, "I don't know. Sorry, I can't help you. I have a tough time remembering last week, let alone that far back."

"There was one other thing - she was drinking a slippery nipple."

"Sambuca and Baileys. I have a faint memory of looking up how to make that. It might have been for your gal. If she likes the drink, then she's not a regular."

I finished the Margarita, thanked him, and threw some bills on the bar. There were dozens of bars down here - maybe this girl was a regular at a different bar. I decided to try my luck at another and then another. I hit paydirt on my fifth bar. It was a place called the Blind Tiger. By then, I was feeling no pain, having had a margarita, two black Russians, and a vodka and tonic. I told myself to slow down. I was kind of on probation with Jacqueline. This was my first day back to work, and if I came home three sheets to the wind, I could just picture the storm. I went up to the bar and asked a blonde woman with a tattoo of an alligator on her arm, "Do you have slippery nipples?"

Thankfully she laughed and didn't slap me. Instead, she said, "One slippery nipple coming up."

I put a business card on the bar. When she returned with the drink, she picked it up and studied it while I sampled the drink. It was surprisingly good.

"You looking for something, Gabriel?"

She had brown eyes. I've always had a thing for blondes, with great figures, alligator tattoos, and brown eyes. She had a slight accent, which just made her seem sexier. I pulled out my notebook but decided not to attempt reading it. I asked if she had a regular by the name of Penn Maddox, who liked slippery nipples.

She looked at me and wrinkled her nose, "Sounds kind familiar. Why?"

"Slim, pretty blonde with a ponytail?"

She nodded and then looked around, shaking her head. "If it's the girl I'm thinking about, she's not here. I wouldn't have said pretty. I guess it depends on how many drinks you've had. She's not a regular, maybe every couple of weeks."

"What do you know about her?"

"Not much – one drink, pays cash, lousy tipper."

"If she pays cash, how do you know her name?"

"I know it's old fashioned. but I introduced myself."

"Does she come in with anyone?"

"Not that I've noticed. Say," she said, holding up my empty glass. "Most people order two slippery nipples. They kind of go together."

Good pitch, how could I say no? "Sure, what the hell."

When she returned, I showed her Dirk Sparrow's photo and asked her if she'd ever seen him.

She gave it a quick glance while she was making my drink. "I don't think so. He's kind of cute."

"What's your name?" I asked.

"Can't read?" She pointed to her left boob, which had the name "Wendy" embroidered on her t-shirt.

"What about the right one? Does it get a name?"

"Funny. You asked if she comes in with anyone. A better question, Mr. Private Detective, is whether she leaves with anyone."

I took a sip of the drink she put in front of me and pointed at her. "Good point, you'd make a hell of a detective." I sat up all of a sudden, "Wendy, do you want to come work for me at the detective agency?"

"No, but it's sweet of you to offer." Wendy smiled. "Are you going to ask me?"

I shook my head to clear some drunken cobwebs, trying to remember my question.

She shook her head and said very slowly, "Does … Penn … Maddox … usually … leave … with … someone?"

"Gotcha! Does Penn …. usually leave …what you said?"

She took my hand and wrote the name Penn Maddox across the palm. "I'm doing this because you won't remember. I've seen her pick up a guy at least two times."

***

I left the Blind Tiger and headed down the street. I took a huge gulp of fresh salt air from the Gulf and tried my best to get a grip on myself. I wondered why it was always the last drink that threw you over the edge. I should just avoid the last drink. I spotted a coffee shop on the next block and stumbled towards it, trying not to bump into too many light poles. When I got there, I ordered a coffee and went to use the payphone. It was almost 5 PM. I'd been boozing for two and a half hours. Thankfully Rachel was still at the office.

"Hey, it's…me."

"Hello, you." Rachel said cautiously. "What's up?"

"Just checking…burb… in."

"Uh….That's nice. How goes the hunt for Bradley and Penn?"

"Flound her. Well, at least I think so."

"Gabriel, are you drunk? You're slurring your words."

"Nooooo. Not drunk, but I like slippery nipples."

"Gabriel, where are you?"

I looked around the coffee shop and asked a man sitting in a booth, "Where am I?"

"You're at Steamed Beans on Beach Blvd," said the man, shaking his head.

"Did you hear that? Beamed Steans on Bleach."

"I'll be right over."

***

I'd consumed two coffees and a bagel and gone to the bathroom twice by the time Rachel showed up. She looked at me with concern. To her credit, she didn't get preachy. All that was said was that she hoped it was worth the effort.

I nodded and took another sip of coffee. I managed to tell her about the alligator lady that had named her left boob Wendy and then showed her my palm where she had written a name, Penn Maddox.

Chapter 14

February 26th, 1985
Talladega, Alabama

Mayor Baxter

I bought this diary after breakfast. I know I'm taking a risk that someone might find it, but one day I might want to write a book about my life and how I've been unjustly accused - framed by the fake news media. Maybe it'll become a bestseller. It would be a beautiful book. It might even be made into a movie. If so, I'd like Chuck Norris to play my part. Since this diary might someday be worth a tremendous amount of money, I'd like it to be used to build the John Baxter Memorial Museum. It would have a huge statue of me out front and a special room with pictures highlighting my accomplishments.

***

Dear Diary

I couldn't get used to the mattress, which, to my surprise, wasn't a pillow top. The ape snored most of the night. Around midnight he got up and took a massive, smelly dump in the toilet just inches from where I was sleeping. I was totally disgusted and made a mental note to speak to Mr. Koenig about better ventilation.

I tossed and turned, thinking about the Aryan Brotherhood and why they'd come to see me. In the past, I've supported causes like the White People's Party. Was this some protection because of that? Or was this Reznikov taking care of me for not ratting him out? I decided to skip the showers for fear that Al Capone and his stiffy might not have seen the memo that I was with the Aryan Brotherhood.

***

I had my first meal - Bran Flakes in one of those single-serve boxes along with skim milk, two pieces of bread, and a banana. Wolf came up to me while I was complaining about the coffee and told me to come to his table. A dozen or so guys were sitting with him, including a giant named Schultz and a skinny guy named Klink. When I was introduced as the mayor, many said they'd voted for me. Others said they were upset about what had happened at the trial. They were so welcoming—lots of very fine people.

Wolf's real name, I later learned, is Earl Gruber. He's from a small town near Vicksburg, and he's been sentenced to twenty years on a bogus drug charge. He was very helpful and suggested I try to get a job in the machine shop where he worked. We went over the prison schedule, and he told me not to lose hope about getting out.

After breakfast, I visited the commissary and bought a bunch of candy bars, some Diet Cokes, and a bag of Lays potato chips. So much for the hunger strike. After that, I used the payphone and called Sexfinger. At first, he was standoffish and claimed he'd been fired. The man has no sense of humor. I asked about the grounds for an appeal that he'd mentioned. He replied the judge should never have allowed testimony from the deceased Hollis Huntley (That's the guy who thought he could fly and jumped off the roof of the tallest building in Gulfport) to be read into the record. By allowing it, the defense never had an opportunity to cross-examine the witness. I asked him why he hadn't objected at the time. His response was, to have done so would have alerted the jury that we felt the testimony was particularly damaging. Still, I don't see why he didn't object. My spirits picked up at the talk of an appeal but collapsed once again when Sexfinger said the process would take months, if not years. Once again, I told him, "You're fired!"

Chapter 15

February 26th, 1985
Gulfport, Mississippi

Gabriel

I couldn't breathe. Everything was dark. I struggled to get my two-year-old son Benjamin off of my face. He was sitting on me, laughing and moving up and down like he was in a bouncy castle. I tickled him off of me and realized that I was lying on the living room couch. I moved my hand over my face, trying to wipe away the size ten headache. That's when I noticed the writing on my palm. Penn Maddox. It all started coming back to me. Benjamin launched a counter-assault, trying once again for the infamous face-sitting maneuver. I tickled him again and then picked him up, putting him on my shoulder.

"How was your night?" Jacqueline stood in the hallway watching us.

"Great, I forgot how comfortable that couch was."

"You smelled like a distillery when Rachel brought you home. She said she would pick you up later this morning. Give you a chance to sleep it off." I put Benjamin down and made my way blindly to the bathroom. "We're you celebrating something?" Her arms were crossed in the 'you're in deep shit' position.

"Not really." I aimed for a kiss as I walked by, but she did the rope-a-dope. "I was working a case. Had a few too many."

"There's some Excedrin in the bathroom. Want me to make you some breakfast?"

"Just coffee." I closed the bathroom door behind me and looked at my reflection in the mirror. My dark hair looked like porcupine quills, and my green eyes were red-rimmed as droopy like an old hound's. Benjamin doesn't like closed doors as he's not quite tall enough to reach the doorknob, so he likes to run into the bathroom door - a two-year-old's version of a battering ram. When I sat down on the toilet, he stuck his fingers under the door and waved. That's what goes for privacy living with a two-year-old.

Jacqueline hadn't asked the question that I had antici-pated, but I was sure it was coming. "Why did you call Ra-chel when you needed help?" I asked my reflection in the mirror. "No big deal," I replied, swallowing a couple of pills. "Because she doesn't judge me. She accepts me for who I am." I turned on the shower and started stripping off my clothes.

"Gabriel … are you … talking to yourself in there?"

"Just singing in the shower."

"I have to go to the art gallery now, but mom will be by to look after Benjamin."

"Alright...have a great day," I yelled as I got into the shower.

"We can talk tonight," she said ominously. Coincidentally, moments later, the water in the shower turned ice cold.

***

Once I'd gotten dressed, I shared a bowl of Lucky Charms with Benjamin. He insisted on eating all of the marshmallows.

Mrs. Chen, Jacqueline's mother, showed up around nine, carrying a couple of grocery bags. "Good morning Gabriel. How was your first day back to work?"

"Fine – nice to be back earning a living." If I know anything about my wife, she had already called her mother and told her about Rachel driving me home.

"I picked up a few things at the Piggly Wiggly. I figured you might not have had time to go shopping."

I helped her put things away, "You didn't need to do that. We have plenty of food."

"I was going to make a tourtiere today."

My mother-in-law is French Canadian. I've always thought my wife's emotional side came from her. Her father, a retired math teacher of Chinese descent, gave her what logic she has. "That sounds wonderful. Why don't you ask Dad to come over and we can have a family meal?"

Her smile was one that you use when you want to humor someone. "Will you be able to find your way home? Or will we send a car?"

I laughed and was thankful to hear Rachel's car in the laneway.

***

As I got into her AMC Pacer with the annoying sun-blinding windshield, Rachel asked, "How's the head?"

"Been better. Thanks for driving me home last night."

"What was worse, the hangover or the questions this morning?" She backed out of the laneway.

"Jacqueline was fine."

"You'll be happy to know that I already spent a couple of hours on your mystery girl, Penn Maddox." It took me a moment to remember who that was. I looked down and saw that the shower had washed away the name from my palm. "There's no listing for Penn, Penny, or Penelope Maddox on the coast."

"Unlisted?" I put on my Ray-Bans and rested my head against the window.

"Not according to Weber. He also checked with motor vehicle. The only Penelope Maddox is an eighty-year-old woman living in a nursing home in Vicksburg. She came up in his search because she has over one hundred unpaid traffic tickets." I nodded and closed my eyes, trying to will away my headache. "Did you hear what I said?" she repeated.

"Yes. She said I had a small penis."

"What?" Rachel pulled into the strip plaza where the Agency was located.

"That's what Sparrow said to me yesterday that was so insulting."

"Why would she be talking about the size of your penis? And more importantly, how would she know how big it was?"

I told her about the fertility statue and how Sparrow had said I should be happy that small penises were the fashion back in those days. "She pointed the thing at me and asked if I needed to borrow it."

I ended up leaving Rachel laughing hysterically in the car while I got out and went into the Agency.

***

I was making coffee in the lunchroom when Rachel came in, still smirking. "That was funny."

"Nyuk, nyuk, nyuk." Coffee in hand, I walked back to the office. I busied myself by reading the morning *Herald*.

The main article was about a white supremacist group called the Sword and the Arm of the Lord and a four-day siege in Arkansas. The heavily armed group had connections to the Klu Klux Klan and the Aryan Nation. Agents with the FBI and the Bureau of Alcohol, Tobacco, and Firearms (ATF) had the two hundred and twenty-four-acre militia camp surrounded. "Hey Rachel, you should check out the story in the paper about this white supremacist camp in Arkansas. Maybe you might recognize some of these names."

Rachel came in and read the article over my shoulder. I caught a whiff of her jasmine perfume and decided it was time to refill my coffee cup.

When I came back into the office, Rachel was just finishing the article. "I'll have to show this to Don. The Church of the Sword and Arm of the Lord sounds familiar. I don't recognize any names, but this sounds like the same group that did the bombings in Biloxi."

"Now that I know Dirk Sparrow is a black man, I was wondering if he somehow got tangled up in the bombings. It kind of fits the timeline."

"Maybe," she said, considering. "But they've accounted for all of the bodies."

I sat down in the chair facing the desk. "You know you look great…" I said, taking a sip of my coffee. She was wearing a navy blue turtle neck and black slacks. Her wavy hair was hanging down and resting on her shoulders. She gave me a questioning look. "... behind the desk. You should be the boss."

"Oh well, thanks, been there, done that." She sat up with her shoulders back and said, "So, what's your plan today, Mr. Ross?"

"I'm going to call the cab companies. The day he disappeared, Dirk got into a cab outside the garage around lunchtime."

"Good idea."

"Then I thought I'd have lunch at the Blind Tiger." A look of concern came across her face. "Relax, I thought I'd offer the bartender a few bucks to call me if she spots this ..."

"Penn Maddox."

"Right, Penn Maddox.

"Good ideas, anything I can do to support you?" She asked in a boss-like tone with a smile.

I took out the photo of Dirk Sparrow and handed it to her. "Do you feel like taking this to the bus station and then the train station? See if anyone salutes?"

"Why the bus station?"

"We need to cover all our bases. I expect Weber wouldn't have done that. Since Dirk's passport is in his dresser, a trip out of the country looks unlikely. And since Dirk's car is in the shop, then he might have hopped on a bus."

Chapter 16

Don

Deputy Weber chewed with his mouth open. I watched as the boxy-headed-brush-cut of a man chomped, giving me an open mouth view of a partially masticated hamburger. After Coogan told me to take a few days off, I'd thought I'd head down to Biloxi and connect with Weber. Something was annoying about him. Was it his penchant for being easily distracted, or was it his insistence on being so by-the-book? Thankfully Deputy Weber had risen to the occasion on Martin Luther King Day and saved Rachel by blowing Jackson Lange to smithereens with his shotgun.

Weber finally finished his hamburger and washed it down with a coke. I ate a couple of fries and looked around the diner. It was busy with the lunchtime crowd. "Well?" I prompted, pointing a fry at him.

"Oh, yeah, well, I'm up to my ass in alligators, so I haven't had much time to think about it. It's been tense around the office since the bombings. Sheriff Pardy called the whole thing a clusterfuck of career-ending proportions. He's up for re-election this year, and I don't think he's even going to run. I know he blames me for a lot of it. There was a time he used to call me the 'sheriff in waiting.' Now he just refers to me as 'that guy.'"

"That's not fair. You saved lives."

"As difficult as it's been, it's nothing compared to what you've had to go through. That board of inquiry sounds rough. You heard that song, *'Take This Job and Shove It,'* by Johnny Paycheck?"

"I hate country music."

"That what I'd say to your boss."

"What kind of cases are you working on?" I changed the subject.

Weber pulled a notepad from his breast pocket and started flipping through it. "Last week, I responded to two 11-54s, that's a cow on the road. We always have our share of 11-84s - that's stolen cars. Since the bombings, we've been busy with 10-73s - bomb threats."

"Have any of them been legit?"

"No, but we need to respond anyway and check it out. The talk is, folks are waiting for the coloreds to hit back after what happened. The start of the race war."

"That's what the bombers wanted."

"I was so busy I sent a case over to Rachel. I just don't have time to work a missing person case." He took another sip of coke, "So, are you just going to hang around until your boss calls you?"

"I don't know. I thought after we stopped the bombings, I'd get a commendation, but instead, I think they want to clean house. My boss has already been transferred to some dead-end department."

Weber reached over and scavenged some fries off my plate. "I have a friend of a friend who has one of those fry trucks for sale. If you bought it and parked it down by the beach, you'd make a killing."

I ignored his comment. "Do you know what bugs me the most? Even more than my career?"

"You're wondering if Paycheck is the guy's real name, or did he just make it up to go along with the song? Sort of like you with Kittyburg."

My choice of alias had popped into my head while I was petting Rachel's cat. I shook my head. "Bubba Lange and the people who organized this will get off scot-free."

Weber nodded. "If a little bird was to tell Lange that you're in Biloxi, I'm sure he'd try to wring your neck for what happened to his brother. Then I could jump out and arrest him."

"You're the one who killed him."

"Right, forget what I said about the little bird."

Chapter 17

February 26th, 1985
Gulfport, Mississippi

Gabriel

Finding the cab company that picked up a fare in front of the Amoco on January 14th should have been simple. About as simple as my relationship with my wife. None of the companies had their records computerized, and all needed time to find their log sheets. I finally started telling them that lives were hanging in the balance. By noon I'd found that South Coast Cab had picked up a customer named David at the Amoco station that day around lunchtime and dropped him off at the corner of Pass and Courthouse Roads in Gulfport. The dispatcher agreed to page the driver, Miguel, and have him stop by the Agency. I wondered if the name the dispatch gave me for the passenger was an error or whether Dirk had deliberately tried to cover his trail. If so, why would he do that?

***

Miguel walked in shortly after 1 PM. He was a short, bulky, dark-haired man with a handlebar mustache - all he needed was the bullet bandolier and a sombrero to match the stereotype of a Mexican bandito.

"Miguel, thank you for coming in." I gestured for him to have a seat in the office and offered him a coffee. In response, he looked at his watch and shook his head. "This is very important," I said. "It has to do with an investigation into a man who went missing on January 14th of this year. Do you remember picking up a fare on that date outside the Amoco Station on Popps Ferry Road?"

"I drive many people - every day," Miguel said in broken English, his hands gesturing wildly. "I pick them up, take them there, pick up someone else, take them there. If they say I pick up man, then I pick up."

"Right," I agreed doubtfully. Like a moron, I felt myself subconsciously speaking slower and louder while mirroring his hand gestures. "I was hoping you might remember the man. He was black." I pulled out a photo of Dirk Sparrow and put it in front of Miguel.

He held the picture for a few moments. "Todos los negros, se parecen."

Which I thought meant 'What park is your negro named after?' "Dispatch says you dropped off the fare at the corner of Pass and Courthouse Roads." Miguel took another look at the picture and once again shook his head, shrugging his shoulders. "The man in the picture's name is Dirk. Dispatch said the passenger record shows David."

"They say pick up David. I say, you, David? He get in."

I asked if he remembered anything about the man, maybe something he said, and he repeated the line about negros and the park. Then he slapped his hands together as if to say, "all done."

I stared at him for a moment, trying to will him into being a better witness. In response, he looked at his watch again.

***

I didn't get to the Blind Tiger until 2 PM. Wendy was working behind the bar. When she noticed me, she gave me a sad look. "Are you addicted to my nipples?"

"I'm still a little hungover. I was hoping for a late lunch. Maybe a coffee?"

She put a plastic menu in front of me as I took my usual seat. "Hang on while I brew a fresh pot." I opted for a grilled cheese sandwich. While we were waiting for the order, she asked, "Find your gal yet?"

I looked at my palm and scratched my head. She smiled and shook her head, then playfully grabbed my palm, seeing that the name had been washed off. I laughed. "I was kidding. You said the girl's name was Penn Maddox. The problem is there is no Penn Maddox, Penny Maddox, or Penelope Maddox anywhere on the coast."

"Maybe she just made that up. Penn kind of sounds like a made-up name. Maybe she didn't want me to know her real name."

"Why would she want to use a fake name?" She poured me some coffee.

"I don't know. But let's see," Wendy put a finger to her chin, suggesting she was deep in thought or maybe just being a wiseass. "Why would anyone out to pick up a guy use a fake name?" She snapped her fingers and pointed at me. "I see you're married. Would your wife approve of you meeting strange women in bars?"

At the mention of my wife, my headache came back. "I don't suppose you happened to notice a wedding ring?"

"No, sorry. Pretty observant, but that would be a whole new level."

She went into the kitchen and came back moments later with my sandwich. "You should put me on the payroll."

"I was thinking the same thing." I took a bite of my sandwich and washed it down with the coffee. "How about I give you fifty bucks if you call me the next time you see her?" I wrote my home number and address on the back of my business card. After a moment, I also wrote Rachel's number. "My office and home number are on this card. I've also written my boss's number."

"Do I get the odd night off?"

"You get the fifty whoever calls. Let me ask you another question. These men you've seen her leave with, do you get the impression they were chance encounters or pre-arranged dates?"

She thought about that for a moment. "Pick-ups, no question."

"What makes you so sure?"

"If it had been pre-arranged, why would the men come in and initially sit at a different table? No, definitely picks ups."

"I guess I've been out of the dating scene for a while. Was she the initiator?"

She chuckled. "Initiator? That's a little harder to judge. From my experience, when I want to meet a guy, I'll smile at him, like this." She flashed a sexy smile, followed by a wink. "Then I just sit back and see how he reacts. If they're interested, they usually come over and offer to buy me a drink."

"That look you just gave me should be illegal."

She ignored the compliment. "If I see her, should I ask to see her ID? Maybe we'd learn her real name."

"That's a good thought, but - no. If you've served her before without asking for ID, it might make her suspicious."

***

I met Rachel around 5 PM back at the agency. We compared notes, and I discovered the momentum I felt yesterday had disappeared.

"I'm sorry, Gabriel, but I struck out at both the train station and the bus terminal. It's been over five weeks, and they see a lot of people. Sometimes they don't even look up at the customer when they're selling tickets." After a moment, Rachel added, "I know you thought the airport was a longshot, but I tried it anyway. You don't need a passport to fly within the country. The ticket agent at the airport was Mexican. When she saw the photo, she said, 'Todos los negros, se parecen,' which translates to 'all black people look alike.'

I told her that was the same thing Miguel had said. I recapped my interview with Wendy and her theory that Penn Maddox might be an alias because she might be married.

"Sounds plausible. If Wendy calls, should I race down to the bar and do what?"

"See who she meets - follow her." I shrugged my shoulders. "I'm grasping at straws." I suddenly remembered something and pulled a baggie out of my coat pocket. "I found this in the backseat of Dirk's car. Someone had thoroughly cleaned the car but forgot about the back-seat ashtray."

"There's pink lipstick on it."

I nodded. "Glenna Sparrow's lipstick color is blood-red. Carl said the girl from the bar was a smoker. What do you think this means?"

"Carl was maybe having an affair with this Penn Maddox?"

"Maybe Weber was right about Dirk being like his bloodhound."

Chapter 18

February 26th, 1985
Talladega, Alabama

Mayor Baxter

Dear Diary

It was unseasonably warm today. A guard came up to me while I was watching others exercise in the yard. "The warden wants to see you."

Finally, I thought I was going to get justice. The warden's name is Robert Harrigan. He's a brown-suit-wearing, middle-aged man with a brush cut. "Mr. Mayor, it's an honor to welcome you to Talladega Federal Prison," he said, standing up from his desk and giving me a two-handed shake. "I had hoped to greet you on your arrival last night, but it was such a nice day; I left early to go play golf." Harrigan had a southern accent that was one-part sweetness and one-part drawl. He pointed to a chair and told me to take a load off. "Can I get my lovely secretary Jamie to bring you anything? Maybe something cold to drink? It's already getting hot in here." He had a small fan on his desk, blowing cold air on him.

"Sure, I'll take a Diet Coke if you have it." While I took a seat, Harrigan stuck his head out of the office, "Jamie, dear, can you fetch the mayor a Diet Coke. I'll have one

too." He turned to me and slapped me on the back, "Have you met Jamie?"

I shook my head, and then the warden added, "She's quite the hottie," making a gesture about the size of her boobs. "You know, we were watching an old interview you did with a reporter from WLOX last year. The reporter asked you about the impact of Hurricane Camille, and you said, Harrigan started to snicker, 'Hurricane Camille was tremendously big and tremendously wet.' That was a good one."

I smiled, pleased that the warden was such a fan.

"We all followed your trial down in Hattiesburg." he continued to chuckle. "I was pleasantly surprised that such a celebrity would be joining us here. I think we're all looking forward to your stay."

"You know, warden, there were a lot of things wrong with that trial - an incompetent judge, poor representation, faulty instructions to the jury. I bet once the news gets out, there'll be riots in the streets of Biloxi. I was a very popular mayor. My last victory, many people said, was one of the largest landslides in history."

"That so?" Harrigan's face showed concern.

"In a nutshell, I have been wrongfully imprisoned. I had to endure the ignominy of a bus ride with wretched, terrible people."

"There must have been a mistake."

"Once news gets to our governor, he'll be issuing a pardon."

Harrigan's concern suddenly changed to a sickly-sweet smile. "This is a federal institution. If you want a pardon, it'll have to come from ole Ronnie."

I was about to explain how I'd been railroaded when we were interrupted by a busty blonde woman who could easily have made the cover of Playboy. She swooshed by me and handed the warden a can of Diet Coke. She turned to me and said, "Sorry, only one left in the fridge." Once she left, Harrigan smiled with raised eyebrows as he opened the can. He took a long gulp. "Sure do appreciate a cold soda on a hot day. So, how are you going to get along with your cellmate? A word of advice, don't say anything about his boobs. He kind of went nuts on the last guy."

"I was hoping you could arrange a private room."

He made a note on a piece of paper and nodded. He then propped his feet up on his desk, taking another long drink of his soda. "Word, I hear, is that you'll be enjoying our hospitality here at the Hilton for quite some time."

"I don't expect to be here very long. My lawyer's working on an appeal."

"An appeal? That so?" He pulled a pair of cigars out of his breast pocket. "Do you like cigars?" He bit the end off one and spat it in the garbage can. I watched as Harrigan lit up. The scent of cigar quickly filled the room. "Nothing like the smell of a good cigar, don't you think?" When I didn't answer, he pointed his cigar at me and said, "I'd really like to hear your thoughts on how we can spruce up the place."

"Right off the top, I think the mattress is a little thin."

"You do?" He drained his soda.

"The food this morning wasn't up to speed. The coffee… well, let's just say I wouldn't even call it coffee. You might want to look into those espresso machines."

Harrigan crushed the soda can with a frown, his jaw clenching, "Mayor Baxter, let me give you a few pointers. To help you get comfortable here." He stood up and hovered in front of me. "One, you ain't getting a private cell. Two, you'd best find a way to cuddle up with your cellmate as he's likely," he winked, "going to be sleeping with you for a long time. Third, you'll be expected to work. We have rewarding jobs in the food preparation field, mopping and cleaning services, toilet and laundry services, as well as our state-of-the-art license plate shop. Sorry there are no openings for mayor. Fourth, I strongly suggest you obey the guards. Obey the rules. If you even think of causing trouble, then don't. I'll find out, and your stay at our lovely Hilton will be very uncomfortable. I'm saying this, Mr. Mayor, with all due respect, of course. You do have a reputation for being a bit of an asshole who thinks the world owes you something. Well, you got that backward. It is you who owe society for what you've done. That's why you're here."

Harrigan went back behind his desk and sat down. "Oh, and I personally would stay away from the gangs. There are lots of people who come here, keep their nose clean, and leave. If you join a gang, then I can almost guarantee that won't be you. Now it's time for you to go. Beautiful Jamie and I have some one-on-one work to do," he winked again. As I was leaving, he called, "Oh, and I hear you about the mattress. I made a note to do absolutely nothing about it."

I was shocked at the rude way this man spoke to me. If any of my staff ever spoke to me like that, they'd be out on their ass.

Chapter 19

February 26th, 1985
Gulfport, Mississippi

Don

"Have you heard any news from the MBI?" Rachel asked as we sat down at the *Lookout Steakhouse* in downtown Gulfport. The choice of restaurants was a concession on her part. She'd taken pity on me because of what I was facing at work.

"I've called for an update. Today, Coogan said it was 2 to 1, but when I asked her which way, she said she had to go. She just said to hang tight."

"Well, at least you convinced one other person. I wouldn't rush out and tell them to shove the job, buy a chip truck, and park it on the beach."

I shook my head and laughed. "You've been speaking to Weber. He's quite the guy. Those were his ideas." I held up my wine glass for a toast. "To Weber, despite everything, he saved your life."

We drank our wine as we waited for the waiter to bring the food. "Have you thought much about what you're going to do if things don't go your way?"

"I was looking at that list you gave me of people who might have organized the bombing. Masters is dying, and Steve Schaffer would recognize me. But that leaves a lot of other names to go after.

"What do you mean, go after?"

"I was thinking about that Dietz character - getting a job in one of his businesses - seeing what I can dig up. Weber says he would try to help, and if I can get anything incriminating, he knows someone at the DA's office we could take it to."

"Don, you saved a lot of lives. You're a brave man. No one else could have done what you did. You don't have anything to prove."

"That's not it. What's stopping me from getting past all this is that 168 people are dead, and no one is being held accountable. I know I tried my best and that together we saved lives. But that's not enough. I owe it to myself to put the bad guys away."

"So, this about saving your job?"

"No. I still don't know if they're going to fire me. Regardless, even if they did, and I get the evidence, then at least that'll be something. Then if they decided to keep me, I'll use Weber's suggestion and say, '*Take this job and shove it.*'

"Why Dietz?"

"Because he's near the top of that list - right after Masters and before Bubba Lange. I figure if someone had anything sensitive, it might be him. What can you tell me about him?"

"There's lots at the library. From memory, he's divorced and paying alimony to three wives. He owns a retail store. He used to be the President of the Chamber of Commerce. I read a piece in the *Herald* that he was involved with the Klan. Oh! And he's good friends with our former mayor." She paused and took a sip of wine. "I'm not sure I like this plan, Don. I understand it must be eating away at you, but you need to walk away."

"I need closure."

"You have to realize your picture has been in the paper. If Lange sees you, he'll kill you."

"That's why I washed off the tattoo and started growing my hair back."

"And I thought you did that for me."

Chapter 20

Gabriel

Dinner that evening was like a game of whack-a-mole, with me as the mole. Jacqueline's mom had baked a tourtiere, and Jacqueline chipped in with a tossed salad. To go with the meal, I opened up a bottle of wine. After a toast to family and good health, Jacqueline picked up the mallet and started swinging. "I read something in the *Herald* today. The local bottling plant is looking for an office manager, someone who knows a little accounting."

I let the comment slide. I asked my father-in-law whether he knew that Benjamin preferred the green marshmallows in his Lucky Charms.

"I observed that recently. He plucked out all of the marshmallows out of the bowl and lined them up by color on the table. You know, being able to sort at such a young age is a sign of higher intelligence."

"I agree." Using his body as a battering ram, on the other hand, was another matter.

Mrs. Chen responding to some pre-arranged signal, then picked up the mallet. "Honey," she said, putting her hand on her husband's arm. "What do you think about the State's plan to raise the legal drinking age to 21? Don't you think there's too much drinking going on? People coming home drunk at all hours of the night."

Mr. Chen gave his wife a confused look. "We talked about this the other day. Maybe you forgot. I said going from 19 to 21 seems like a big leap. All that will do is fuel the underground economy."

"What do you think about that, Gabriel? You're a big drinker." Mrs. Chen shoveled some tourtiere into her mouth.

"I haven't given it much thought – and I'm not a big drinker." I punctuated my comment by taking a big sip of wine. Then, in an unusual move, the mole grabbed hold of the mallet and started to do his own whacking. "You know Jacqueline, isn't it great when a person finds a job that they enjoy. Like working at the art gallery. It must be so reward-ing for you." When she didn't respond, I turned to Mr. Chen. "Did you feel fulfilled as a math teacher?"

"Yes, the kids were not always the best students, but I enjoyed those that wanted to learn."

I looked over at my wife with a satisfied look.

"You're right, Gabriel," Jacqueline countered, now pull-ing out a sledgehammer she had been hiding. "I like my job. It's safe and interesting, and there's never a question about whether I'll come home in one piece."

"Or drunk," chipped in Mrs. Chen.

I think that last shot might have clipped me on my little mole head, so I decided to duck. "Speaking of art, I was at a client's home yesterday, and she had several distinctive African masks and statues. I was wondering how expensive that type of... collection might be." I felt like saying crap but didn't want to be crass in front of Jacqueline's parents.

"It varies. The real stuff imported from Malawi is usually made of ebony," Jacqueline replied. "They can be very expensive. Sadly to say, some knock-offs might look expensive, but they're usually just cheap wood painted black."

"You have a new case?" asked my father-in-law, jumping in.

"Yes, I usually can't talk about my cases, but since it's been in the papers anyway, I've been hired by Glenna Sparrow to look into her husband's disappearance."

"Sparrow, I read something about that a month ago," said Mr. Chen. "It had fallen out of the headlines, so I just assumed he'd been found."

"Not yet. He's been missing five weeks. I'm just starting to look into it...."

"I bet the wife did it," interrupted Jacqueline. "She found out her husband was having an affair with someone at his work, so she killed him. Smashed his head in with a wine bottle." For effect, she grabbed the wine bottle and filled her glass.

"Uh. Thanks, Jacqueline." I smiled uncertainly. "The police always look at the spouse first. Since she was the one that hired me, it doesn't fit this case."

"Maybe she did that to throw suspicion off of her," said Mrs. Chen. I conceded that she had a point.

"Is it too early for you to have found anything?" asked Mr. Chen.

"Nothing at the train station, bus terminal, or airport. No one remembers seeing him. I've spoken to his neighbors, his family, and the people at his work – and learned nothing. But I may have caught a break - a man at his garage told me that Sparrow got into a cab around noon on the day he disappeared. I found the cab company and spoke to the driver. He doesn't remember Sparrow, but his log sheet says he dropped him off on Courthouse Road in Gulfport."

"That's a pretty busy intersection. Have you found a motive for his disappearance?" Mr. Chen asked.

"There's no obvious financial motive, but that still leaves the possibility of a more romantic motive."

"I read somewhere that it was an interracial marriage," said Mrs. Chen. "In Chicago, you wouldn't bat an eye about that, but this is Mississippi. Could that not be a motive, especially after what happened earlier this year with that reporter for the *Herald*?" She was referring to the reporter who'd been found slain in his home on Christmas day. The deputies still had not found the body of his wife.

"There was a bit more to that than just race. Most people believe the reporter was about to blow the lid on the plot to bomb the NAACP rally in Hiller Park." I finished my glass of wine. "Anything's possible, but I uncovered two other pieces of the puzzle. When he called for the cab, he gave them a phony name."

"Logically," said Mr. Chen, "That would suggest he left on his own, and he knew people might come looking for him. What is the second piece of the puzzle?"

"He left his car at the garage. When I checked it out, it was immaculate except for the ashtray in the back seat. I found a cigarette butt with pink lipstick. Sparrow's wife, my client, wears blood-red lipstick."

"Sounds like he was cheating on his poor wife with some tramp," said Jacqueline.

***

Later that evening, after the Chens had gone home, we were getting ready for bed. Jacqueline opened the bathroom door where she was brushing her hair, dressed only in her bra and panties. "Gabriel, Rachel is a beautiful girl. Is she still seeing Don?"

"I don't know. She says it's complicated. They were to go out tonight to talk about what's happening with his job. I can't believe it, but the top people are trying to blame Don for all the people who died at the park that day. I'm so glad I'm not working for some big company and all of the bullshit."

"You find her attractive. Don't you?"

There you have it—the game continues. I could tell her the truth, and so would begin World War Three, or I can do the smart thing and lie my ass off. "Not as attractive as you, sweetie." A fleeting thought occurred to me. Was Rachel one of the reasons Jacqueline wanted me to get another job?

"I think she's lovely in a kind of plain Jane way."

My wife is not usually a bitch. Asking Rachel to drive me home must have gotten under her skin. "I guess I was lucky to have run into her the other night when I needed a ride. Otherwise, I would have called you - and you would have had to wake up Benjamin - bundle him up in the car seat. The whole production."

"Or called a cab. I should call her tomorrow, maybe invite her out for lunch."

Chapter 21

Mayor Baxter

Dear Diary,

Terrible day. It started okay but went downhill quickly. Wolf, my new best friend, got me out of a day-long job orientation and right into a cushy job in the machine shop where they make license plates. He said the pay was a whopping 10 cents an hour and that once I got used to the machines, the work wouldn't be hard. Today they were working on Alabama plates, which are white with the dark blue Heart of Dixie screened in the top left. They use large sheets of metal, which are stamped by an enormous press. Wolf, who showed me the ropes, also showed me how to make a shiv out of the scrap metal and then use black electrical tape to make a handgrip. He wanted me to start making them and said that it was a good idea to hide them in my mattress just in case my cellmate got any ideas.

So, here's the bad news. My lovely wife, Madge, came to visit me. Visitors need to be approved, and it surprised me when the guard asked if I wanted to see her. The only reason I consented was out of morbid curiosity. She hadn't returned any of my calls, and the last time I'd seen her was before my arrest. Our last conversation hadn't gone well. We were in our kitchen, and she was making a federal case about her little fuckbuddy, William Friesen, being found hanging by his necktie in a motel closet. I made a joke about him being too stupid to tie a proper knot. She didn't think that was funny. For the record, I told her I had nothing to do with his murder. She wouldn't let it go and followed me around the house, ranting about having had sex with a dead man. That's when I reminded her that he was likely alive at the time.

***

Madge and I met in a room with a long table divided in half by a glass wall. There were little air holes so you could hear what the other person was saying. I got there first and was surprised to see that we had to share the room with a half dozen other prisoners meeting with visitors.

I looked up as the guard ushered her in. She looked pretty hot. Her shoulder-length brown hair has always been a turn-on. I like pretty women with beautiful hair...and big tits. She has tremendous tits. Everybody says she does. Hers were even bigger than my cellmate's.

"Hello John," she said, taking off her coat and looking around the room. I looked up at her, but she avoided eye contact. Was it the sight of seeing her husband in an orange jumpsuit? Was she filled with remorse for not returning my calls? Surely, she's not still angry over Friesen?

"Hello, Madge. You look very nice. I like that dress…it accentuates your…" She harrumphed the compliment away and sat down. She was holding a brown legal-sized envelope. Maybe documents from Sexfinger on my appeal?

"How are you doing, John?"

I let out a deep sigh. I wished I could hold her and bury my face in her breasts. I wanted her to tell me that everything would be okay. I wanted to tell her the food sucks, my cellmate was a psycho, my only friend was a Nazi, and that some guy who looks like Al Capone wanted to show me his stiffy in the showers. "It's okay," I said bravely. "I hope Sexfinger is working on the appeal. The trial was rigged. Would you believe it? I should never have had Poncho Villa as my judge."

"The name is pronounced Sechfinger – And, he says he's not your lawyer."

"I'll call him…I was just kidding. The old man has no sense of humor."

"He asked me to tell you to stop calling him. He wants you to find another lawyer."

"Another lawyer? How come you know all this?"

"Well …," she paused and chewed her bottom lip. "As it turns out Larry, and I …. Well, he's working for me. On the divorce papers."

"You and Sexfinger?" I asked, making a nasty face. "Wait, wait, what did you say about a divorce?"

"I can't stay married to a convict. It's not who I am. I brought a copy of the divorce papers for you to look over."

"But … I'm going to be getting out any day now."

"Larry says they're going to throw the book at you. They want to set an example. He says maybe twenty years."

"Twenty years?" I couldn't believe my ears. "More like twenty days. Did you say Larry Sexfinger is your lover, and he drafted your divorce papers?"

"Sechfinger, and yes. He's quite good in bed."

"How could he be? He's an old Jew."

"Did you notice the size of his hands?"

Chapter 22

February 27th, 1985
Gulfport, Mississippi

Gabriel

It was another bright sunny day when I pulled into the strip plaza. I parked beside Rachel's Pacer and thought about my plans for the day. I was considering taking a drive down to Courthouse Road to see if any middle-aged black men were just hanging around. When I walked in the door, I found Rachel in the office meeting with someone.

I went into the lunchroom and watched Mr. Coffee do its thing. A thought flashed through my mind about warning Rachel that Jacqueline might call. I needed her to back up my story that I had just bumped into her the other night. Taking my coffee, I sat down at Rachel's desk and wondered who she could be meeting with this early. Her daytimer was on the desk, and I scrolled through it until I got to February 27th. There was an appointment scheduled with an RS at 8 AM. I thought about who RS could be. Red Skelton? Roger Staubach? Rod Steiger? I was thinking of why Ringo Star would want a detective when the phone rang. I answered, and my mood dropped when I heard Glenna Sparrow's voice. "How can I help you, Glenna?"

"It's been three days. I want to stop by and get an update. Will you be there in thirty minutes?" She sounded a little agitated.

"I'll be ..." Just then, the office door opened, and Rod Smith, the lawyer, came out. He gave me a quick smile and a wave as he left the building.

"Mr. Ross, I'll be there in thirty minutes," Glenna said before hanging up.

As I was putting down the receiver, Rachel was coming out of the office. Before she could say anything, I said, "I need to move my car."

"Why?"

"I'll tell you in a minute," I said, rushing out the door.

***

"You moved your car because you don't want Glenna Sparrow to think less of you because you're driving a pink bug?"

"I led her to believe that it wasn't mine. I moved it to a spot in front of the travel agent."

"Gabriel, if you're so embarrassed, then maybe that should tell you something."

"What was Rod in for?" I asked, changing the subject.

"I called him. My brother Jacob rented a house in Mobile near where he works. His partner, Louis, is a black man from Jamaica. He's here on a legal work visa. Even though Louis has a separate entrance and is not on the lease, a neighbor called the cops, and now it looks like my brother will get evicted. I called Rod because his law license allows him to practice in Alabama."

"And what did Rod say?"

"What it comes down to is, we can file for an injunction, and we might win this round. The risk we take is angering the local cops and making the situation worse. Homosexuality is still a crime there, and it could end up even worse. Rod said he'd be willing to file the injunction for free if that's what they want to do."

"What are you going to tell them to do?"

"He knew the risks. Jake's pretty stubborn. It wouldn't surprise me if he took this to the Supreme Court."

"Sorry, not to change subjects, but before I forget, Jacqueline might call you today, maybe offer to take you for lunch as a thank you for driving me home the other night."

"That's nice. She doesn't need to do that."

"Believe me, there's an ulterior motive. She has it in her head something is going on between us. She's upset about me calling you for the ride instead of her. I told her last night we were friends, and we just bumped into each other, and you offered me a ride."

"So, if she calls, you want me to tell her that I'm madly in love with you and that we've been carrying on this affair for months? How did this come up?"

"We had her folks over for dinner last night, and the subject of Dirk Sparrow came up. I told them we were thinking he was having an affair."

"Gabriel, did you ever tell Jacqueline about how we went out for a while when she left for Chicago?"

I looked at Rachel for a moment. "Are you insane? Don't get me wrong - I love my wife and have no desire to hurt her. Maybe, if I had said something when we initially got back together. To say something now... I know she'd be upset that we kept something from her. She already suspects there's something between us. So please - whatever happened in the past is no one's business but our own." Suddenly it occurred to me. "Did you tell Don?"

"No, but that's different. You're married. I'm still not sure Don and I are exclusive."

"Have you been seeing other guys?"

"No. But he might have hundreds of girlfriends. He's not very forthcoming. I've tried to bring it up a couple of times, but he can be so shifty." After a moment, she changed the subject. "And now Glenna Sparrow is coming here. You're not going to tell her that you think he was having an affair, are you?"

"You don't think I should?"

"I'd suggest playing your cards close to the vest for now. It's only been a couple of days, and that cigarette butt might have been in the backseat for months. What plans did you have for today?"

I told her my plan to cruise Courthouse Road. "After that, I wanted to call some people from the Rotary Club. I understood from Glenna that Dirk was a member."

***

"It's been three days. I take it you haven't found my husband," Glenna said, sitting in her usual seat.

This time she was wearing a one-piece floral jumpsuit with what looked like a chef's hat. Benjamin has one almost identical that Jacqueline calls a onesie. It looked expensive. "You'd be the first to hear if I did. To be precise, I never said I could find him. I said I was confident that we could find out what happened to him. Different thing."

She pulled out a pack of Benson and Hedges from her purse and lit up. I felt a sense of pride that I might have gotten her hooked again,

"Surely, you've done something in the past three days?"

Her tone was almost as annoying as her jumpsuit. "I'll have a preliminary report for you by the end of the week." I was tempted to tell her about her husband having an affair. Not because it was a good idea, but just because I thought it would make me feel better.

"Did you find the man from the bar?"

"His name is Bradley, and I have a line on the woman who called your house. Her name is Penn Maddox."

She looked impressed, "Did they have something to do with Dirk's disappearance?"

"It's too early to derive any conclusions. I hope to learn more soon." I stood up, signaling the meeting was over and that she should leave. Except, she didn't get the message. She continued sitting there, smoking her cigarette. I moved the ashtray closer again. "Have you thought of anything else that might help us?"

"I told you everything."

There was an awkward moment when I hovered over her waiting for her to leave. "I enjoyed meeting with your boys the other day. They're both handsome." I felt like saying they must be adopted. I decided to save that for another day.

Chapter 23

February 27th, 1985
Gulfport, Mississippi

Gabriel

It took less than ten minutes to get to where Dirk Sparrow had gotten out of the cab. It was a few miles north of the waterfront and had a strip mall on each corner. There were dozens of spots Dirk could have met someone and gone for lunch. As I drove south, I saw an occasional black man strolling down the road, but no one resembling Dirk. When I'd traveled the three miles to Ken Coombs Pier, I turned around and headed back - this time taking note of restaurants.

I let my mind wander. I'd spent most of my time trying to get a line on this Penn Maddox when she might not have had anything to do with Dirk's disappearance. My thoughts shifted to Glenna Sparrow and her annoying act in the office. The real reason I hadn't wanted to give her a progress report was because there hadn't been much. I had a lot of questions but wasn't closer to getting answers.

It would be understandable for any woman to freak out if her husband had been missing for five weeks. The problem was, she was acting. Her behavior didn't seem real. It felt like she was playing a part written for an upset spouse. The question was why? Was hiring me just a way to make it seem like she was upset about her husband? Was she worried that people were quietly whispering behind her back? Was that the reason she slammed the door in my face when I asked about insurance? Was she worried about what I might say to Weber?

I thought I was building a pretty good case against my client when I suddenly realized I had been driving north and hadn't been paying attention to the restaurants. Frustrated, I pulled into a strip plaza and was preparing to turn around when something caught my eye. It was a warehouse that had been turned into a fitness club called the Weight Date. Carl had said he thought Penn Maddox worked in some kind of club. Glenna also commented on Dirk's love handles. Could this be where he was going when he got out of the cab? I parked the bug and decided to check it out.

A very tall Swedish-looking blonde was at the reception desk. She was wearing an extra-small white t-shirt despite having Arnold Schwarzenegger's arms. "Welcome to the Weight Date! My name is Sonja," except it came out "Velc-ume-a-tu-zee veeeght dete."

"Thank you, Sonja." I took a quick look around. Off to the right, there was a room with a bunch of women doing yoga. Directly in front of me, the gym's main part had a smattering of people pumping iron.

"Are you looking to get rid of that winter flab?" She pronounced it fleb. I looked down and subconsciously held in my stomach. "Our motto is hustle to gain muscle."

"Listen, Sonja," I ignored her and put my business card down in front of her. "I am here on official business. A man by the name of Dirk Sparrow disappeared five weeks ago. I've traced his steps to this gym." Sonja looked at me with a slightly tilted head as if she was trying to decipher what I'd said. I put the picture of Sparrow in front of her and finger-stabbed the man in the photo a few times. "This is Dirk Sparrow. Is he a member here?"

"Hoo du yuoo knoo he-a ceme-a here?"

"I have a witness." I didn't want to tell her that I had just made it up.

"A veetness?"

"Can you look up his name on your computer and see if you have anything on him?" I felt like adding that it was important to American-Swedish relations.

"We don't have a cumpooter. Ev'rythin' is in files locked in th' owny's office."

"Can you ask him for the key?" I said, looking around. How many members could this place have? Fifty?

"He is on vacashun …in Erooba."

I decided to try a different tact. "Do you have a therapist by the name of Penn Maddox, white, blonde hair, kind of pretty?" She shook her head. Sonja was starting to rain on my parade. "Do you mind if I look around? See if I recognize anyone?"

"I can give you trial membership."

"I'll think about it." I walked by the room where the women looked like they were playing Twister. Of the dozen or so women, none matched Penn's description. I ventured off to where people were lifting weights. I could see that the building was much longer than I had thought. There was a bank of treadmills and ellipticals, as well as a bunch of nautilus machines. About three dozen people were working out. A quick survey yielded four black faces, one female and three males. The first two men I approached grunted that they didn't recognize the man in the photo. I finally hit pay dirt with the woman.

"Yeah, sure, I recognize him. I think he's a new member." The woman looked to be in her early forties, with a mahogany complexion. She was short, heavyset, and muscular with a ski jump for a nose. I looked at her camo sweats with the arms ripped off and then noticed she was wearing army boots.

"When was the last time you saw him?" I watched her change the fifty-pound weights on the bench press.

"It's been a while. Some people join and burn out quick-ly. I just figured he wimped out." She lay down on the bench and told me to spot for her.

"Did you ever speak to him?"

In between lifts and grunts, "Said hello … a couple of times…. he was cute …., but I'm not his type."

"Why, because he was married?"

"Don't care…about that."

"Then why wouldn't you be his type?" A dozen reasons came to mind.

"Because…." She suddenly told me to grab the bar. I was surprised at how heavy it was. I barely got it back on the bar catcher. "… I'm not a snow bunny." Looking at the strain on my face, she added, "Not used to lifting?"

"No problem. I lift all the time. What's a snow bunny?"

"White women who like black men. Snow bunnies."

After a moment, she started lifting again. I prepared myself to catch it. "Why do you think he was interested in snow bunnies?"

"There was…this chick. … I haven't… seen her lately." She concentrated on the weights for a moment. "Maybe she works here… you know with new people… how to use the equipment." She paused again before continuing, "I could be wrong …but I thought something … was going on."

Once again, I labored to get the bar on the catcher. "Women can tell when men have a thing for other women."

A thought flashed into my mind about that conversation with Jacqueline about Rachel. "Can you describe her?"

"Mid-twenties, kind of pretty, good figure. Oh, and she wore her blonde hair in a ponytail."

"Know her name?"

"Nope."

I thanked the woman and got her name and number just in case I had more questions. I showed the picture to a couple of more people and got a couple of more grunts, and head shakes.

Stopping by the front desk, I approached Sonja. "A woman inside recognized the man. He's definitely a member here. I need to see his file."

"Sefen days. Oovner veell be-a beck in sefen deys."

"She also described a woman that was helping him and thought she might work here." I repeated the description, adding, "She might have recently quit because the woman hasn't seen her for a while. Her name is Penn Maddox."

"Ve-a oonly hefe-a svedeesh gurls."

Chapter 24

Mayor Baxter

Dear Diary

The conversation with Madge enraged me. I thought about what happened and came up with all the things I should have said after she left. She's an extremely low IQ person. She was nothing but a little gutter slut until she met me. I gave her a life fit for a queen. Now she's getting schlonged by a Jew. I wanted to throw up at the thought.

I'm starting to think everything that is happening to me is a vast conspiracy. The left-wingers out there got together and somehow corrupted the legal system against me. That Ben O'Shea and his little midget friend testified that I had embezzled money. They even said that I had arranged for Friesen's murder.

I called my friend Dietz. He told me that Corbin Masters was dying of cancer. That's too bad. Corbin always donated to my campaigns. A true patriot. Oh, well. I asked Dietz about the riots over my conviction in Biloxi. He said he had heard some grumblings but that the town's mood had been weird since the bombings. It was like the whole town was waiting for the niggers to hit back.

He was referring to a few bombs that went off at Hiller Park. Apparently, some disgruntled MBI agent went rogue. If I had been allowed to continue as mayor, the bombings would never have happened. My view as mayor has always been that to control crime, you had to allow it to breathe. If you try to clamp down too hard, you end up with a city where people are too scared to go outside.

I told Dietz about Sexfinger and Madge and how I felt betrayed. He said I should never have trusted a Jew. I told him that I had left numerous messages on Sexfinger's answering machine, saying I would write to the Mississippi Bar. I think fucking your client's wife should be enough to get him disbarred. Dietz said he would ask around and send me a real lawyer.

Big news about Al Capone. Wolf told me it was now safe for me to use the showers. Apparently, someone stuck a shiv up his ass.

Chapter 25

Gabriel

When I got back to the Agency, Rachel was eating her lunch in the office. I went straight to the chalkboard and drew a line down the middle. On one side, I wrote <u>Reasons Why I Think Glenna Is A Murderer,</u> and on the other, I wrote <u>Reasons Why Dirk Took Off with A Floozy.</u> I started jotting down points on both sides.

"You can't put she's 'butt ugly' under both headings," protested Rachel.

I wiped off 'butt ugly' and replaced it with the word 'divorce.' "I think he finally woke up and realized that the kids weren't his. I think he asked her for a divorce. She'd be too embarrassed to let that happen and didn't want to lose half of her money."

"You're just assuming this, right?"

"It all makes sense."

"Why would she hire us?"

"To throw suspicion off of her. Hear me out. If this were a murder case with a body, the cops would stay on this as a cold case for as long as it took. But what did Weber do when he got busy? He punted the ball to us and said he thought Dirk just skipped town with a floozy. Glenna decided to go along with this and hired a shlep to look into it because she knew I'd never find the body. This morning she barged in here demanding an update. You should have seen her act."

"You're convincing me that you don't like her."

"I think she arranged that whole taxi thing and deliberately gave the dispatcher a phony name to make it look like he was running away. Then she got her accomplice to get in the cab."

"Didn't you say Carl saw his boss get into that cab?" When I didn't answer, Rachel got up and grabbed the marker away from me. She wrote 'cigarette butt' under the floozy column.

"Alright, I'll admit I have no idea what's going on here." I told Rachel about the visit to the Weight Date and finding a woman who could positively identify Dirk as working out as a member with another woman matching Penn Maddox's description.

"That's wonderful, Gabriel. You've traced his steps to this gym. That's something concrete you could put in your report."

"How about this. Let's say he discovers that another guy was plowing Glenna's cornfields and decides that what's good for the goose is good for the gander, or vice versa. I keep forgetting. They have a huge fight, and she kills him."

"Oh, my God! I want to be here when she reads that in your report."

"I also learned a new term from that witness at the gym. 'Snow bunny.' Have you heard that before?

"It's what you call a white woman who prefers black men."

"Why haven't I heard about this? We have Dirk and Glenna, Dirk, and this Penn Maddox, and remember that guy from the *Herald* who was murdered last Christmas?"

"Green."

"Why is there so much of this?" I asked, throwing my hands in the air.

"Probably because it's legal. The laws in Mississippi have changed."

"Why would a woman choose a man outside her race?"

"You did."

Hmm. I hadn't thought about that. "Touché."

"There are probably all kinds of reasons. Because they're in love comes to mind. In high school, this would have been before the law changed, one of the girls, a white girl named Janet Pettibon, dated a black football player from another school. It was quite the scandal. People were on her like white on rice. I remember seeing 'slut' spray-painted on her locker. Of course, there's the sex thing. And that goes both ways. White girls might be curious about black men and rumors about them being better endowed. Black men might think snow bunnies are more sexually available. As for Janet, I always thought she was the type of girl that craved attention, and this was her way of saying, 'look at me."

"So, in Glenna's case, what do you think?"

"I've never even met the lady, but you did say she had that statue..."

***

The rest of the afternoon was a bust. I spent two hours waiting for a man named Preston Merrick of Merrick, Merrick, and Merrick's law firm to call me back. There might actually have been four Merricks. I got his name from the Chamber of Commerce, where he was listed as the President of the Rotary Club of Biloxi. While waiting for the callback, I started drafting a report for Glenna.

Dear Mrs. Sparrow,

The results of our preliminary investigations into your husband's disappearance are, as of this date, inconclusive. We have made significant process in retracing your husband's footsteps before his disappearance. We have determined that he was a member of the Weight Date Fitness Club. We've uncovered both the female caller's identity and the individual who created the disturbance at the bar called Shaggy's.

It's our current theory that Dirk Sparrow was the victim of foul play. Our working notion is that Mr. Sparrow communicated his desire for a divorce. We believe that you used the penis statue you prominently display on your mantle to bludgeon him to death. We also believe that you and an unnamed individual buried him beneath the Star Wars swing set you have in the yard.

Yours truly,

Gabriel Ross

***

I shook off the stupid thoughts and threw the paper in the trash, trying to concentrate on what might help me with this puzzle. I got a sudden brainwave and picked up the phone. A voice I recognized as belonging to Carl answered.

"How are you making out, Mr. Ross?"

"Making some progress. I haven't found Dirk yet, but I'm getting closer every day. Listen, Carl, I thought of another question."

"I'm kind of busy on account of Kenny not showing up for his shift."

I paused for a moment letting the silence creep into the conversation. Finally, Carl said, "Ah, what the hell, what can I do for you?"

"When I was there earlier this week, I commented on how clean Dirk's car was, and you said he was fussy that way."

"Yeah, I remember."

I decided to take a calculated gamble. "Who told you to clean the car?"

A long moment of silence prompted me to repeat my question. "Carl, it's a simple question. Who told you to clean the car?"

"Mrs. Sparrow told me to clean it up for him."

"That's what I thought." It was time to twist the knife a bit further. "Did you find anything interesting?" *Like a bloody knife?*

"No, as I said, he was pretty fussy about his car."

"You forgot to clean the ashtray in the back seat. I found a cigarette butt. It had pink lipstick. What shade of lipstick does Glenna wear?"

"I don't know."

"Let me help you, Carl. She wears blood-red lipstick."

There was silence on the line. Carl then started to sound defensive. "So what? I missed a cigarette butt. Are you going to tell Mrs. Sparrow or something?"

"No, of course not, but I have one final question. It won't take a minute." I didn't wait for him to throw up the stop sign. "Ever hear or see anything that made you wonder about the Sparrow's marriage? That maybe one or the other, or both, might be having a fling?"

Carl's tone was a little edgier when he replied. "I told you the other day. Glenna Sparrow was all the woman Dirk needed."

Interesting. He didn't say it worked the other way. "Alright. Did you say Kenny didn't show up for work today?"

"I called his house, and there's no answer, so I figure he's probably on his way."

"I hope so. I know you're busy, but I need to ask him a couple of questions about the report I'm preparing for Glenna. She's really anxious for it. Can you ask him to call me back when he has a moment?"

***

Kenny called me back about thirty minutes later. I told him I only had a few questions about the incident at the bar on January 8th.

"We were there because I proposed to my girlfriend, and the guys wanted to buy me a couple of rounds to celebrate."

"Congratulations. Let's start by describing the table, where everyone, including this girl, was sitting."

"Well, let's see, there was Dirk and then the girl, I don't remember her name. Then there was Mitch and then Carl and then me."

"Do you remember much of the conversation at the table?"

"No, not really. It was pretty loud in there. Someone asked her about the guy who had started everything, and she said he couldn't take no for an answer. I think Mitch asked her where they'd met, and she said something about a club. I assumed she meant nightclub, but Mitch told me later she meant fitness club. Mitch's not here right now, but he was closer and might be able to tell you more."

"Maybe you can ask him to get back to me. Can you describe her, maybe what she was wearing?"

"Plaid shirt and blue jeans. She had blonde hair...like in a ponytail. Oh, and she wore those big hoop earrings because I remember thinking they'd be heavy."

"Did you think she was pretty?"

"Pretty enough, I guess. Not as pretty as my girlfriend, though."

"You'd better start calling her your fiancée."

"Right."

"One last question, Kenny, are you black?"

"That's Mitch. I'm the white guy."

Chapter 26

February 27th, 1985
Gulfport, Mississippi

Gabriel

I should never have taught Benjamin to throw snow-balls at his mother. That was the argument Jacqueline was using as Benjamin hit her with another pea in the face. Dinner was meatloaf, courtesy once again of Mrs. Chen. Benjamin was sitting in his high chair, and while he liked the meatloaf well enough, he didn't like his mother telling him to eat his peas. His response was to hurl one after another at her. Of course, I thought it was funny. He had remarkable precision for a two-year-old. With each new strike, he would kick out his feet and laugh hilariously.

When I saw the steam coming out of Jacqueline's ears, I showed him a new trick. Holding a pea in my hand, I slapped my forearm while launching the pea into my mouth. Benjamin's eyes lit up as if it was magic and tried to replicate. I finally gave up and said 'yum-yum,' showing him the mushed-up peas in my mouth. Once again, he started to laugh.

"That's great, Gabriel. First, you teach him to throw his food, and now you teach him to eat with his mouth open."

"I didn't teach him to throw his peas, he figured it out for himself. Your dad thinks he has above average intelligence."

"If he does, he didn't get that from you."

***

Thankfully the mood improved later in the evening after we took Jelly Bean to the park and let him chase the squirrels. Next, a bath and a bedtime book, and he finally fell into a deep sleep. Jacqueline and I relaxed on the couch. I had the latest edition of *Time Magazine* while she was reading *Soap Opera Digest*. Since she'd started back to work, she was worried about missing *Another World*.

"Did you have a good day?" I asked, testing the waters.

"Fine...I sold a painting. It was a John Armistead. Remember the one of Sun Studios?"

"Sure, nice." Emphasizing nice as if I was impressed. To be honest, I had no idea what an Armistead was or about the painting.

After a moment, she asked, "Any developments on the case?"

"Some. I think we said we wouldn't discuss my work. You didn't want me to bring it home."

"Right. It's just that you talked about it at dinner yesterday."

"That's because your father asked. I was being polite."

"Fine. What's on the cover of *Time* magazine?"

"Bernard Goetz, the subway vigilante in New York - the one who shot those four muggers. The writer thinks he's going to be acquitted."

"As well he should. Just like in that movie with Charles Bronson."

I was just about to suggest that we head to bed and have a game of Jeopardy. When we'd first started seeing each other, we'd adopted a code for having sex. One, because she was a married woman whose husband was a crazed lunatic who later tried to murder us, and two, because I liked to hum the theme song while we were fooling around. Now, when we're out at a party, and she wants to go home, she'll start humming the theme song.

We were interrupted by the phone. Jacqueline was sitting nearest and answered. "Who'd be calling at this time of night?" she asked before answering. I watched as a cloud quickly came over her face. "Can I ask who this is?"

She handed me the phone. "It's a woman named Wendy."

I raced to grab the phone, tripping over one of Benjamin's toys and falling flat on my face. Jacqueline gave me a pitiful look as I held my hand up for the phone.

"Wendy, is she there?"

"Was that your wife, Gabriel?"

"Yes."

"She seems a little frosty."

I ignored the comment and repeated myself, "Is she there?"

"No, I just wanted to test the system." There was silence on the line before she added, "And I thought of something else."

"What's that?"

"You said she was a blonde. The last time she was here, I stood over her table, waiting for her to fish some money out of her purse, and I noticed brown roots. I think you should be looking for a brunette."

"A brunette?"

"Yeah, I thought you'd want to know. That is if you haven't already found her."

"Thanks, that's great. I'm still looking for her."

"Is everything okay, Gabriel? You seem a little pre-occupied. I hope I didn't ruin your evening."

"No, it's okay, just sitting around waiting for you to call." I was pre-occupied. While I was talking to Wendy, Jacqueline steamed to the hall closet, got down the spare bedding, and dumped it on the couch. I watched as Hurricane Jacqueline veered off into the bedroom.

"How's the search coming?" Wendy asked. I could hear crowd noises, so I figured she was at the bar.

"I'm getting closer, I think. I traced the missing man's movement to a fitness club called the Weight Date. He's been working out with a woman that matches the description of this Penn Maddox."

"That's something. What's next?"

"I have a couple of more leads."

"Have you staked out any of the other bars?"

"No, but the girl at the Weight Date said I looked flabby. I might sign up for a trial membership and see who shows up."

"Great idea. You don't look flabby to me. Listen, I better let you get back to frosty."

Chapter 27

February 27th, 1985
Talladega, Alabama

Mayor Baxter

Dear Diary,

The evening meal was supposed to be meatloaf and mashed potatoes. I'd call it bullshit with a side order of instant glue. Wolf told me the cost of feeding an inmate was less than a buck a day. He also said that if a warden can save money on Alabama's food budget, they get to keep the cash tax-free. And to think, I'm in prison for taking a few bribes.

Sexfinger didn't want to take my call. I heard him tell the operator that he didn't know a John Baxter. Finally, after the third try, he accepted the call but said he had nothing to discuss as he wasn't my lawyer. I told him I'd been joking and that I needed to know what progress had made on the appeal. After a little back and forth, I reminded him that he had said there were grounds. Sexfinger tried to play dumb, so I asked about Judge Ramirez. "He's not a real American. Shouldn't I be entitled to have a real judge?"

"Judge Ramirez is a third-generation American who just happens to be of Mexican heritage. He's well respected in the legal community."

I told him that many people at last night's dinner had said he wasn't qualified. He probably got his law degree in Tijuana for fifty bucks. Plus, I saw him eating a burrito on the bench. Sexfinger said something stupid about everyone at dinner being a criminal and that, for some reason, their opinion didn't matter.

I instructed Sexfinger to get me released right away, preferably before my next meal.

Chapter 28

Gabriel

By the time Rachel got to the agency, I was sitting in the office with a coffee and a box of Krispy Kreme donuts.

"Good morning. Aren't you the eager beaver?" She slung her coat over her chair and came into the office. She was wearing a green cowl neck sweater and a cream-colored pleated skirt.

"I snuck out early. I didn't want to wake anyone."

She watched me swallow half a honey donut. "Did you know the guy who made those was a Nazi?"

"I happen to know her name is Shanice, and she's not a Nazi."

"I meant the company. A former Nazi founded it. Look it up, Larry Bremmer, the editor of the *Herald*, told me."

I continued chewing my donut and nudged the box closer to her.

"I only eat those when I'm upset." When I didn't respond, she gave me a funny look, "Is everything alright, Gabriel?"

"Everything is wonderful," I said, in between chews. "I made coffee,"

She started to walk to the kitchen and then turned, "I forgot to tell you. Jacqueline called; I'm meeting her for lunch in Ocean Springs tomorrow. Any tips?"

'I'm not qualified to give advice where she's concerned. I slept on the couch again last night."

"She still hasn't forgiven you over your drunken episode?"

"Wendy called last night."

"The bartender from the Blind Tiger? Did she spot the girl?"

"No. she remembered something about the girl that might be important. Penn Maddox might be a brunette. While she was serving her, she noticed the girl had brown roots. Anyway, Jacqueline happened to answer the phone, and I think it might have inflamed her jealousy bone. The next thing I knew, I was couching it."

"That's too bad. I'll try to put a good word in for you at lunch."

"What about Don? Has he heard anything?"

"No, he thinks they're dragging it out, hoping he'll quit. I'm worried about him. It's eating him up. He feels he has to go after the people responsible for the bombing and make them pay."

"Did you want me to talk to him? I got let go from Ford by a bunch of knuckleheads, and I got over it."

"Good idea, maybe the four of us could go for dinner. But it'll have to wait. He's gone bass fishing in Arkansas."

"Sounds like a good thing to do to get himself straightened out."

"What about the case?" Rachel asked, taking a bite of my donut.

"Carl said that Glenna told him to clean the car."

"And that is important …why?" She asked with a quizzical smile.

"Because, maybe she killed him in the car."

"Pretty thin if you ask me. I bet his car, like the business, and the house, is in her name, and she just wants to sell it. It's been over five weeks."

"That's cold. If something happens to me, I want you to make sure that Jacqueline doesn't sell the Bug for at least three months."

***

I was still eating a donut when I told Rachel my plan to join the Weight Date and get rid of the flab.

"What are you trying to do - fatten up first so that you can say you lost weight?"

"Something like that." We were interrupted by the phone. "It's Preston Merrick of Merrick, Merrick, Merrick, and Merrick," said Rachel, handing me the phone.

"Hello, Mr. Merrick, thanks for returning my call."

"I'm sorry about yesterday, Mr. Ross. I was in back-to-back meetings. You know what that's like."

I didn't. "That's okay. I only have a few questions."

"You told my secretary this has something to do with Dirk Sparrow. I spoke to a deputy a while back. Nice chap. He was some kind of expert on the Rotary Club."

"Sorry if I cover some of the same ground you've discussed with Deputy Weber. He has referred Mr. Sparrow's disappearance to me. I'm not that familiar with your organization, so maybe you can enlighten me."

"What would you like to know, Mr. Ross?"

"Forgive me for speaking bluntly. My impression of the Rotary Club is it's a bunch of wealthy, old white guys." I had just finished reading an article in the *Herald* about Birmingham's Rotary Club and how they were steadfastly refusing to allow African American businessmen to join.

Merrick paused for a moment, and I thought I'd offended him. "I've heard that before. We're trying hard to have our membership mirror the community. We were quite proud that a colored chose to join our club."

"How many...African American members do you have?"

"Dirk's our first. But once you see one. If you know what I mean."

I'd thought that saying was about cockroaches. "How long has Dirk been a member?"

"Not long, maybe a year."

"How did his membership come about?"

"His wife, Glenna, made the introduction. She's a client of mine and suggested that her husband get to know some of the other business people."

"I'm trying to get a sense of Dirk. It might help me find out what happened to him. How would you describe him as a member?"

"You know, I didn't really know him. Other than to say hi. He seemed to be an affable chap."

"Did he have any special friends at the club? Someone I could talk to about him?"

"No one special comes to mind. But feel free to contact anyone in the club. I can have my secretary fax you the current roster."

***

As I drove to the fitness center, I thought about Preston Merrick of Merrick, Merrick, Merrick, and Merrick. I didn't think that he had anything to do with Dirk's disappearance, but the conversation had served to remind me that this was Mississippi. On the one hand, he said he was proud of his token black man in the club, but on the other hand, a year later, he still hadn't taken the time to get to know Dirk and couldn't think of anyone who had. I thought about snow bunnies and wondered whether Dirk's interracial marriage was a factor in whatever had happened to him.

Chapter 29

February 28th, 1985
Little Rock, Arkansas

Don

I slipped into the booth across from Jethro. We were in a fast-food diner in Little Rock.

"What the fuck?" asked Jethro, stopping mid-bite of his beans and wieners.

"Hello, Jethro. How you been keeping?"

"I can't do this, man." His eyes darted around the diner.

"How are the beans?" I smiled. Jethro, who couldn't have been twenty-five, looked scared. I'd had no problem finding him once Rachel showed me the *Herald* article about the FBI siege in Elijah, Arkansas. The siege had wound up a couple of days ago, with the leaders taken into custody. The other fifty or so members of the camp scattered. I just had to wait and tail Jethro to the diner.

"I don't want to be seen with you, man."

"Alright, I hear you.

"What do you want?"

"Not here. Finish your beans. I'll be waiting in that black pickup." I pointed to my truck parked in front of the diner. "We'll go for a little drive."

"What if I don't want to?"

"I have no desire to hurt you, Jethro. I owe you my life."

***

Fifteen minutes later, I was driving south on Highway 65 towards Pine Bluff. "So, you never answered my question, Jethro. How have you been keeping?"

"Oh fuck, what a mess!" He looked out the window, breathing a deep sigh.

"Do you mean the clusterfuck that just happened at the camp or the clusterfuck you were part of in Biloxi?"

"I wasn't part of that, remember? I was just there for the march. I tried to warn you."

"As I've learned recently, Jethro, trying isn't good enough."

"I heard they're hanging it all on you."

"Well, trying to. We'll just see about that."

"They told us the bombings were all your idea - you're some disgruntled MBI agent."

"Well, I am a little disgruntled, but the bombings were all Jackson Lange, his brother, and that Fender guy."

We drove in silence for a few minutes. I needed to find a way to enlist Jethro's help if I wanted to bring Bubba Lange and the others to justice. If I pushed too hard, I risked losing him. "I never properly thanked you for what you did at the camp. By covering for me, I was able to stop the killing from being even worse than it was." Jethro didn't respond, instead, he just looked out the side window. "I remember you saying you didn't sign up for killing people."

"I said I didn't cotton with killing people, even niggers."

"Right. You know, I don't think they like being called that."

"What the fuck do you want?"

"As I said, I wanted to say thank you. What you did was brave and saved lives."

We drove through the town of White Hall, neither of us saying anything. Finally, Jethro spoke up. "People gonna recognize you. There are lots of the militia hanging around here after what happened at the camp."

"Thanks for the warning. I don't understand why you're involved with these idiots if you aren't into killing people."

"We need to protect our race," he said as if quoting from some training manual. "There are more and more brown and black people in this country. As Bubba says, by the time the next generation comes around, we'll be in the minority."

"So, the answer is killing everyone that isn't white?"

"I said, I'm not into that."

"How did you ever get involved in the militia and that phony-baloney church?"

"I met Barry MacGloyn, and he introduced me to his father." Barry MacGloyn was the bomb maker who I'd killed that day in the park. His father was a Baptist preacher who had not only promoted the event to his black parishioners - he'd rented a bus for them.

I looked over at Jethro and figured I wasn't going to deprogram the young man. He probably had been fed a steady dose of hatred since he was young. "Where are you going to go now, Jethro?"

"I don't know. I might go back home."

"Where's that?"

"Beattyville, Kentucky. My folks have a double-wide. I can probably stay there for a spell."

I turned the truck around and headed north on Highway 65 back towards Little Rock. I knew that once Jethro got out of the truck, I'd likely lose touch with him. A few miles from the diner, I decided to go for broke. "How do you feel about the people responsible for the bombings getting off scot-free?"

"Jackson's dead. You killed McGloyn. Fender, he's in jail."

"I was referring to the men who organized it."

"I reckon it's not right, but if the Government decides not to arrest them, then there ain't nothing Jethro Coyle's got to say about it."

They drove to the diner, and surprisingly Jethro didn't rush out of the truck. "Got a place to stay?" I asked, turning off the ignition.

"I usually sleep in my truck."

I grabbed a pen from the dash and wrote my home address and number on a scrap of paper. "If you want, you can bunk at my place."

Chapter 30

February 28th, 1985
Talladega, Alabama

Mayor Baxter

Dear Diary

I'm in a bit of a funk. I keep thinking about Madge and that Jew in bed laughing at me. But I don't want to dwell on the negative. Koenig told me that he thought I had lost weight. I think I have. I'm not sure if it's the stress or the lousy food.

I'm getting a new roommate tomorrow. The ape was sent to solitary. I have to come clean about something. I'd gotten a head's up from Wolf about a cell inspection. When they came, they said they were looking for weapons because of a man being hurt in the showers. They tore our cell apart. They didn't find anything on my side, but they found a homemade shiv under the ape's mattress. Of course, he denied any knowledge and said I had put it there.

Koenig asked me if the shiv was mine, and I said no, but that I had seen the ape with it more than once. I whispered to the guard that he'd said he was going to stick some homo in the showers with it.

Chapter 31

February 28st, 1985
Gulfport, Mississippi

Rachel

I put the phone down, growing increasingly frustrated. I'd spent the last hour calling car rental companies. If Dirk Sparrow didn't catch a plane, hop on a bus or board a train, he might have left by car. Since his car was at the garage, then calling the rental companies sounded like a brilliant idea. I still thought it was a good idea when Alamo said they had no rentals for a Dirk Sparrow. It dropped down to a fair idea when Avis said the same. When I hung up from Budget, I thought the idea was looking shaky. When Hertz said they had nothing on Dirk Sparrow, I realized I'd wasted my time.

This brought to mind the mystery girl and how we seemed to be spinning our wheels, trying to find someone who might have had nothing to do with the disappearance. Weber had said there was no Penn Maddox in the state, but there was a Penelope Maddox up in Vicksburg with over a hundred traffic tickets.

I picked up the phone and dialed Weber's number. "Hey, it's Rachel. Got a minute?" I asked once Weber came on the line.

"For you, of course." He munched on something.

"Did I catch you at the wrong time? It sounds like you're eating."

"Just a Krispy Kreme."

"I'm surprised you didn't go fishing in Arkansas with Don, seeing how you two are so buddy-buddy these days."

"I would have if I wasn't so busy. You know, I'm quite the angler. I probably could have given him a few pointers. I remember one time I was bass fishing up north..."

"Listen, Weber," I interrupted. "I was calling about the woman with the hundred traffic tickets up in Vicksburg."

"Oh yeah... Penelope Maddox. You don't have to worry about her. I already notified the Warren County Sheriff's Department," he said officiously. "You can't let people get away with not paying their tickets."

"Can you just get me the address? I want to ask if she has a family member named Penn Maddox."

"Oh, I get it."

Luckily, I was able to get the woman's address without having to hear the fishing story.

***

The number for Gettinger Gardens was easy to find, and after a brief delay, I was put through to a feeble-sounding woman who identified herself as Penelope Maddox.

"Hi, Mrs. Maddox, my name is Rachel…"

"What-r-ya-selling?" she interrupted in a loud voice.

"I'm not selling anything…."

"Then, you the police?" She interrupted again. "I'm not paying those frikin tickets. You already took my license, so what do you want now… blood?"

"I'm not with the …"

"You know, I don't care what you do," the woman said, raising her voice. "I'm gonna drive my Jeep every Sunday down to the Dairy Queen and have me a shake. I don't give two shits about having a driver's license."

This wasn't working, so I tried a different tactic. "I love milkshakes. What's your favorite?"

"Chocolate, of course," she said indignantly as if daring me to say otherwise.

"I'm not with the police, and I don't care about your tickets." I was about to say I was a detective but decided it might be wise to approach things differently. "I was trying to get in touch with Penn Maddox."

There was a pause on the line. I could almost hear the rusty wheels of the old lady's mind start to turn.

"And who the hell are you to be asking about my granddaughter?"

I tried to keep the excitement out of my voice. "School…I knew her in school. I wanted to reconnect."

"You the blonde with the big coconuts?"

I laughed. "Well, you got me, Mrs. Maddox."

"I used to be known for my hooters. They were a hell of a lot better than you see in those titty magazines. Still are. I oil them up every night. I still get them out now and then and flash the orderlies. They don't pay those poor nigras anything, so what the hell, might as well give them a show."

I tried to blank out the image from my mind. "Do you still stay in touch with Penn?"

"Her name's Penny or Penelope," the old woman corrected. "She lit out of here when she was fifteen years old. Took up with the pervert who ran the funeral home. There's no way I want him running his hands over me, even if I'm dead."

"Is she still with him…. the funeral home guy?"

"I don't know. He skipped town on account of everyone talking about what they caught him doing to one of the bodies."

"What did they catch him doing?"

"Let's just say he was using his own brand of embalming fluid."

"You think Penny might be mixed up with him?"

"I don't know. I got a postcard last year," Mrs. Maddox said. I heard what sounded like papers rustling. "I think they threw it out. The people here are terrible. They call it Gettinger Gardens. I call it Get-me-out-a-here-Gardens. I remember the picture on the postcard was of Mo-beehl."

"What can you tell me about Penny?"

"You said you knew her from high school. Y'all probably know her better than me. She lived with me for a few years after her mamma threw her out. Come to think about it, that girl was messed up even before she took up with the pervert."

"I didn't know she was thrown out of her home."

The old lady's tone grew softer as she whispered. "I don't rightly know what all went on over there - likely something to do with Penny's mother. You ask me, that woman weren't never been right in the head. But this here is all ancient history, on account of the farm burning to the ground. Penny should be glad she got out before that; otherwise, she'd probably be dead too."

"Can I give you my number in case you happen to hear from her?" I gave her the agency number. Before we ended the call, she made me promise to take care of my coconuts.

Chapter 32

February 28th, 1985
Gulfport, Mississippi

Gabriel

I stumbled back into the Agency at 4 PM. Rachel was immediately alarmed when I collapsed on the couch in the office. "My God, Gabriel, your face is all flushed. What happened?"

"Sonja, that woman from the club, tried to kill me. She probably killed Dirk the same way."

"Oh! I get it. You overdid it. You're going to feel it tomorrow."

"I feel it now." I groaned. "She said we'd start slow with some simple 'eerubeec' exercises to get rid of my 'fleb.' Then, each time I got tired and stopped, she ordered me to do five pushups. I couldn't even do one because she kept putting her big foot on my back."

"Sounds like the fitness club was a good idea. Maybe a little overdue."

"Ugh...then came the frickin' weights. She was supposed to be my spotter but wouldn't until I had done like...a thousand sets."

"Um…sounds like an exaggeration."

"It was at least ten. I'm not going back."

"I don't suppose you saw Dirk or Penn Maddox?"

"Who? Uh, no. I asked Sonja if you and I could split the membership. You could go during the week, and I could use it on… Sundays."

"Hey! Don't I get a say in that?"

"Let's discuss it later. I think I need to lie quietly for a while. Can you turn off the light on your way out?"

Rachel turned off the light and covered me with a blanket, which I promptly kicked off. Before leaving, Rachel said, "Don't forget tomorrow's Friday. You promised your girlfriend you'd have an update for her."

What seemed like a minute later, Rachel came back into the office and turned on the light. "I know you're resting, but I thought you'd want to know that I haven't been sitting around wasting time. Remind me to tell you about the rental cars." I opened one eye and looked at her. I let out a deep groan. She then turned around and switched off the light again.

A few minutes later, she was back and turning on the light again. "And, I think I have a fresh lead on your mystery girl."

"What lead?" I whined.

"Never mind, you need your rest." Rachel turned the light off and went back to her desk. She was demonstrating a tactic women have been using since there were cavemen. Tease out something important, then watch as their caveman falls all over themselves to find out.

I got up. "Start with the rental cars."

"Okay, I was thinking, if Dirk and this mystery woman left town and didn't take a plane, train or bus, how would they do it if his car was at the garage. So, I called Hertz, Tilden, and Alamo. None of them have any record of either Dirk Sparrow or Penn Maddox."

That hardly seemed worth waking someone up over. "They could have just taken her car. What about the girl?"

"Do you remember, or maybe you don't…after your drunken episode, I told you Weber ran a search for Penn Maddox? The only name he could find was some little old lady in Vicksburg with a hundred tickets, named Penelope Maddox.

"I remember you telling me this."

Rachel explained about speaking to Penelope Maddox and what she had said about her granddaughter. "So at least we know where to look for her."

Chapter 33

February 28th, 1985
Talladega, Alabama

Mayor Baxter

Dear Diary,

Charlie Manson is my new roommate. I called him Charlie, and he corrected me and said his name was Robbie Bintwater. He told me he was arrested in Houston on a drug rap, and his mistake was dealing on some spic's turf. A rich, white kid who was buying from him bragged to some friends about his great dealer. Before he knew it, a bunch of spics caught wind and threatened to cut his eyes out. Charlie, thinking one alley was as good as another, just moved. The spics found him and told their crooked cop friends that someone was muscling in, eating into the profits. That's when the DEA agents broke down his door and hauled him off to jail.

Charlie got his hair shaved off as part of the 'Welcome to Talladega' pitch. He looks even more like a crazed psycho. He won't ever be cellmate of the year, but at least he speaks, and I don't have to worry about him going nuts on me in the middle of the night.

I should explain about the gangs here. Not everyone is in a gang, only about a third of the inmates. From what Wolf told me, there are four major groups. The first, of course, is the Aryan Brotherhood. He tells me that the AB has chapters in every prison, both State and Federal, in America. Roughly half of the AB members are in prison. The others are on the outside but still taking orders. Officially they all share an ideological desire for the white race's purity, but I suspect it's more about money. The Brotherhood controls the thriving drug trade here. Certain guards are paid to look the other way while others make even more by bringing cocaine and meth into the prison.

Next is the Mexican Mafia. For the past few years, there's been trouble between the AB and the Spics – mainly over drugs. I include the Cubans as a subsection of the Mexican Mafia because a spic is a spic, right? There are over a hundred Cubans here - boat refugees. A few work in the metal shop with me, and they're nasty little bastards. Wolf told me to stay clear of them.

Third, are the niggers, or as they're called here, the ants. Most are former gang bangers belonging to the Bloods or the Crips. As long as you don't cross them, they leave you alone.

Lastly, there are the wops like Al Capone. They're mostly older guys who keep to themselves and play bocce ball in the yard.

A word about homos. They're called girls in here. Just like on the outside, they sell their services. Gangs get protective of their girls - just like on the outside. If you want to visit them, you need to make arrangements. Wolf said Charlie would make a good girl and asked me to talk to him about it.

Chapter 34

February 28th, 1985
Gulfport, Mississippi

Gabriel

I thought about Penn Maddox all the way home. I decided to call Weber tomorrow and press him for another search of driver's licenses, this time in Alabama. I still hadn't made up my mind that Penn Maddox was even involved. A good part of me remained convinced that Dirk Sparrow was shacked up somewhere. If he was a victim of foul play, then Glenna Sparrow was still my prime suspect. I decided to call my partner Ben O'Shea tomorrow morning and get his counsel before giving Glenna an update.

***

Dinner was a subdued affair. It was as if the cone of silence had come down over the dinner table.

"Did you have a good time with Mamma Chen today, Benjamin?" asked Jacqueline. Benjamin hadn't mastered talking yet but understood most of what was said to him. He answered her question by making a squawking noise and pointing excitedly at the bowl of green Jell-O on the table. To counteract the infamous pea throwing, Jacqueline had made green Jell-O and put the peas in it. It was a cruel, evil trick.

"Eat your Jell-O, Benjamin," I said, making a gagging face which, of course, made him laugh. The gesture earned me a look of irritation from Jacqueline. I made up my mind that I needed to talk to Jacqueline about the case and the purpose of last night's call from Wendy for the sake of my marriage.

***

Once we'd finished cleaning up, Jacqueline bathed Benjamin, and I read him a bedtime story. After, I went into the living room where Jacqueline was sitting engrossed in the latest romance novel. "Honey, we need to talk. I want to tell you about the case and that phone call last night. I'm thinking you might be thinking it's something that it isn't."

"I put it out of my mind. Haven't given it another thought," she lied, keeping her eyes focused on her book. I knew she was lying - the book was upside down.

"That's good because once I tell you about it," …., *you'll see how foolish you've been*. I caught myself and added, "You'll understand."

"I thought we weren't going to discuss your work?"

"I know we said that, but I'd value your thoughts on the case. I'm due to give the client an update tomorrow, and I'm torn about what I've found out so far."

"Are we in any danger in this case? Is there a serial killer here?"

"No, nothing like that. It's a simple missing person case."

She finally lifted her eyes from her book and nodded for me to proceed. I took the next twenty minutes to summarize what we'd learned about the disappearance of Dirk Sparrow. I left nothing out, including Wendy recognizing the woman known as Penn Maddox, to my visit to the Weight Date and Rachel's conversation with the grandmother.

"Have you reached any conclusions about what happened?"

"The wife is a little odd, and part of me thinks I've been hired to make it seem like she's concerned about her husband. My theory is that he discovered that she was having an affair and asked for a divorce. That's when she killed him to protect her money."

"And I suppose you think the cigarette butt was planted to lead people to think he was having an affair? She figured a good detective would discover it."

"I hadn't thought about that, but maybe."

"This is all fine, Gabriel, but don't you need evidence?"

"Yes, of course. This brings me to the second theory and this mystery girl who called Dirk's house and spoke to their son. Let's say Dirk started an affair with this woman after the altercation in the bar. Maybe they decided to run away together."

"If that's the case, what's he doing for money? You said he hadn't touched his account or used his credit cards since he disappeared."

"Fair point. So, Wendy's call last night was to tell me she remembered something about the girl. Since she's met this girl and could recognize her, I've kind of deputized her."

"She sounded a little flirty on the phone."

I was amazed; they couldn't have said five words to each other, and Wendy thought Jacqueline was frosty, and Jacqueline thought Wendy was flirty. Neither was wrong. "There you have it. I know you're having lunch with Rachel tomorrow, so now you have some lunchtime discussion material. Any preliminary thoughts?"

"Mother asked whether this could be a racial thing, and you dismissed her quite rudely, saying you didn't think so. After what happened with the reporter, I think you should keep an open mind."

"I haven't discounted anything. Have you ever thought about being with a black man?"

"If I found one who treated me right, who respected and loved me. Who wouldn't lie to me or hide the truth from me, who wouldn't endanger my life or the life of my son...absolutely."

I smiled and waited for her passive-aggressive rant to be over. After a suitable pause, I brought it back to the case. "About the case..."

"I think the wife did it," she interrupted. "Your instincts are probably right, but you need proof. That part is not your problem. I would give the client her money back and then tell your friend Weber what you've discovered."

I was amazed at how clear everything was to her. I, on the other hand, had been dithering around for days, even when my gut told me Glenna Sparrow was a murderer.

Chapter 35

March 1st, 1985
Talladega, Alabama

Mayor Baxter

Dear Diary

I was told at breakfast that I needed to be in court for sentencing. They said a document had been left in my cell. I kind of remember seeing something, but frankly, reading's not my thing. Once again, I was taken by bus to Biloxi to be lectured by the Spic Judge. It didn't go well.

He started by asking me where Sexfinger was, and I told him that he had been fired for gross incompetence. I also said I had written a letter to the Mississippi Bar asking if they supported lawyers having sex with their clients' wives while they were supposed to be defending them.

The Judge totally ignored what I had to say and asked if my new lawyer was present. "I'm representing myself." He gave me some bullshit about someone representing themselves having a fool for a client.

I told him that I had a massive IQ, which I do. Many people say I'm a stable genius. I told him I was well educated and that I had the best words….

The Judge just banged his gavel and told me to be quiet. He then went on a rant about how I had let greed and evil lead me down the wrong path. He said he felt my sentencing was particularly tragic. In his little mind, I had been given so much, only to throw it all away —what a load of crap! A massive majority elected me, an incredible majority of the voters. A beautiful majority. People said it was probably the biggest single landslide in the history of elections. It was me, and only me, that turned Biloxi into the fastest growing city in the world. No one else could have done that. No one else had the connections to make that happen.

The so-called judge droned on and said he had decided to show leniency and not give me the maximum sentence of twenty years. He said something about nineteen. I looked around and asked the guard, "Did he say something about nineteen. Nineteen months?"

The judge, hearing my confusion, repeated the sentence. "You'll be confined to a federal penitentiary for no less than nineteen years," he paused for a moment before adding "and eleven months, and twenty-two days."

I went nuts and started yelling and throwing stuff. There were a few spectators in the crowd. They, too, started to scream in shock. I made a lunge towards the judge. I just wanted to get my hands around his neck and squeeze it a little. Before I could get a few feet from him, a swarm of cops jumped on me.

Chapter 36

Gabriel

My back was killing me. I popped a couple of Excedrin and washed them down with a coffee. Jacqueline had already taken Benjamin to her mom's for the day. After a quick shower, I called Ben O'Shea on the chance I might catch him before he headed to work. His wife Chevon called him out of the shower. "Good morning Ben," I said. "Sorry to call so early."

"That's okay, Gabe. How are things?"

"Moving along. Rachel's still not sure she wants to be the boss. How does Arnie feel about things?" Arnie Sims was an investigator who had volunteered to move to New Orleans when Ben went on vacation.

"You know him, he takes everything in stride. We talked about it the other day, and he said he was fine with whatever I decide to do."

"Which is…?"

"Why don't you give me a shout at the office."

"Is Chevon right there?"

"That's correct."

"Jacqueline and I are still dancing around the issue. Do you think Jacqueline and Chevon are talking?"

"Absolutely. It's Friday. Why don't we meet in Slidell this afternoon and grab a beer?"

"I need to get your thoughts on a missing person case." I summarized the case as I had last night for Jacqueline. When I was done, I asked him for his thoughts.

"My first thought is you've accomplished quite a bit in four days. Second, I wouldn't let the client pressure you into anything. If the guy's been missing for five weeks, then the ground's already cold. Third, forget about giving her a conclusion. It's too soon for that. When you give her your summary, just stick to the facts. What you've learned from her kids, from her neighbors, how you've progressed in chasing down the people, the fitness club, the grandmother. If after that, she wants you to keep looking, then tell her you'll need more money."

***

I drove to the Agency, remembering to park the Bug in front of the travel agency. When I got into the office, I found Rachel on the new computer sending out invoices to some insurance companies for whom we'd been doing reference checks.

"Good morning, boss!" I said enthusiastically.

She flashed me a smile. "Morning, boss, yourself!" She returned her gaze to the monitor. Her silky brown hair rested on her shoulders. "How are the muscles?"

"Excedrin works. All set for your lunch date with my wife?"

"Looking forward to it."

I told her about my conversation with Ben. "I've made notes on what we've found so far. Do you think you could type them up?"

She rolled her eyes, looking up at me. "I hope I can decipher your handwriting."

***

I went into the office and called Weber, getting his voicemail.

He returned my message about a half-hour later. "Good morning Gabriel, you called?"

"Rachel has a lead on Penn Maddox. She's traced her to Mobile, Alabama."

"*Stuck Inside Mobile with the Memphis Blues Again*," crooned Weber. "Are you a Dylan fan?"

"Sure, whatever…"

Weber interrupted me, "I saw him in concert back in Mobile in 1978. It was great!"

"When you did your check the other day, did you happen to look at the surrounding states like Louisiana and Alabama?"

"*Going down to Louisiana where that green river runs,*" he sang.

"Let me guess, another Bob Dylan?"

"Yes, siree. I saw him that same year in Baton Rouge. In answer to your question, yes, I did. I always like to go the extra mile. I think being thorough is important. There was nothing on Penn Maddox."

***

I put my notes in a brown envelope and labeled it Glenna Sparrow. At 11:30, Rachel left to meet Jacqueline while I was speaking to a couple of Rotarians from the list that Preston Merrick's secretary had faxed over. The gentlemen said they knew Dirk Sparrow was a member in both cases, but neither could remember ever speaking to him.

A few minutes before noon, the agency door opened, and in flew Glenna Sparrow. She was wearing another pantsuit, this one pink with yellow polka dots. She nodded to me and settled into her usual chair in my office with a look of consternation on her face. "It's Friday – you've had this case for a week - have you found him?"

"No. It's been four days. He's been missing now for almost six weeks."

"What "have" you found out?" she asked, using air quotes.

I handed her the envelope. "Quite a bit."

She took out the sheets and started to read the summary. When she was done, she put the sheets down on my desk. "So – what – happened – to - him?" She asked slowly, pronouncing each word separately.

"I - don't - know – yet." But if you want me to keep looking, I will need more money."

She gave me a thoughtful look, and for a moment, I thought she was weighing the pros and cons of continuing to look for the man she had been married to for twenty years. Finally, I couldn't stand it anymore, and my dislike of the woman bubbled over. "To be honest, Glenna, before I agree to spend any more time on this, there is something you haven't explained."

"What's that?"

I pulled the black and white polaroid of Dirk Sparrow out of my file. "The kids don't look like their father very much."

Chapter 37

March 1st, 1985
Biloxi, Mississippi

Don

I arrived back from Arkansas, disappointed at not being able to recruit Jethro. Despite the failure, I was determined to infiltrate Dietz's business interest and look for evidence that could tie him and the others to the bombings. I spent the morning at City Hall doing research and found out that Dietz's holdings were varied. They included a shoe store, a popular hotel, a couple of nightclubs, and a part-ownership in Bubba's Shrimp Emporium. I started calling around to the businesses asking to speak to him. By mid-morning, I found him in his office at the Tivoli Hotel. Rather than speak to him immediately, I decided to check the place out first.

As I walked into the lobby, I was impressed by a crystal chandelier and fancy staircase. Brass gleamed everywhere, and the wood oak trim of the reception desk was polished to a shine. Porters in red uniforms wearing little black hats were scurrying about looking after guests. I made my way to the front desk. A middle-aged bald man with a red three-piece suit and a haughty look was talking to a man who was wearing pajamas and a bathrobe.

"Do you work here?" asked the man in the bathrobe.

"No, I just like to dress like this and hang around hotel lobbies wearing a name tag," he replied, sarcasm dripping onto the counter.

Bathrobe man looked puzzled as he scratched his unkempt hair. "I want extra towels, pillows, blankets, toilet paper, coffee, and shampoo."

The desk clerk paused for a moment before snapping his fingers. "I get it. You're having a pajama party. Did you want me to throw in some candies for the other kiddies?"

"No, it's just me." The clerk gave him a blank stare before writing his room number on a piece of paper. Once the man left, the desk clerk threw the piece of paper in the trash. He looked over at me and shook his head. "We get all kinds." The look of scorn was quickly replaced with a phony smile. "Now, what can I do for you?"

"Is Mr. Dietz available?"

"Who wants to know?"

"A friend."

His shoulders dropped as he sighed deeply. "A friend with a name?"

"James. James...Kirk." It was the first name that popped into my mind.

"Oh! Mr. Kirk, welcome to the Tivoli." He craned his neck, looking behind me. "Did you park your starship with the valet?" Will Mr. Spock be joining you?" Before I could answer, "Well, sorry, Mr. Dietz is unavailable."

"Why not?"

"Because he's busy. That's what unavailable means. I'll tell him you beamed in."

"So what? Is he in a meeting?" I persisted.

The clerk arched an eyebrow, "He's busy and too busy to tell you why he's so busy."

***

I walked away from the desk and decided to wait in my truck. There was a silver Jaguar XJ6 parked in a spot marked, 'Reserved for Mr. Dietz.' While I sat and waited, I thought about my last conversation with Rachel. I hated lying to her about the Arkansas trip, but nothing was to be gained by involving her in what I was trying to do.

A coffee, two twinkies, and a package of Juicy Fruit later, I watched as an older man carrying an attaché case got into the Jaguar. I tailed the car into downtown Biloxi and watched as he pulled into a parking space out front of Dietz Designer Shoes.

***

I waited thirty minutes outside the store, resisting the temptation of going in for a closer look. Instead, I went into a variety store and bought another pack of gum and some more twinkies. There was a phone booth outside the shoe store, and I dropped a quarter and called Rachel at the office. The call went to the answering machine. I blurted out a request that she call me back that evening. While I was about to leave the phonebooth, Dietz left the store and glanced over at me. We made eye contact for a brief moment, and I thought there might have been a glimmer of recognition before the older man looked away and got into his car.

I tailed him and watched as the Jaguar pulled into a walled stone mansion in Biloxi's exclusive area.

***

I stopped at Kelly's fish market on the way back to the apartment, picking up some bass steaks for dinner. As I was putting the key in the lock, I heard the phone ringing. I raced in, dropping the packages on the floor. As soon as I picked up, there was a click on the other end. *Had I been too slow, or had the person waited just long enough to see if I was home?*

A shiver ran up my spine. I had an unlisted number. Other than Rachel, Weber, and my old boss, the only person who knew my number was Bubba Lange. I went to my dresser and got the revolver I'd hidden under my jockey shorts. I tried to put the call out of my mind and listened to the Allman Brothers performing *The Whipping Post* as I put the groceries away.

***

The phone rang again thirty minutes later. I was relieved to hear Rachel's voice, asking me about the fishing trip.

"It was great. Just what I needed. I caught a mess of fish. I brought some home. I hope you like bass."

"Great. Any news from Jackson?"

"No, you know how they say no news is good news? Well, not in this case."

"Try to put it out of your mind."

"Did you happen to call about thirty minutes ago?"

"No, I just got in and heard your message. It might have been your boss. You should call them. Maybe they made a decision."

"Whoever called hung up before I could get to it. You're probably right. But, it's Friday after 7 PM. I'm sure every-one's gone home."

"Are you okay, Don? Do you want some company?"

"Let's leave it. I'm a little bushed. You never get a good night's sleep in those tents. How about Saturday night?"

"Are you going to make me supper?"

"7 PM and wear something sexy."

***

Once we hung up, I remembered I hadn't checked the mail. The MBI might have sent me a pink slip. As I left the apartment to check the mailbox, I saw I'd left my gun on the end table. Ignoring a little voice alarm going off in my head, I headed for the stairs and the basement. The building was deserted - the silence was unnerving. When I got to the basement, I saw the landlord, Mr. Sharma, had not fixed the overhead light. *How does he expect people to check their mail?*

I shone the miniature flashlight on my key chain on the mailbox. As I pulled the mail out, I thought I heard a noise from the shadows. "Is someone there?" I called out. *Likely a cat.* I chuckled nervously at the thought of Agent Kittyburg being spooked by a kitty cat.

A familiar male voice broke the creepy silence. "I was wondering when you'd get home."

Chapter 38

Gabriel

"I'm paying you to find my husband, not to question my family tree."

"I don't believe those two boys are Dirk's."

"Well, congratulations, Detective. You solved a big mystery," she made a grandiose gesture with her hands. She shook her head in disgust and stood up. "They don't look like my husband because they're not his." She made a rude gesture as she flew out of the office.

***

I was making a list of all the reasons I hated Glenna Sparrow when Rachel walked in the door. "How was it?" I asked.

"Good, she had salad, and I had soup."

"I didn't mean what you ate. I meant; how did you get along?"

"Fine. You know, Jacqueline loves you and is frightened about losing you. She knows you guys aren't getting along, and she knows you probably think she's been a little over the top lately. All of that is leading to a feeling of insecurity about your relationship. I think that's at the root of her jealousy."

"That's interesting. You came away knowing more than me, and I live with her."

"Don't misunderstand - she has very strong feelings about you endangering yourself and your family. She thinks you should leave this to the police. She made that clear."

"Did she ask you if something was going on…you know, between us?"

"No, but I think she thinks there's…I don't know. Something - I can't explain it."

I thought about that for a moment. "Did it end well?"

"Sure, we left saying we should do it again. Oh, and she wants to go back to putting little notes under your windshield."

"Maybe I should start selling Mary Kay, seeing how our client just fired me."

"You didn't say you thought she bludgeoned her husband with that thingy? I said I want to be here for that."

"No, I gave her the report you typed up."

"That's it, and she fired you?" Rachel wrinkled her brow.

"I said I thought her kids weren't Dirk's."

Rachel nodded her understanding. "Ah! I see."

"Soon as I said that, she freaked out and said she wasn't paying me for that kind of detective work. As she was leaving, she said the boys weren't Dirk's. Then she gave me the finger."

"They're not her husband's kids?"

"That's what she said."

"What does that mean?"

I gave her a quizzical look, "It means someone else's sperm...

"That's not what I meant," she interrupted quickly. "Was she implying they were adopted, or maybe she was artificially inseminated...?"

"I don't know. She wasn't in the mood to ask a clarifying question."

"She can't fire you for making an observation. Did she actually say you were fired?"

"No, just gave me the finger. Anyway, before she blew up, I told her that I would need more money if she wanted me to keep working on the case. Since she didn't write me another check, then I'm saying I've been fired."

"So now what?"

"Let's fax Weber a copy of what we've uncovered. Then I'm meeting Ben for a beer."

Chapter 39

March 1st, 1985
Biloxi, Mississippi

Don

"Jethro?"

"Yeah, I've been waiting for you to get home. Is it still cool for me to bunk with you for a spell?"

"Absolutely, stay as long as you like. Say, did you call my apartment about 45 minutes ago?"

"Nope."

"Okay, grab your gear, and we'll head upstairs." Jethro had a U.S. military duffel bag, which he hoisted and carried on his left shoulder as they climbed the stairs. "Sorry, it's kind of a crappy building. No elevator. It's all I could afford. But I have a couch and a stereo and lots of beer." I led the way to my apartment. When we got there, I held the door open, "Welcome, Jethro. Were you in the military?"

"One hundred infantry Division, Fort Knox, Kentucky. How about you?"

"Did a stint in Nam and saw action in Cambodia." I got Jethro a beer. "Make yourself at home. I don't have a lot of furniture. I've got this whole business with the job hanging over my head."

"Still haven't heard anything?"

"No, I was just checking the mail to see if there was news, but all I got was a phone bill."

Jethro picked up the phone bill, "Don Kittyburg. What's your real name?"

"Don Kooper." Don pressed play on the stereo. "Like the Allmans?"

"Whipping Post. The best of Southern Rock."

"I'm glad you decided to come back. I may need help in case Bubba Lange decides to come over for a visit."

Jethro eyed my revolver on the end table. "Is that what this is for?"

"I think a man named Dietz might have recognized me today. He's a friend of Bubba's. Before you got here, the phone rang, but it was a hang-up."

Jethro looked a little uncomfortable. "If they come here and find me, then I'll be just as dead as you."

"Good, then if I'm in the shower and they barge in, feel free to shoot them." Jethro nodded uncertainly.

"I was going to order a pizza. That sound okay?"

"Yeah, I haven't had anything since the diner."

"What do you want on your pizza?"

"Meat, no vegetables."

"Don laughed, remembering a fight he'd had with Rachel, who only liked vegetarian pizza. "There's something you can help me with, Jethro. My girlfriend Rachel is coming over tomorrow night. I told her I was bass fishing up in Arkansas. I even bought some fish at the market to make her dinner. Do you mind not spilling the beans on what I was really doing in Little Rock?"

"Sure. You want me to take off?"

"No, I'd like you to meet her. She's cool. You'll like her."

"I don't want to get in the middle of anything."

"Don't worry. If things get steamy, we'll go into the bedroom." After his shower, Don, and Jethro ended up talking music and girls until the pizza came. When the pizza guy knocked on the door, they both made a move for the gun.

Chapter 40

Gabriel

The bar was called the Hideout. It was located in downtown Slidell, a small community east of New Orleans. As I opened the door, the sounds of Lynyrd Skynyrd's *Gimme Three Steps* brought back memories of what had happened last year. Ben saw me walk in and waved me over. Things hadn't changed much. The same John Deere hat-wearing men were crowding the bar. Even the cloud of smoke hanging in the air looked the same. The long-haired pony-tailed bartender was gone - doing a stint for his part in what happened. In his place was a cute young girl wearing the skimpiest of halters and jean shorts.

"Hey, I ordered you a Bud," said Ben, who waved me over. "Should have ordered two - this place is packed. Bring back memories?"

I nodded and took a sip of my beer. "Everything's the same, except the bartender." I'd been drugged, beaten, and left in an alleyway behind the bar the previous year.

"I hear he's serving five years for his part."

We sat for a moment, watching the bartender. Her red hair hung loosely on her shoulders. She had a cute face, if you didn't mind the freckles. I didn't.

"Did your client show up?" asked Ben, signaling that our leering-at-the-bartender time was over.

I told him about Glenna's visit. "I don't feel good about dropping the case. I felt we'd made progress."

"I probably would have asked the same thing, maybe even earlier. You wouldn't be doing your job had you not asked."

"And I called it. Those kids aren't Dirk's."

"Could be lots of reasons for that," Ben took a handful of peanuts from the bowl on the table and did the slap-the-arm maneuver I had shown Benjamin.

I guzzled the last of my beer and was about to signal the waitress when Ben said, "Maybe we should take it easy. Chevon told me about you calling Rachel for a lift on Monday instead of Jacqueline. I guess you stirred up a hornet's nest."

I nodded. "Jacqueline can be a little judgy, and I just didn't want that."

"I hear you. How has she been about you working?"

"She has strong opinions. Strong opinions about a lot of things. If I wanted to change her, I would have had to have done it when we first married. Now she won't even let me change the television channel."

"Goes with the territory. Listen, have you heard the latest about Baxter?"

I waived the waitress down and ordered another round. "No. I hope he's enjoying the prison experience."

"I got a call from the DA today. He's been sentenced to twenty years."

"Sounds reasonable. If they could have proven his involvement in Friesen's murder, he'd have gotten more. In his mind, he probably thinks he's done nothing wrong. He's a narcissist and completely delusional – I bet he feels like he's a hero. I wonder how he's getting along with the other inmates?"

"The DA said he's in with the Aryan Brotherhood. There was a stabbing in the showers the other day, someone who crossed paths with him. They found the shiv in Baxter's cell but under his cellmate's mattress. They think Baxter is manipulative enough to have planted it there."

The waitress brought our beers, and Gabriel raised his beer in a toast. "To Mayor Baxter, let's hope he rots in prison." The music on the jukebox switched to Dr. John's *Right Place, Wrong Time,* and I started feeling nostalgic about Ben and how the agency had initially started. I had been down from Detroit with a vague notion of working on the oil rigs when I'd met Ben in a bar. He'd been thinking about start-ing a detective agency and wanted someone to run it until he retired from the Biloxi P.D. Six years later, he's taught me the business, and together we've had a fantastic run.

"So, have you made up your mind about the office?" I asked, coming out of my daydream.

"I'm fine letting Arnie run it, and that will free me up to work on cases, maybe leave early a little more of-ten and keep Chevon happy. Unlike Rachel, Arnie doesn't care. 'Whatever you want me to do' is a direct quote. What about Rachel?"

"Much more complicated. She's still mixed up with that Kittyburg character, and his job is up in the air. It's looking a little dark because the Governor wants to hang everything that happened on him. If he stays with the MBI, I expect she'll want to move to Jackson to be with him."

"If she stays, she'll run the office?"

"I think so. She's getting her confidence back, and her customers rarely give her the finger."

Ben ignored the comment and surprised me by put-ting his hand on my arm. "There's something else the DA told me. Not such good news," he took a deep breath. "Sounds like Reznikov might end up going free. The trial isn't going very well. The judge has ruled several things inadmissible."

"That's bullshit." Ben nodded and took another handful of peanuts.

"Does Baxter know?"

"I don't know. It's not official. He'll be furious when he finds out. Consider the irony. He was a bit player compared to Reznikov. Because he wimped on the DA's deal, he gets 20 years to regret it. Had he turned state's evidence, then the real crook would be there, and he'd be in some country club prison."

"Serves him right for being in bed with the Russians."

Chapter 41

Mayor Baxter

Dear Diary,

I got a letter today from the Mississippi Bar. They said they took my complaint with grave concern. They wrote that they were pleased to advise that Mr. Sechfinger acted within the guidelines set out under the Mississippi rules of professional conduct. They went on to write that my wife had been consulted. She had assured them the marriage had been over for years. Further, the relationship with Sechfinger had only begun after he had been fired. I threw the piece of crap in the garbage. Jews protecting Jews.

Partway through the day, the guard passed me a business card and told me I had a visitor. A Sam Fitzgerald from the firm, Low, Ball, and Lynch, was waiting for me in the interview room. I figured that Dietz had come through. When I got to the room, I did a double-take. Sam was actually Samantha. She was shaped like a snowman, a small, round white head wobbling on top of a large round body.

"Mr. Baxter, I'm Sam Fitzgerald of the firm of Low, Ball, and Lynch." She shook my hand with fat little fingers that

looked like little breakfast sausages. I couldn't believe it. I looked around the room at the other prisoners to see if I was being pranked. This must be Dietz's idea of a joke.

"I've been asked to offer you representation. My firm and I have quite a bit of experience in these matters. If you're interested, I can conduct a preliminary interview on representation."

"Seriously, Dietz sent you?"

She ignored the question. "I'm up to speed. I read the transcripts."

"Then you know I'm being railroaded."

"I think the DA offered you a reasonable way out. Did your previous lawyer advise against taking the plea deal that was offered?" she asked, narrowing her eyes.

"He assured me that we would get an acquittal. Once the charges go away, I can resume my life as Mayor of Biloxi."

"Really?" She had a smirk on her fat little face.

"I think the appeal should be based on the Mexican judge being unqualified and that Sexfinger was incompetent."

"The likelihood of a successful appeal is less than 10%," she frowned. "How are you enjoying life here? Would you consider someplace better?"

"Is that a joke? I hate it. The food sucks, the work pays pennies, and I'm constantly worried that someone will stick a knife up my ass. I don't understand if you aren't talking appeal - were you planning to bust me out of here?" The snowman wasn't making any sense.

"Let me explain something to you." She lowered her voice to just above a whisper. There's no Low, Ball, and Lynch. I just made that up. I work for the State Attorney's office."

I started to get up, and she growled, telling me to sit down. Once I did, she said I should hear her out. "Frank Reznikov's trial isn't going well. There is a chance that when it goes to the jury, we might not get the result we were hoping for."

"I don't understand." I held up her phony business card.

"Sorry about the misdirection. Frank Reznikov has a lot of friends here. Some of them, I believe you know. If he suspects that you've been meeting with a prosecutor, then your life would be …well, I wouldn't bet the farm on being alive tomorrow."

"You're here to offer me a deal?"

"In a nutshell, if you cooperate and help us secure a conviction, we'll see to it that you get transferred to a low-security federal institution. Maybe in Yazoo City. We could then, say in five years, consider you for a work-release program."

"You don't get it. Nothing short of the witness protection program is going to work. I want relocation, dismissal of all of these charges, and maybe a little plastic fucking surgery."

"That's just not possible with someone like you. You've been convicted of serious crimes – and I might add, got away with others on technicalities. How are you going to feel if Frank gets acquitted and you spend the next twenty years here?"

"I'd be furious. But what the fuck am I supposed to do about it?"

She pulled out a glossy picture of a beach and palm trees. "This is Honolulu. There is a Federal Penitentiary on the island. Tennis courts and a mini-putt. I can't promise you, but I can see what I can do."

"The Aryan Brotherhood runs this prison. They run all the prisons. They are all across the country, including in fucking Honolulu. Once I testify against Frank, I'm dead."

Part 2

Chapter 42

March 2nd, 1985
Gulfport, Mississippi

Gabriel

I looked down at the welts on the man's back. There were at least a dozen puffy raised sores. "Can you tell how old these whip marks are?"

"I can't be sure," said Abrams, making a note on his clipboard.

"They look fresh," I said to Weber, who nodded in agreement. "I think this man was whipped and drowned in the bayou."

"Could be," replied Abrams as if any plausible explanation was acceptable to him. "No bullet holes, though."

I turned to Weber, "Have you seen this type of thing before?"

He nodded. "Man named Kunte Kinte. It was a mini-series called *Roots*. They whipped him because he tried to run away."

"That was a great show," chipped in Creepy. "There are still whipping posts out on some of the farms around here."

***

We huddled under our umbrellas outside the building. The wind had shifted, and the rain was coming down on an angle. "Well, what do you think?" asked Weber from under his Smokey the Bear hat.

"I think we should talk in my car before we drown."

We huddled in the Bug, and I put on the gas heater. "I always wanted to drive one of these." Weber looked around and checked out the backseat. "Can't say I like the color."

"Are you thinking the stiff is Dirk Sparrow?"

He made a funny face as if I was stupid to ask. "Don't you?"

"I don't know. The face was all puffed up. I wish I could unsee that. Glenna said he had love handles. With all that bloating, it's pretty hard to say. Why did you get me out of bed for this?"

"You're investigating his disappearance. I think there's a good possibility that," he thumbed in the direction of the building, "you found him."

"I've only ever seen a grainy, black and white polaroid of the man. You should have called Glenna."

"I did, and she told me to call you."

I asked him again if he had ever seen those types of whip marks in real life, and Weber said no, but that he'd put out an inquiry to neighboring counties.

***

I drove straight to Glenna Sparrow's house, the rain making the wipers work overtime. I didn't know what game she was playing, but I'd had enough. She'd given me the finger, done the enraged wife routine, and couldn't even be bothered to see if the stiff lying at the medical examiner's office was her husband?

As I pulled into her driveway, I honked the horn. I didn't give a damn if she saw me driving a pink VW. I leaned on the horn for a minute before I realized I was likely waking up the neighbors. I got out of the car and fought my way through the driving rain to Glenna's front step, where she was waiting for me with a smirk on her face. She held the door open and told me to come in out of the rain.

I did the wet dog routine in the hall, and she brought me a bath towel. "I knew that was your car all along. I saw it was parked in front of the travel agent the other day."

"You did?"

"Pretty hard to miss."

I mentally told her to go to hell. "Alright, Glenna, I want answers."

"You mean, why are my kids adopted, or why did I ask Weber to call you?"

"Let's start with the latter."

"Is it my husband?"

"I don't know. The medical examiner said he'd been in the water for some time… and well, his face was all puffy, so I can't be sure."

"Weber seems to think so."

"Maybe you could go and make a more positive identification. You being familiar with your husband's body." I thought about the statue. *I have to admit, I did glance at the man's flaccid penis. It didn't look like anything special to me.*

"I think that would be very disturbing."

I let out a deep sigh. *Dead bodies usually are.* "It doesn't matter. The ME is going to do some tests. He'll want the name of Dirk's dentist so they can be sure."

"Well, then we'll have to wait to celebrate."

I did a double-take. The words celebrate, and dead husband didn't seem to go together. "What do you mean by that?" I asked, an edge creeping into my voice.

"Just that we can't close the case until we know it's him."

Amazing. She didn't give two shits about what happened to her husband. She just wanted to know if he was dead. "About the kids being adopted…"

"It's not something I usually tell people, but if it's bothering you." She lit up a cigarette, and we sat in the living room. "My parents never approved of my marriage. It was 1965, two years before interracial marriages were made legal. I loved Dirk, so we went to another state and got married. When my parents found out, they were furious. They threatened to have Dirk arrested and to disown me. We settled in Biloxi and lived in a dumpy apartment while Dirk worked in a hotel. Once my father died, my mother wanted to reconcile. In return for gaining access to a trust fund my grandparents set up for me, I agreed to sign some legal papers. One of the clauses of the agreement was that this money could never be Dirk's. Everything, the house, the cars, the business, had to be solely in my name. Another clause forbade miscegenation. At the time, we wanted the money more than a family, so it didn't matter. But later, I changed my mind. I pleaded with Mother, but she wouldn't change the agreement. Since I wasn't allowed to have Dirk's baby, we decided to adopt two young - very white boys. My mother made all of the arrangements with the help of the church."

I started to understand why Glenna was the way she was. Her mother sounded like a nasty piece of work. A thought flashed through my mind about whether her mother might have somehow gotten rid of her son-in-law. "That's quite the story."

"We all have our crosses to bear."

"Do you still want me to find out what happened to Dirk?"

"I'm not sure it matters. Surely Weber will get off his ass and investigate now that he has a body. I can tell you that Dirk would not voluntarily go swimming. Like most coloreds, he couldn't swim."

I hadn't heard that before. It sounded like bullshit. "When I looked at the body, there were scars on his back from being whipped. Do you know anything about that?"

"Whipped?" For the first time, I detected an emotional reaction from her. She recovered quickly, "He didn't … I don't know anything about that." She looked at me for a long moment. This time she won the staring contest. "I think your work here is done."

Not by a long shot.

Chapter 43

Mayor Baxter

Dear Diary,

I spent my spare time today writing letters. I wrote one to Ronald Reagan. I told him I was his biggest supporter and a fan of all his movies, especially the ones with the monkey. I told him that I was a longtime Republican and had contributed to his election campaigns. I made it clear that I supported all his policies, including his stand against the civil rights act and, more recently, against the voting rights act.

I went on to explain that a tremendous majority of voters had elected me and that I, in turn, had transformed Biloxi, Mississippi, into one of the fastest-growing cities in America. Now, I was asking for his help. I had been wrongfully imprisoned merely because of a few indiscretions and some connections I had with some business developers.

***

Wolf told me we were going to have a business meeting after our break for lunch. He must have connections because we got to use the private room where the guards usually meet. I joined about thirty others in the back of the room. Wolf was upfront, along with Klink, telling everyone to pipe down. I was passed a clipboard and told to sign in.

Klink was talking about dues. "For the newcomers, dues are $20 every month plus 10% of your take from the hustles you have on the go. Be it drugs, the girls, gambling, anything."

"Now, before we get down to business, join me in saying our oath," said Wolf.

The men in the room joined him in reciting the pledge. I hadn't memorized the words, so I just mumbled my way through it.

"An Aryan Brother is without care. He walks where the weak and heartless won't dare. For an Aryan brother, death holds no fear. Vengeance will be his, through his brothers still here."

"Take a seat, men," said Wolf. We have a couple of important pieces of business to cover— first, an initiation. I am nominating John Baxter for membership in the Aryan Brotherhood. Most of you have already met the former Mayor of Biloxi. His nickname will be Luger. He assures me that his blood is pure and that he has read and agrees with our constitution."

"I will now give Luger a copy of Mein Kampf, our bible." Wolf walked over and shook my hand. "At our next meeting,

assuming the council agrees, you will become a brother, and you will need to show us your ink." There was a round of applause from the crowd and some cheers. I hadn't expected or prepared myself for the ceremony or that I'd have to pay for membership. I had no idea how I would contribute.

"Okay, guys, I have a second piece of business that we need to cover. Brother Klink tells me that a spic named Hector Lopez spit on him over an issue in the dining hall. We can't allow any of our members to be disrespected. An insult to one is an insult to all. Tomorrow when Lopez gets up from his lunch, the guards will ensure that the doors are closed after he leaves, locking in the rest of the spics. I want Klink, Burkhalter, and Schultz to join Luger and me in cellblock 2. Luger, you're to bring enough shivs from the machine shop for everyone. We'll each land a blow for the Brotherhood."

Chapter 44

Gabriel

The wipers on the Bug were going almost as furiously as my mood as I left Glenna's. How many times can a person be fired? When I got back to the house, Jacqueline was watching a Betamax movie called *Herbie Rides Again*, coincidentally about a man who drives a Bug. She'd put it on for Benjamin, who quickly lost interest and went to play with his trucks. "Where did you run off to so early this morning?" Jacqueline asked.

"Weber called. I met him at the Medical Examiner's." I told her about Abrams, the body, and the subsequent visit to Glenna Sparrow.

"Sounds like you're officially off the case," she said, turning off the television.

"Seeing that body with the whip marks is going to haunt me."

"Why don't we do something to get your mind off of it then."

I immediately thought of something naughty, but as if reading my mind, she added, "I meant as a family."

"Not a very nice day for a picnic." I looked out the living room window.

"We can play a game, help Jelly-Bean build a fort. Maybe invite my parents over for brunch?"

She was right, of course. I sat down on the couch and closed my eyes, trying to make the image of the black man lying on a gurney disappear. It was too late. I was already waist-deep in the funk bayou. I pushed myself to get up and go into the kitchen for the sure-fire cure for the rainy-day blues—a massive breakfast of blueberry pancakes, bacon, and coffee.

I felt better after we ate, and we spent the next hour building a pillow fort on my bed. Benjamin "Genghis" Khan sprung a surprise attack wielding a wooden salad spoon and had to be tickled back.

***

Later in the afternoon, I called Weber and asked him when we might hear news about other bodies with whip marks. He went on and on about something called VICAP, which allows police officers all across America to search a crime database by keywords. "Revolutionary - it will allow police departments to work together to bring criminals to justice…blah, blah, blah."

"That sounds great. Can you use it to see if other bodies with whiplashes have turned up?"

"No, I read about it in a magazine called *Police Beat*. I think they're still building the database. But I sent out an inquiry this morning that will go to all the sheriff's in neighboring counties."

I felt myself slipping back into the funk. "How long before we get an answer?"

"They'll start to come in dribs and drabs next week."

"How about the dental exam?"

"That would depend on Abrams. He's pretty busy. The dogcatcher moved away, and he agreed to help out until someone else gets hired."

Chapter 45

March 2nd, 1985
Gulfport, Mississippi

Rachel

I stood in front of the door to Don's apartment with nervous anticipation. He'd said to wear something sexy, so I was wearing an old beige trench coat over my red velvet bustier, ready to flash him when he opened the door. An image of my mother popped into my mind - a look of disapproval written on her face. Oh well, it'll be funny to see his expression.

I knocked on the door a few times - I could hear *Mississippi Queen* on the stereo, so I knew he was there. Suddenly the door was opened by a strange man wearing a bath towel. He was over 6 feet tall with tight curly dark hair, cut short. He had the thick body of a man used to physical work. We stood looking at each other for a long moment before I looked around and said, "I must have the wrong apartment. I'm sorry."

"That's okay. Who're you looking for?"

I felt a little flustered. I…. "Don Kittyburg." Then I realized the towel the man was wearing was just like the one I'd given to Don last Christmas. It had a bunch of kitty cats on it. "Is this Don Kittyburg's apartment?" I cocked my head.

"Yeah, Don just stepped out for something. You must be Rachel, I'm Jethro." He held the door open and smiled at me.

I figured he was in his twenties. "Don never mentioned that he had a friend staying with him. Jethro who?"

"Coyle, come on in. Sorry about the towel. I just had a shower." I took a tentative step into the apartment and then followed him into the living room. He was leaning back on the couch with his outstretched arms on the back.

"What are you doing here?"

"I'm bunking with Don for a few days. You're even prettier than Don said."

The comment creeped me out. I noticed a copy of *Playboy* open to the centerfold on the couch beside him. "I'm sorry, am I interrupting something? Maybe I should leave."

"No, no," he said, seeing I was looking at the magazine. He quickly put the magazine away. "Please take your coat off. Grab a beer – there are lots in the fridge."

I didn't know what bothered me more. The fact that I had next to nothing on under my coat or that a half-naked man, wearing a kitty cat towel, wanted to have a beer with me. "Where's Don?"

"As I said, he had to step out for a couple of supplies. You looking forward to those bass steaks we caught up in Arkansas?"

"Wait a minute, how do you know, Don?"

"We met up at the camp, and he said I could bunk with him for a few days."

"I'm sorry, can you put some clothes on?"

"Sure, I guess I'm used to hanging with the guys." He got up and walked down the hall to the bathroom. He turned around before going into the bathroom, "You're the prettiest girl I've seen in a while. You know, not counting the ones in the magazines."

While Jethro was getting changed, I went into the kitchen and paused in front of the fridge. *Should I leave? Maybe change into something and come back.* I opened the fridge, and sure enough, I spied a plate with two good size bass steaks covered in Saran Wrap. I was shutting the fridge door when I noticed the Kelly's fish market bag in the garbage can.

Calling out to him, "Hey Jethro, I saw the fish ready to grill in the fridge...looks yummy. How many fish did you guys catch?"

"I don't remember, but it was a mess of them." He came out of the bathroom wearing blue jeans and a plaid shirt. "Yeah, Don's quite the fisherman. He caught a couple of whoppers."

"What did you do with the rest?" I asked as he passed me on the way to the living room.

"The rest? We ate 'em?" Jethro's tone was sounding a little unsure.

"Really? You guys must like fish. And there's only two left? I always thought Don was more of a meat-eater."

"He'll be home soon. You can ask him. Hey, do you like Lynyrd Skynyrd?" He went to the stereo. Soon the guitar riff in *Gimme Three Steps* filled the room. Jethro started playing air guitar.

I revised my estimate - the man was a lot younger than I'd initially thought. "Were they largemouth bass or smallmouth?"

"Don would know for sure, but I'd say ...medium. Yeah, that's it, medium ... medium mouth."

"Jethro cut the bull. I'm a private detective, and I happen to know you knuckleheads didn't catch anything."

"We did. Big whoppers." He started pantomiming wrestling with a fish using the imaginary guitar, now miraculously transformed into a fishing rod.

"Big whoppers, all right. I saw the Kelly's fish market bag in the trash."

"Oh!"

"What were you guys doing in Arkansas?"

"...We went to see the Cardinals play." He was now swinging an imaginary bat.

"The Arkansas Cardinals? There's no such thing."

He just shrugged his shoulders and said, "Grand Canyon?"

"Arizona!"

"Visiting my granny?"

***

Spending ten more minutes with Jethro seemed like three hours. Finally, a knock at the door interrupted the stare down.

"That must be Don." Jethro jumped up from the couch.

"Sit down!" I ordered. "Why would Don knock on his own door?" I went to the door and asked, "Who's there?"

"It's me, Travis." Travis Franklin was a friend of the Agency since it had opened in 1979. He had helped Gabriel solve his first case. I opened the door and said hello to the 16-year-old.

"Hi, Rachel. Are you going somewhere? It's not raining out."

"Long story."

"Where's Don? He invited me to come for dinner." Travis walked into the living room and gave Jethro a wave, and sat on the couch.

"How is it you guys know each other?" I asked, hands on hips, frustrated at having to play catch-up.

"We went for lunch today," said Travis. "It was crazy. We went to the Tivoli where my Mom works. I had a shrimp cocktail." I looked at Jethro.

"Porcini mushroom omelet. It was ok. The place was a little hoity-toity for me. That's why I took a shower, get that rich person smell off me."

"Were we all supposed to wear raincoats to dinner?" Travis said, looking at Jethro.

"Don didn't say anything about a raincoat party. He just said we were going to cook up the fish we cau...." his voice trailed off as I glared at him.

"Yeah," said Travis, his eyes as wide as saucers. "Don said he caught a couple of beauties, four-footers..."

Jethro interrupted. "It's ok, Travis, she knows."

There was another knock at the door. This time when I opened the door, Deputy Weber said, "Hello, Rachel. I'm sorry, I didn't think to bring a raincoat."

I gave them all a suspicious look as Weber joined the others on the couch. I had a lot of questions. Why hadn't Don told me he had a roommate? What was he really do-ing in Arkansas? Why the elaborate lie about fishing? Why would he take these guys for lunch, let alone to the Tivoli, a place he said was not his style? "Someone had better start giving me some answers...." I was interrupted when the front door opened, and Don came in carrying a bunch of parcels.

He took one look at me, "Hey hon, was it raining earlier?"

Chapter 46

March 2nd, 1985
Gulfport, Mississippi

Rachel

I followed Don into the kitchen, steam coming out of my ears. "What do you have to say for yourself, Kittyburg?"

"Just wait until you taste those bass steaks I caught." He did a little dance until he caught my glare as he was putting away his purchases. "Oh! wait a minute, are you upset about something?" In response, I pulled the Kelly's fish market bag out of the garbage can and showed it to him. "I can explain that. The fish was so good, Jethro and I had eaten most of it. Have you met Jethro?"

"Quit it, Don. The game's over. He already admitted that Arkansas wasn't a fishing trip. Now quit lying. I want the truth."

Don looked at me. "Settle down. I'll tell you, but first, why the raincoat?"

"You didn't tell me about all these people being here. You said you want me to wear something sexy."

"Oops, I'm sorry." He smiled. "I forgot I'd said that. So, what do you have on underneath?"

"Forget it, buster. You've no hope of seeing what's under here. The only reason I'm not walking out of here is because you owe me an explanation, many explanations. And if you try to spin it on me, I'm gonna take your fucking fish and beat you with it."

"Okay, okay, but once I tell you everything, will you let me take a peek under the raincoat?" he asked playfully.

I ignored his question, pushing him into the living room, where Travis, Weber, and Jethro sat quietly on the couch. "Let's start with the real reason you went to Arkansas."

"To find him." Don pointed at Jethro.

"Don, you are two seconds away from a butt-kicking," I threatened.

"You showed me the article about the white supremacist meeting up there. Jethro and I met at the camp near Saucier before the bombings. He helped me get away. It took a while to convince him, but he's agreed to help me get Dietz and the others."

"Why didn't you just tell me?"

"You were against me getting involved. What's more, I didn't know what to expect up there. I was worried about involving you."

"And just how is Jethro going to help you?"

"Dietz is the owner of the Tivoli Hotel. That's where Travis comes in. His mother, you might remember, works in the accounting office there. Travis thinks he can get his mom to play along."

"Go on." I stood with my arms crossed.

"Travis said that the hotel was looking for cleaning staff. Jethro was to see Dietz today after we had lunch. How did it go, Jethro"?

Jethro cleared his throat and then gulped his beer. "Dietz kept me waiting a while, but when I told him who I was and that Bubba Lange would vouch for me, I was all set. If everything checks out, I start on Monday."

"So, the plan is," Don continued, "Travis' mom will copy whatever she can and find a way to give it to Jethro. He'll bring it home and give it to me. Hopefully, we will find something that we can take to Weber."

Weber then picked up his part of the plan. "I've spoken to an ADA, that's Assistant District Attorney," he said, deepening his voice. "I asked her if she'd be interested in something that would implicate Dietz and the others in the bombing. She said to bring it on."

"Hold on, for anything you find to be admissible in court, it would have to be discovered through a subpoena."

"I know that. I'm a deputy sheriff." Weber pointed to his name tag. "That's why we're only taking copies. Once we have something, then I'll get the subpoena."

"What if Mrs. Franklin doesn't want to play ball?"

"I'm pretty sure I can convince her," said Travis confidently. "She was horrified about what happened at Hiller Park."

Chapter 47

March 3rd, 1985
Talladega, Alabama

Mayor Baxter

Dear Diary

I'm not sure about getting involved too deeply with the Brotherhood. I don't want to do anything to make my legal problems worse. As it stands now, I can look forward to getting out of here at the age of 73. If you add an assault or a murder charge to that, I might never see the outside of this prison again. I decided to talk to Wolf about my dilemma. Surely, he'll understand that a man of my experience can be of great help to his organization. As mayor, there were times when something needed to be done. A counselor who needed help to understand the big picture or a landowner who was holding up development. In those cases, I just called Reznikov, and the matter went away.

***

After breakfast, I told Wolf I wanted to speak to him alone. We went out in the hallway. He asked me if there was a problem getting the shivs. "No problem. I've got a stockpile in my mattress just like you asked."

"Great, and what about your cellmate? Does he want to make a few bucks?"

I laughed uncertainly. "I broached it, and he said no thanks."

"Well, one of you has to do it. Are you going to get on your knees and suck cock, Luger? Because if he doesn't, then you'll have to. Now, what do you want to talk about?"

"I'm not sure Frank would be happy with the way you're speaking to me."

"Reznikov doesn't give a shit about you. What's more, I haven't told him about the prosecutor you met with, but if you don't do as you're told, I will."

I stared at Wolf and decided that I wasn't on the firmest of grounds. When I didn't say anything, he pointed at me, "You wondering about what kind of a tattoo to get?"

"I was thinking a little bulldog tattoo, maybe on my ankle."

He laughed and undid his jumpsuit, lifting his white T-Shirt. He had a tattoo of an iron cross that covered most of his chest. "That's pretty funny. I'd say go big or go home. Make a statement showing your commitment to the Brotherhood. Talk to Schultz - he's the ink man. Now, what did you want to discuss?"

Chapter 48

March 4th, 1985
Gulfport, Mississippi

Gabriel

After spending a quiet Sunday with Jacqueline and Benjamin, Rachel and I spent Monday visiting some businesses in town and offering our reference and investigation services. Towards the end of the day, I called Weber. He was out of the office but returned the call about forty minutes later.

"Want to take a drive to Wilmer, Alabama?" Weber asked.

"What's in, Wilmer?"

"Unknown black male turned up in Big Creek Lake about three months ago. Severe lacerations on his back. The medical examiner labeled this another drowning but with suspicious circumstances. I spoke to the sheriff up there, and they've hit a dead-end in the investigation. The stiff's name is Reche Tines. He works for Northrup. His family is from some town in Mississippi."

"That the only one?"

"So far. There are plenty of counties I haven't heard from."

"Getting back to our stiff, did Glenna Sparrow ever go in and identify him?"

"She did and gave us a solid maybe. We're going ahead with the dental examination anyway."

I shared what I'd learned from Glenna about her family, breaking pretty much every rule on client confidentiality in the book. The only saving grace was that there was no such book in Mississippi. "I bet she's been pestering you for an update."

"Haven't heard from her."

We made plans to drive together to Wilmer the next day. "Leave the Mary Kay. I'll pick you up with the cruiser."

Chapter 49

March 5th, 1985
Gulfport, Mississippi

Connie's mother was fond of saying, a person was as nervous as a long-tail cat in a room full of rocking chairs. That's precisely how she felt driving into work Tuesday morning. Her boss had given her a job when she needed one. After her husband died, they'd been forced to live with her family up in Hattiesburg. Travis's father was a corrupt deputy sheriff and had left them with a stack of bills, an old car, and a large mortgage.

Travis had told her that Dietz helped organize the bombings at Hiller Park that had killed so many people. *Was he a racist? Leader of the Klan in Mississippi?* She'd walked in on him one time, just to give him a budget report he needed, and she overheard him on the phone. She didn't know who he was talking to, but she remembered him saying that he'd taken care of that little problem and that they were good to go for the 21st at Hiller Park. That was Martin Luther King Day, the day of the bombings.

"It's easy, peasy, Mom," Travis had said, "All you need to do is to wait for Dietz to leave. Then sneak into his office and root through his desk. It should be easy for you. You're always snooping through my stuff."

"I do not."

"Yeah, sure. You're going to look for anything that would implicate Dietz in what happened. Once you find it, take it back to your office and photocopy it. Remember to put the originals back precisely where you found them before he gets back. Then just put the copies in an envelope and put it in the trash for Jethro."

Dietz had taken Jethro around yesterday and introduced him. He said he would start in garbage collection, and he'd be by once a day to pick up the trash. Dietz's office was down the hall, and Connie would have to walk by one other office. Travis had said that if she happened to get caught, "Just make up some excuse about how Dietz forgot to give you something."

She didn't have Dietz's schedule for the day, but he was a creature of habit. He usually got in around 10 AM, stopped to say good morning, and then disappeared into his office. He routinely had appointments with suppliers and people working in the hotel until noon. He then would disappear for a couple of hours, sometimes longer, depending on whether he planned to visit one of his other businesses.

Connie looked up as Adele walked by the office. Adele was Dietz's personal executive assistant. "Good morning, Adele. Do you know the boss's schedule for today? I have a couple of items." Adele was a blonde, twenty-something intern whose elevator didn't quite reach the top. She had an annoying habit of ending every sentence on an upward inflection, making everything she said sound like a question. She was hired because she was inexpensive and had big tits. Dietz had already been divorced three times. In each case, his wife caught him with his secretary. Everyone in the company thought it was only a matter of time before history repeated itself.

"I think he's got an urgent call this morning?" Adele looked up at the ceiling as if the answer was written there. "After that, I think he's meeting with the Teamsters. Lunch probably at noon?" she said, biting her lip. "In the afternoon, I think he's got back-to-back meetings? Maybe I can slip you in this afternoon, in between his appointments?"

"Thanks, Adele." Lunch it is. Sometimes Dietz took Adele to the club for what he euphemistically called a working lunch. That would be perfect. She tried to keep herself occupied but jumped every time the phone rang, or someone walked by. At 10, Dietz strode by and said, "Good morning Connie, it's gonna be a great day!"

A smile crossed her face as she returned the greeting.

About an hour later, Adele walked into her office. "I told the boss that you wanted a word? He wants to know what about?"

"It's not that important. I noticed the sales at the shoe store for the last two months were really low."

Her eyes widened, "They're having a sale?"

Connie smiled at her and wondered how her bra size compared to her IQ. "No, I meant, the purchases have been low."

"Oh, well. Maybe they should have a sale? Don't ya think?"

Connie nodded. "You should mention that to the boss. Maybe he'll give you a special bonus."

"Really? He told me that I was wasting my gifts. Do you think?"

"Absolutely, Adele,"

***

Dietz dialed a familiar number and waited a long time before someone picked up.

When he finally answered, Dietz, wanted to know why the phone hadn't been picked up promptly.

"Fuck off, Dietz."

"Yeah, same to you." The man was the mover and shaker in the party now that Masters was on his last legs. That didn't mean Dietz had to like him any better. He didn't trust him – that's why he had insurance. Lange was the link to the Aryan Nation and other white supremacists groups. Similarly, he knew that Bubba thought he and his Klan friends were dinosaurs.

"Thanks for the reference on Jethro Coyle. He started yesterday. He already told me he wasn't a union man. I think I might tell these Teamster crooks to go to hell."

"You're wise to look into everyone you hire these days. The people up in Jackson told me that Kittyburg is getting fired this week."

"Speaking of Kittyburg. I thought I saw him the other day outside my shoe store."

There was a moment of silence on the call. "You sure it's him?"

"Yeah. His hair is growing back."

"I'll have to check it out."

**

When noon came, Connie watched Dietz head out to lunch by himself. That still left Adele at her desk. She decided to check on her. When Connie went into her office, she found Adele watering the plants. "Hey Adele, I know you're kind of in charge when Dietz is gone. I heard there was a big disturbance down at the front desk. Likely a couple of Teamsters causing trouble."

Adele's eyes went wide as she processed what she had heard. "Should I call the club?"

"I would check it out first. Show your initiative. Maybe you can take care of it."

"Oh! Okay. Thanks, Connie. Can you watch the phone for me?"

Depending on what Adele found, Connie might have ten minutes. "Take your time Adele, I'll handle the phone. The boss might be impressed if, while you're down there, you did a little inspection. Observe how that front desk manager looks after things. He seems a little snarky to me."

Once Connie saw Adele go down the hall to the elevator, she quickly slipped into Dietz's office. It was a huge room with an oak desk near the picture window overlooking the beach. There was a computer, a fax machine, and a Dictaphone on the desk. Connie quickly went to the desk drawers. Sitting in his leather chair, she looked through the file folders in the drawer. In addition to the one labeled Tivoli, there was another for Dietz Designer Shoes. Another thick file was marked Lucky's Casino, and then another for Bubba Shrimp Emporium. She quickly went through them and found they were mainly financial information and notes about employees.

She quickly checked her Casio. She had already wasted ten minutes. There was a file labeled Teamsters in the center drawer – it too held little of value other than his notes about union-busting. On the other side of the desk, the top drawer was locked. *If there was anything juicy, it would be in there.* Using the letter opener, she wedged it in the drawer and tried to pry it open. To her surprise, the lock gave way. She opened the drawer, but other than one of those mini-cassette recorders, all she found was Tivoli letterhead and a bunch of pens. *Why would he lock it if there wasn't something important in it?* She took out the letterhead and spotted a clear plastic sleeve containing a bunch of mini cassettes. On each cassette, there was a date and then a bunch of letters she didn't recognize.

She had three problems. One, and she had already been fifteen minutes. Surely, Adele was on her way back, Two, she didn't have the faintest idea how to copy a bunch of cassettes, and three, she'd scratched up the drawer with the letter opener.

Chapter 50

March 5th, 1985
Wilmer, Alabama

Gabriel

It was a cloudy day, with more rain showers expected as we drove to Wilmer. It took the better part of two hours, given that Weber insisted on driving five miles per hour below the speed limit. He rattled on nonstop, regaling me with all of his police exploits. Occasionally I would throw in an 'uhuh' or a, 'that right?' just to be polite. I was deep in thought about Glenna Sparrow's mother. Discovering another body seemed to cast shade on the thought that her mother might have gotten rid of Dirk.

Wilmer was a small town with a population of 9,998. "I wonder why they didn't round it," I said as we drove through the downtown.

"The population numbers are all off in these little towns. Back during the last census, some mayors didn't want to count the blacks, fearing it might discourage investment."

"Pretty racist."

"Folks around here would say you'd be better off counting the hogs." I looked at Weber, trying to figure out if he was joking. It was 1985 - surely people didn't think that way.

***

Weber turned into the parking lot for the Mobile County Sheriff's office. It was a long two-story structure that looked more like a high school. "Thanks for coming with me, Gabriel. I know you're not getting paid for this, but I thought you'd want to be included. The sheriff's name is Harker, and he's expecting us. Better let me do the talking. You know, cop to cop."

"Sure." I got out of the car and followed him up the steps and into the building. There was a reception desk staffed by a heavyset black woman. Weber stepped up and flashed his badge asking to speak to Sheriff Harker. "He's expecting us."

A few moments later, a tall white man came out of an office and waved us over. He looked middle-aged and could have moonlighted as a beanpole. He gave us a warm smile, and Deputy Weber did the introductions as we went into the office. Once seated, Harker got right down to business and asked us about our case.

"We've got a black male," said Weber. "Found in the bayou. The ME says he might have been in the water for a couple of weeks. The body had lacerations on the back consistent with the man being whipped. We're pending dental records, but we do have a man named Dirk Sparrow who's been missing for six weeks now."

"You must be thinking foul play. Any suspects?"

Weber looked over at me and nodded. "We have the name of a person of interest," I said. "We've recently tracked her to your neck of the woods. Her name is Penn Maddox. Deputy Weber has already searched, and there are no listings with that name in either Alabama or Mississippi."

"She a colored?" He pulled out a legal pad and started taking notes. I shook my head, and he followed up by asking what else we had.

"Not much. We have a description which isn't worth much. Mid to late twenties, somewhat attractive, physically fit."

"What makes you think she's around here?"

"My colleague contacted a Penelope Maddox, who lives in a nursing home up in Vicksburg. As luck would have it, she has a granddaughter who goes by that name. She recalls getting a postcard from her granddaughter with a picture of Mobile on the front."

Sheriff Harker leaned back in his chair, thinking about what I'd said. "I'm not grasping something. Why would your associate have called the woman in the nursing home?"

I filled Harker in on the backstory of how we'd connected the woman to the missing man.

"And what's your role here, Mr. Ross?"

Deputy Weber answered for me. "He's a private detective who's looking into the disappearance. The missing man's wife hired him."

After a moment of indecision, Harker opened a file folder that had been sitting on his desk. He extracted a black and white glossy picture of a naked black man with lacerations on his back. "This look like the same thing?"

The marks were almost identical. I nodded and passed the picture to Weber.

"The body was found mid-December in Big Creek Lake. You probably passed it if you came up highway 98. It's a huge freshwater reservoir, about 3600 acres. The marine police found the body on the north shore near the bridge. There's no missing person report, so we figured he was a vagrant. We caught a break with the fingerprints. Turns out, our man used to be in the Air Force. His name is Reche Tines, with a last known address in Utica, Mississippi. We contacted the Sheriff up in Warren County," continued Harker, "And they said the Tines family moved a while back. We were able to locate what was left of the family in Moss Point. They said that they'd been concerned about Reche but thought he had likely taken up with a girl."

Harker took a sip of coffee before continuing. "When he finished his stint in the Air Force, Tines got hired by

Northrup and moved in with his sister in Moss Point. She was the one that came to claim the body. She was pretty broken up. She said some shit about the Klan, made some accusations but didn't have any evidence. We looked into it, of course. There ain't much Klan here, but we have trouble makers who might do something if provoked. That's pretty much sums up where we are."

"Would seeing a white woman with a black man be enough to provoke these people to do something?" I asked.

"Hard to say. I suppose if they were liquored up enough. You know the expression; he only has one oar in the water? Well, that would describe a few of them. But we checked on them, and there wasn't anything to say that's what happened." Sheriff Harker paused for a moment and then asked, "Assuming that this Penn Maddox killed both men, have you any idea why?"

"Not really. We're concentrating on finding her. But the obvious motives are either racial or maybe sexual," I replied.

"Maybe a combination of the two, like one of those sado-mechanics." offered Weber.

"I think the term is sadomasochist," corrected Harker. "Well, what's the plan, boys? You gonna solve this for me?"

"I think we need to find Penn Maddox. She's the link." I said.

"I can put the word out about her. Maybe speak to the people in Mobile," offered Harker.

***

"So, we have ourselves a female serial killer who likes to torture black men before she kills them," Deputy Weber said on the way back to Gulfport.

"Maybe. Female serial killers are rare."

"In that Glenna Sparrow fired you, are you going to keep looking for this woman?"

"Are you going to open a homicide investigation?" I countered.

"I'll talk to Sheriff Pardy as soon as we get back."

I stewed for a minute, wondering whether Weber would be able to solve the case on his own. I also knew that I couldn't just drop the investigation. "Her grandmother lives in a nursing home in Vicksburg, and this latest body used to live in Utica. I'm wondering if Tines and Maddox knew each other."

"About the same age. Want me to call the sheriff up there?"

"Sure. I'm going to check with Rachel. She's spoken to the old lady. I'd like to drive up there and meet the grandmother."

***

We stopped at a fry truck along the side of the road. Once again, I heard how much money could be made. It was almost 2 PM when I got to the Agency. I opened the door and found Rachel hard at work playing Pong on the office computer.

"Now I get it," I said as I walked in.

"It's my break. How was your trip to Alabama?"

I told her what we'd learned from Sheriff Harker and my plan for the two of us to drive up to Vicksburg.

"Can we do it tomorrow? I'm kind of busy." When she saw my skeptical look, she added, "Not with Pong. I'm waiting on a call back from Don. He has something going on at the Tivoli." She filled me in on Don's plan.

"Sounds dangerous."

"I'm also waiting on a call from Rod. He got the injunction, so Jacob doesn't have to move. But the jerk neighbor who ratted him out has organized a protest, and there's a mob out front of his house carrying signs saying terrible things. Rod was supposed to go visit the sheriff to see if anything can be done."

"Do you need to go?"

"No, I'm going to let Rod handle this."

"I'll keep my fingers crossed," I said, walking into my office. Rachel got up and followed me in. "Wendy from the Blind Tiger called about twenty minutes ago, but she said it wasn't important."

I picked up the phone and called Wendy. She answered right away. "Is that woman really your boss?"

"Rachel? It's complicated. Next time I'm in, I'll tell you about it. Listen, Wendy, I meant to call you. You'll probably read about this in the *Herald*. They pulled a black man out of the bayou. It might be the man we're looking for."

"Oh, I'm sorry, Gabriel. That poor family. So, does that mean I don't have to keep an eye out for that woman?"

"No, it's even more important that we find her and see if she had anything to do with what happened."

"Rachel said you were on the road in Alabama - is that for another case?"

"No, same case. We have a lead that Penn might have moved to Mobile. And we might have another body."

"You think there's a connection?"

"I think so. You were calling me?"

"It's nothing. I got this brain wave, and I thought you should know. You said this girl likes my slippery nipples, so I have an advertisement out front of the bar. Two slippery nipples for the price of one. I thought it might draw her in.

I have some flyers made up. I was going to drop some off. What do you think?"

"It's a good idea."

"Then I'll stop by and show you my slippery nipple flyers. I drew a picture of my … well, you know." There was something distinctly flirty about her tone.

Chapter 51

Mayor Baxter

Dear Diary

Lunch today was sandwiches, cut into little triangles. It was some kind of mystery meat, but I was so pre-occupied with what was about to happen, I ate them anyway. I had the shivs in the pocket. I was at a turning point. In mere minutes, my life could change forever. I didn't care about the spic, but what if something went wrong. I looked over at the table where the Mexican Mafia was sitting. I whispered to the guy next to me, who they call Hochstetter, "Which one is Hector López?"

"He's the fat fuck facing forward at the end of the table." López seemed oblivious to what was about to happen, laughing with his buddies. I had thought about passing a message to a guard warning them. It would be just my luck to give to the wrong guard. Besides, Wolf was watching me closely. I had no choice but to play this out.

Wolf gestured for us to meet outside the hall. He told me to hand out the shivs and said that after we took care of Lopez, I was to gather them and trash them in the machine shop. We made our way to Cell Block Two and hung around and waited.

We didn't have to wait long. When we saw him heading towards his cell, Klink stepped out from behind a pillar. "So Hector, tell me again about why it's okay for a dirty spic like you to spit on my food?"

Hector looked around and smiled when he saw no one but Klink. "You want a piece of me?" He approached Klink, his fists up in a boxing pose. Klink was about half his size. "Prepare to die, Nazi," the spic said, circling Klink. Lopez must have sensed something because he turned just in time to see Schultz, who was as heavy as Hector but taller, come out of one of the cells. Schultz punched Hector on the side of the head and then slammed him into the bars. Hector was stunned and fell. Schultz then jumped on him and pummeled him with a half dozen blows to the head.

Hector was finally able to push Schultz off and staggered to his feet. That's when Klink jammed his shiv into Hector's back. Yelling in pain, Hector reached back to where he'd been stabbed. Wolf used his left hand to pull him forward by his neck as he thrust his shiv into Lopez's belly. Hector was now bent over and screaming for help, holding onto the bars. Burkhalter stepped forward and jabbed his shiv into the man's side. What I was watching was brutal. I looked around for witnesses, and I saw a guard watching. Hector was now on the floor, blood oozing all over the place, crying. Schultz used his shiv this time, jamming it into his cheek. I watched as blood dripped. Wolf gestured to me, signaling it was my turn. I knew it was too late to turn back. I thought about Madge and Sexfinger in bed, the spic judge, and then shoved my shiv into Hector's left ear.

Chapter 52

March 5th, 1985
Gulfport, Mississippi

Connie slammed the drawer back in place. Hesitating for a moment, she took the plastic sleeve containing the mini-cassettes as well as the player. She quickly made her way to the door and peeked out in the hall. When she saw the coast was clear, she strolled past Adele's office.

"Were there any calls, Connie?"

Shit! Connie craned her neck back, holding the plastic sleeve and recorder out of sight. "No, all clear. How did you make out at the front desk?"

"The desk clerk, you know the man in the red suit? I asked him if something big was happening and he said there hadn't been any problems. Just the usual crowd – no complaints, so it must have been a false alarm. That guy's really friendly. We were joking around, and he said he had something really big he'd show me later."

"Don't forget to tell Dietz about that."

Connie went back into her office and tried to decide what to do. She eventually put the recorder and the cassette in her purse and headed off for lunch.

**

She sat on a park bench alone, slipped the first cassette into the recorder, and pressed play. The cassette was labeled January/85 and had the inscription JD, CM. The first voice she heard on the tape she recognized as her boss. "Meeting in this parking garage makes me feel like Deepthroat."

"Not sure we have much choice," said another voice. The voice sounded like an older man. "It wouldn't surprise me if the Feds haven't bugged all our phones."

"Fuck this. We should call it off." Dietz again.

"We're just a few weeks away, and I'm not going to call it off," said the older man. There was heavy coughing.

"You might want to give those up." Dietz again.

"Fuck you. You should know better than to lecture me. If you'd been a little more careful in your hiring, we wouldn't be in this position."

"I dealt with that," said Dietz.

"Like you dealt with Green?"

"What the fuck does that mean?" said her boss.

"It means that your guy fucked up. Don't you listen to the news? We don't know what happened to the wife. She was supposed to be hanging from a tree. There was supposed to be a swastika on the door. Now it doesn't look like a race thing at all. Because he took all the stuff out of the den, it looks like he was killed because of what he was working on."

Connie suddenly realized what she had just heard. Then Dietz said, "Gordie said she was dead."

"Well, of course, Dietz," said the other voice. "I'm sure he thought she was. She probably popped up like a fucking terminator, dragged herself to her car, and drove to the airport. Maybe she's on her way to fucking Disneyworld right now." There was a pause for a few moments before the voice asked, "Who's this Gordie anyway?"

"I know a guy who knows the guy," Dietz said. "He's the one that took care of the state cop in November."

"Let's hope that this one stays dead. Listen, Dietz, it gets worse. Some chick named Rachel handed a floppy disk to the sheriff. She says it was stolen from Green's house by the killer."

"He was supposed to put everything in the locker," her boss was whining now.

"Supposed to? Listen, Dietz, you and your guy created a mess. People were supposed to see this as a race thing. Swastika, Luger, nigger hanging in the backyard? A lot of people went to a lot of trouble to coordinate things. My contact in the sheriff's office said the floppy has everyone's name on it. Mine, yours, everyone's."

"So now, this Rachel dame knows everything?"

"She told the sheriff she didn't own a computer."

"Then she might not have seen the stuff."

"You're a fucking idiot, Dietz. She obviously did. Why else would she give it to the sheriff?"

There was more hacking, then Connie heard Dietz say, "I'll fix it."

The last thing Connie heard on the tape was the older man saying, "Fix this Gordie thing, or I'll be looking for a tree for you."

Oh! Good gravy! Connie thought to herself. She knew what she had. They were openly talking about having that reporter from the *Herald* killed. And this was just the first of a dozen mini-cassettes. Dietz must have been secretly recording his conversations. Surely this would be even better than some handwritten memos. She could authenticate Dietz's voice. The letters on the cassette must be initials. JD stood for John Dietz. She wondered who CM was.

She went to a payphone and called Travis, who had said he'd be home if she ran into trouble.

"Travis, I'm glad you're home," she blurted out once Travis picked up.

"Anything wrong, Mom?"

"Yes and no." She told him the search for notes hadn't turned up anything but then told him about the mini cassettes and what she had just heard.

"Great, Mom! That's better than we'd hoped. Let me call Don and see what he has to say. I'll call you back at your office number."

She looked at her Casio. Dietz would be back from lunch in less than an hour.

***

The phone was ringing when she got back to the office. It was Travis.

"Okay, Mom, this is what we're going to do. Jethro will be by to pick up your garbage in the next couple of minutes. Do as we said. Put what you have, including the recorder, in an envelope, and put it in your trash. Jethro will pick it up and take it out to the parking lot, where Don will be waiting with another cassette recorder. He'll record the mini-cassettes, and then Jethro will get it back to you."

"There's a dozen tapes, Travis. How long is this going to take? Dietz is expected back from his club in less than an hour."

"Don't worry, Mom, we have all that covered."

***

Dietz got into his Jaguar, having had a filling lunch, a couple of Manhattans, and gotten the phone number of the cute waitress. He was feeling pretty set to do battle with the Teamsters. Dietz planned to play hardball with them. He could just picture their faces when he told them to get the fuck out of his office. *Maybe I should take Adele for a picnic this weekend.* He put the key in the ignition, and all he heard was a click. He tried it repeatedly but got the same noise. "Fuck, I just had it serviced," he said, taking his anger out on the steering wheel. He was about to get out and call the auto club when a deputy sheriff's cruiser pulled up beside his car. A tall, boxy-headed deputy strolled over to the car. He was making a note of the license plate in his little spiral notebook. He then stood back and held his fingers up as if he was framing the car for a photo. "What are you doing, Deputy?"

The deputy smiled and held up a finger as if to say just one minute. Dietz was getting frustrated and tried the car again to no avail. Finally, the deputy approached his window. "This is some car."

"Yeah, It's a nice car. But for now, it's not working, and I'm late for an important meeting."

Deputy Weber leaned closer. "Does it have gas?"

"Of course, it has gas!"

"Daddy always told me that if I was ever to be broken down, I should follow a checklist. That way, I won't miss anything. Why I remember a time when a fellow's Pinto broke down out on Highway 10. He swore it was some major technical problem. Well, you guessed it. He just forgot to fill up." Weber started laughing.

"It's got lots of gas."

"What about the lights. Did you perchance leave the headlights turned on? Stuff like that will drain the battery right dead. Why I remember a time…"

Chapter 53

March 5th, 1985
Gulfport, Mississippi

Connie had no sooner put the sleeve of cassettes and the recorder in a brown legal envelope when Jethro rolled in his garbage cart into her office. He was wearing a black t-shirt with the saying; *one man's trash is another man's treasure.*

"I like your T-Shirt, Jethro." Connie gave him her waste paper basket.

"Thank you, ma'am." Jethro pouring the basket contents into his cart and turned around.

About five minutes later, Adele came into the office. "Was that Jethro picking up garbage?"

"Sure was," said Connie, not looking up from her reports.

"Isn't he supposed to pick up the garbage in every office?"

"He didn't? Must be because he's new."

Adele looked down the hall, her hands on her hips. "Have you heard from the boss? He was supposed to be back ten minutes ago."

"No, I wonder what's keeping him?"

***

"One time," said Weber. "I remember the starter going on me when I was out on patrol. It would make that clickety, click, clickety, click sound just like yours."

"Listen, Deputy. I don't know what you're doing, but you need to get out of my way. I'm going to go back inside to call the automobile club."

Weber didn't move, continuing to block the door. "This sure is a mighty fine car. Mighty fine. 1982, right?"

"Yes, now, can you?"

"You know one day I'm going to get myself a car like this. Of course, that'll probably be in the next millennium, but you know these cars hold their value, don't they?"

***

Don

I listened to all the tapes Jethro had brought. It was enough to put Dietz, Lange, Steve Schaffer, and Reverend MacGloyn away for a long time. Thankfully the recordings were short, so it didn't take that long to tape everything onto Weber's full-size cassette. Just as I thought, the bomb-ings were supposed to initiate a race war. Green had gotten too close. His killing was supposed to look like racism and was coordinated with bombings of synagogues throughout the state. Additional assassinations were discussed, includ-ing taking out a couple of well know African-American politicians.

Now, months after the bombings, the city's black lead-ers were begging for peaceful dialogue. They were fighting a losing battle. Protests had become more violent, with mobs looting and vandalizing. When I finished with the last tape, I put everything back in the envelope and went into the ho-tel. I saw Jethro emptying the trash can in the hotel lobby. I walked over to him and said, "I think you dropped some-thing, young fella."

***

Weber now had the Jaguar hood up, and he was playing around. He asked Dietz to try it now, only to get the same clicking noise. "It might be the alternator. I remember a time a car driving right down Beach Boulevard around this time of day, and it just died," he said, snapping his fingers. "Try it again.

"Fuck off, Deputy Weber. I have your name. Sheriff Par-dy is a friend of mine, and I'm going to make sure he hears about this. I don't think you know shit from Shinola about cars. You've wasted almost forty minutes of my time."

Just then, Weber reconnected the sparkplug wires and said, "I think I got it this time. Give it a try."

Dietz tried the ignition, and it started right away. He still couldn't leave because of the way Weber had parked the cruiser. Weber walked over to Dietz, "You see, it's that checklist thing. I had to make it down the list before I realized the spark plug wire had fallen loose. Why I remember one time…."

***

Jethro ran up the stairs and into Connie's office, handing her the package.

"Just one thing. I want you to go into Adele's office and distract her while I put this back. She said you forgot to empty the garbage cans in all the offices."

Jethro nodded and walked down the hall, and knocked on Adele's open door. "Connie said I missed something?"

"Yes, Jethro, don't you need to check each office for garbage? Maybe that wasn't explained to you?"

"I wish I had someone like you show me the ropes." He looked at the nameplate on her desk. "Wow, Executive Personal Assistant. Are you like in charge?"

"Yes, I am."

***

With Jethro blocking Adele's view, Connie slipped into Dietz's office and put the cassettes' sleeve back, along with the recorder. She took one last look around before sneaking back to her own office.

Jethro followed her into the office moments later, smiling.

"Well?"

"I have a date for next Saturday night."

Chapter 54

March 6th, 1985
Gulfport, Mississippi

Don

The phone rang me out of a confusing dream. A woman in a red bustier was slapping me repeatedly with a large fish. It was 4:30 AM, so I hunkered down under the blankets and cursed whoever it was that was calling so early. The celebration had gone on into the early hours. Connie, Travis, Weber, Jethro, and I had met up after work for a celebration. Even the assistant district attorney had stopped by to offer her congratulations and to listen to the tapes. Upon hearing everything, she said she would speak to Judge Ramirez about the subpoena.

Whoever is calling is being very persistent. A sudden thought occurred to me. My former boss, Bubba Lange, used to call me each morning around this time to give me my daily assignment. The thought crept over me like an icy chill. I sat up quickly, staring at the black rotary phone.

"Holy crap!" Jethro was standing in my bedroom doorway, scratching his head. "Tell whoever that is to go to…"

"Hello," I said, putting a finger to my lips and picking up the receiver.

"Rise and shine, buddy." After a moment, the voice added, "Do you know who this is?"

"What do you want, Bubba?"

"I heard you were in town. Is someone with you? I thought I heard another voice."

"No, just me."

"Kittyburg, or should I say, Agent Kooper? I guess I won't be able to say that much longer. The word is the Bureau will give you the old heave-ho, as we say in the oyster business. I was just about to set sail when I thought - who's going to help me bring in the catch? I thought about my brother...you remember Jackson, right? He's dead now, thanks to you. Then I thought of Fender, who's in Parchment, also because of you. Wanna come down to the pier and make things a little easier for me?"

"You're funny. You know the truth of what happened."

"I remember a line from some movie, '*One man's truth is another man's lie*.' I've kind of missed our calls. How does it feel to be the mastermind behind the murder of 168 people? How are you able to sleep?"

"I'm bored with this," I answered, yawning.

"Listen, Kooper, I just wanted to say hello, and to tell you that we have a few more tricks planned. It doesn't look like the niggers got the message. We might have a few more bombs out there with your prints on them. If the MBI thought you were disgruntled before, once they fire you…"

I was about to hang up when he said, "We're coming for you."

I hung up the phone and looked at Jethro.

"Who was that?"

"Wrong number."

Chapter 55

March 6th, 1985
Talladega, Alabama

Mayor Baxter

Dear Diary

Today brought a mix of emotions, mainly fear that some-one saw something and that what happened with Lopez was going to blowback on me. Luckily, I got rid of the shivs that night because the warden and some guards raided the ma-chine shop the next morning.

"Mayor Baxter," said Harrigan, coming up to me. "Were you involved in this unfortunate incident yesterday?"

"You talking about Lopez? I just heard about it."

"That so? It looks like he was stabbed to death with home-made knives, coming out of this machine shop." I shrugged, and he asked if I'd heard anything.

I looked around and then lowered my voice to a whis-per, "I don't know anything about that, but if you ask me, that Cuban over there," I gestured to a guy named Santiago, "was spouting off about some Mexican the other day."

"That right?"

We all had our own cubby holes to store our gloves and goggles. The Warden searched Santiago's and found a bloody shiv.

***

Wolf came up to me at lunch and said no one was to be alone in the yard. "It was pretty smart to leave a shiv in Santiago's cubby. Keep your eyes open. If the Cubans find out you fingered him, they'll be coming." He told me to stick close to Schultz.

***

Later that night, once the guards turned out the lights, Charlie and I were lying in our bunks, "Hey, Charlie, do you ever think of sex?"

"Sure, had me a girl in Houston. She says she might come visit."

"Was her name Bruce?"

"Listen, I told you I'm not into that."

"Just asking, Charlie."

"The name's Robbie."

"How are you getting along here?" I asked, changing the subject.

"The food kind of sucks, but I've had worse. I'll just have to get used to it."

"How's working at the laundry?"

"Okay, I guess. At first, I had an issue handling other peo-ple's stuff. But you get used to it. It helps pass the time. I never thought I'd be working for a fuckin' nickel."

"I hear you, man. Say, I know you used to sell dope. If you ever want to earn a little extra, maybe I could hook you up."

"Nah, I'm done with that shit."

"I heard some spic got killed a couple of days ago. Any-body ever hassle you, you know, like try to bully you?"

Chapter 56

March 6th, 1985
Vicksburg, Mississippi

Gabriel

Another overcast day. Rachel picked me up at home in her Pacer, and we headed to Vicksburg. It was going to be a long drive, so we headed out early. Thankfully, Rachel drives faster than Deputy Weber. On the way, we talked about what had happened at the Tivoli and the incriminating tapes that were found. "Sounds like that should be enough to put people away for a long time."

"Don's already given the tapes to the District Attorney. She said she'd make sure Don's boss got a copy."

"It sounds like an episode of *Mission Impossible*, with that white-hair guy who also does the 'Man from Glad' commercials."

"I don't think that's the same man. The guy in *Mission Impossible* was Peter Graves."

"Whatever, it doesn't sound like Don will be losing his job." I said something about calling to congratulate him. I was selfishly thinking about how it would impact me if Rachel left the Agency to live with Don in Jackson. We drove in silence for a good half hour.

Finally, she looked at me speculatively and asked what I was thinking.

"Nothing."

"I saw your lips moving back there. Mom used to do that. When we were on a family outing, Jacob and I would be in the backseat acting up, and she'd be muttering away to herself."

"Just thinking about the case, I guess. It feels like we're missing something."

"You found the connection between the two men. It's too much to be a coincidence."

"What if we're wrong? Like with your brother, some people don't want homosexuals living in their neighborhood. What if others don't like snow bunnies?"

"Dirk Sparrow was whipped and drowned because some redneck saw him with a white woman? And these same people whipped the man in Alabama?"

"It's just a thought," I said, feeling less sure. "Ben always warns me not to go down the rabbit hole. Not to be too quick to narrow the investigation to one suspect."

Rachel didn't look convinced. "Maybe grandma will help shed some light on this girl. I called her yesterday afternoon just to say we would be by for a visit. She's quite the character."

"How so?"

"You'll see." Rachel went on to explain about the fish dinner, the raincoat, and everyone showing up.

"Just a minute, what were you wearing?"

"Remember a few months ago, this crazy guy broke into my apartment and ruined my clothes?"

"Yeah, I remember you telling me about that."

"Well, Don went out and bought me some new clothes. See-through blouses and mini-skirts. One of the things he bought me was a red velvet bustier."

"No!!! And you wore that to dinner? With Weber and Travis and this Jethro guy?" I started laughing so hard I thought I was going to cry. Rachel's face was the color of a tomato. I laughed probably more than I should have, but she had laughed at me when I'd told her about the penis statue.

***

I was still chuckling as we arrived at Gettinger Gardens, a one-story structure in the shape of a "U," with a flower garden in the middle. When we checked in at the front desk, the orderly said Mrs. Maddox was waiting for us in the party room. As we walked down the hall, Rachel confided she never liked coming to places like this. Despite having worked in a psychiatric hospital, she always felt sad for the residents. At the party room, we found a silver-haired woman sitting alone drinking juice with a straw and watching a rerun of *Barnaby Jones*.

"Mrs. Maddox?" asked Rachel. The woman was dressed in a fancy print dress with a frilly white collar. She turned towards us and gave us a once-over. "It's Rachel Henderson. I called and asked if it was okay to stop by?"

"Yes." The woman cast her eyes in my direction and gestured.

"This is my associate Gabriel Ross."

"Kind of tiny, aren't ya?"

"I make up for it in other ways." I smiled.

"What?"

I raised my voice and spoke as clearly as I could. "I said I make up for it in other ways."

"No need to shout. I heard you the first time. In what ways do you make up for being so short?"

"Oh...personality, heart, intelligence."

"Sure, you do," she said, dismissing me and turning back to Rachel. "You said you were Penny's friend from school, the blonde with the big coconuts." She pointed at Rachel's chest. "They ain't coconuts." She then reached down and grabbed hold of her breasts. "These are coconuts. Who are ya, and what do you want with my granddaughter?"

"We're private investigators - not the police." Rachel handed her a business card. "We've been asked to find your granddaughter."

"Is lying to little old ladies part of your way of doing business?"

"Ma'am," Rachel said, speaking firmly. "I didn't say I was the woman with the coconuts. You just assumed it, and I didn't deny it."

The woman nodded her head. "Kind of spunky, aren't ya, girl?" She turned to me. "I like her. Now, what's your story, little man?"

"Rachel and I work together." The old lady made a face like she didn't buy it for a second.

"I'm not stupid, young man. You ain't from the South, are you?"

"I was born in Detroit…that's in Michigan."

"I know where Detroit is," she said dismissively. "Lot of short people up there?"

Before I could answer, Rachel jumped in. "Mrs. Maddox, I thought we could talk about your granddaughter."

She continued to glare at me. "What do you want to know?"

"Whatever you would care to share with us. Something that might help us locate Penn," I replied.

"Her name is Penny, not Penn," she spat out at me. "Penelope Pearl Maddox. She lived on a farm over in Utica. My son's name was Braxton Maddox. I named him after a Confederate General. That's about it."

Rachel pulled her chair closer to the woman, "Please, Mrs. Maddox, tell us what you remember about her growing up."

She took a deep breath and looked up at the ceiling. "My son was a good man. He'd give you the shirt off his back. When she was young, I told Penny that she got all the goodness in her heart from her daddy. He owned a very successful pawnshop in Vicksburg," she said proudly.

"What about Penny's mother?' I asked.

The woman's face grew stern. "I told Penny that any evil in her soul came from that side of the family. Penny hated her mother so much she swore never to say her name, so I won't either."

"What made her feel that way?" Rachel asked, putting her hand on the woman's arm.

"Because she was a terrible mother. Nothing Penny ever did was good enough. Sometimes, words weren't enough. One time my son brought Penny to my house. She was all bruised up. I went and got my squirrel gun and was fixin' to go over there, but lucky for her, my son stopped me." The old lady paused for a moment to drink some juice, making a loud, slurping sound. "Penny wasn't my son's natural daughter. That slut got herself knocked up and then got all fired up to get hitched. She tried to tell Braxton the baby was his, but I knew."

"Do you know who the real father is?" asked Rachel.

"You'd be better off figuring who she hadn't slept with. Braxton once told me that she said she knew a real important fella down in Biloxi before they met. Supposedly met him at a party with a bunch of high falutin a-holes."

I smiled at the expression. "Was Penny a good student?"

"Did you bring me any candy?" she said, looking around.

"No, I'm sorry. Would you like me to bring you candy?"

"I forgot you're a Yankee. Down here, you come chatting up a woman - you best be bringing something sweet."

"Thanks for the tip." I looked over at Rachel, who was suppressing a laugh.

"You asked if Penny was a good student. Not especially. She got suspended a lot. Mostly for fighting. Her mother taught her how to fight, how to kick someone after they'd given up. There were times when Braxton used to bring her to work with him just to save her from her mother."

"That sounds terrible, Mrs. Maddox," said Rachel.

"Don't get me wrong, young lady, Penny could be a handful. She had no Maddox blood in her and could lie like a two-legged dog. I guess you could say she also learned that from her mother."

"When did your son die?" I asked.

"January 12ᵗʰ, 1970. Penny was called to the principal's office. Mr. Hooger, the kids, called him Booger, told Penny that her Daddy got killed in a robbery at the pawnshop. Cops said it was some motorcycle gang. They never did catch the bastards that shot my boy."

"Losing her father, then having to live with that kind of mother, must have been hard," I said.

"It went from bad to worse. That woman wasted no time inviting another man into her bed. Judging by the speed of things, he was already in the on-deck circle, if you know what I mean. I think Penny tried to make it work, but eventually, she ran away and came to live with me. She never said anything, but I think there was some funny business going on over there. Penny was developing into a woman." In case we didn't understand, she lifted her breasts again. "As I said, I think her mother's new boyfriend was dipping his wick, so I called Sheriff Giddins and had him go out there. Of course, everybody denied it, including Penny. But I ain't no fool. Something was going on."

"Did Penny have friends that she might have stayed in contact?" asked Rachel

"She didn't have girlfriends. She wasn't that kind of girl. There was, of course, the blonde with the coconuts, but that was maybe one time. There was one little darkie girl named Nia. I remember her on account of her bum leg. Her folks lived on a farm out in Utica. Penny used to go on and on about how welcoming and fun they all were. Nia had a big family, and Penny'd get invited to stay for dinner all the time."

"Do you remember Nia's last name? Maybe we could talk to her." I asked.

"Tines, but they moved away after some trouble."

I flashed a look at Rachel. "Can you tell us about that?"

"Penny's mother never forgave me for calling the sheriff on her boyfriend. When she got wind that Penny was sweet on Nia's older brother, she called Sheriff Giddins and claimed the boy had raped Penny. I suppose Giddins was just doing what he had to. He went to the school and arrested the boy in front of everyone. Had there been the slightest evidence, then that boy would have been lynched. The sheriff dropped the charges once he looked into things, but people had started talking by that time. Not long after that, Tines sold the farm and moved."

Rachel was about to ask a question when Mrs. Maddox raised her hand. "We've been at this for too long, and this old bird is tired. Best you two love birds get moving. Next time you come, bring me some candy."

"One last question," said Rachel as she stood up to leave, "On our call, you said that Penny left and started to work at a funeral home."

"She was fifteen and just took a notion and moved to Vicksburg. I think the business with Tines upset her almost as much as what happened to her daddy. As for how she got along with those people at the funeral home, best you speak to Sheriff Giddins."

***

"Seriously, you went over to Don's apartment wearing a coat over a red velvet bustier?" I asked as we sat down at a nearby diner in Vicksburg.

"After everything, Penn's grandmother laid on us, that's what you're thinking about?"

"I'm sorry. I just got this image in my mind."

"That's a little creepy. What do you think about what she said about her granddaughter?"

"Hard not to feel for the girl. Her father murdered like that, then her abusive mother, possible sexual abuse, and then when she finally finds a friend, her mother screams rape."

"It made me want to cry."

I nodded, looking at the menu. "I think I'll have the southern fried steak."

"I could go for a salad. Are you feeling better about Penn as a suspect?"

"There's definitely a connection to the body in Alabama. But there's still something that I don't understand. Reche Tines is dead, likely tortured, and murdered. If she liked him so much, why is he dead?"

"Maybe this Sheriff Giddins can shed some light on that."

Once our meal came, Rachel asked, "I know Penn Maddox was described as physically fit, but do you believe a woman could torture a man and then drown him all by herself?"

"You haven't met Sonja yet."

Chapter 57

March 6th, 1985
Vicksburg, Mississippi

Gabriel

The Warren County Sheriff's Office was located in a stately old building in picturesque downtown Vicksburg. It was a large brick building housing the sheriff's department, the county jail, and the medical investigation unit. We went in, gave the woman at the desk a card, and asked if we could speak to Sheriff Giddins about Penn Maddox. We must have pressed the right button, as moments after she spoke to someone on the phone, a tall, older man with graying hair, a long face, and droopy eyes lumbered out of one of the offices.

"I'm Sheriff Jim Giddins." He extended his hand.

Once introductions were made, he ushered us into a vacant meeting room and asked what this was all about.

"We're looking for Penn Maddox in connection with a couple of homicides, one in Alabama and another in Biloxi." I gave him a summary of the victims and how we'd come to believe that Penn Maddox might be involved.

"I remember the family. This office has had quite a bit to do with them. Some folks called them white trash - others just said they were crazy. Braxton Maddox, Penn's father, seemed normal enough to me. If you've been out to see Mrs. Maddox at the nursing home, you likely know the story. I always thought her granddaughter got dealt a bad hand and then went about making things even worse."

"Can you tell us a little bit about Braxton's murder?

"That was over a dozen years ago. He had a pawnshop over on Washington Street called *Braxton's Guns.* He called it that because that's pretty much eighty percent of his business. People around these parts like their guns. He told me once that folks would come in at the end of the hunting season, pawn their long guns and then come back and get them back the following season."

"Were the guns the reason he was robbed?" asked Rachel.

"Spect so. I got a call from a man who lived kitty-corner to the shop. It was mid-afternoon on a Friday. He saw a couple of motorcycles ride up, and the riders went into the shop. He decided to call us because he heard what sounded like firecrackers going off from inside the store. We scrambled and got there as soon as we could. But we were too late. We found Braxton with about a dozen holes in him.

"Was the witness able to identify them?"

"He got a sudden case of amnesia and said he didn't get a good enough look. We get all kinds of gangs come through here. The Feds got lucky about six months later. The ATF raided the clubhouse of a gang called the Pagans. They're a bunch of low-lifes affiliated with the Aryan Brotherhood. It was a drug bust, but they found a stash of guns that still had the pawnshop tags on them. The leader, a man named Earl Gruber, is in Federal Prison on a drug charge. Without the witness, they didn't have enough for the murder charge."

"That must have been difficult, Penn," I said.

"It was. Losing her father, who she adored, and then having to live with that woman was hard. I think her mother was the crazy one. Things got kind of weird. Penny started acting out and getting into trouble at school."

"You just called her Penny. Did she go by that name?"

"When she was born, she was Penelope. When her daddy got killed, she became Penny. She even told her principal that she had it legally changed. She gave him the name of some lawyer in Vicksburg. My, that girl could lie. It's funny now that I think about it…Penelope, Penny, Penn …It was like whenever something bad happened, she would reinvent herself and change her name.

"Her grandmother said something about sexual abuse."

"There was definitely something hinky going on out there. Her mother took up with another man, then Penny's grandmother claimed that Penny and this man might be involved in something sexual. I investigated, but everyone denied it. If I had to bet money on it, I'd guess Penny was playing around with her mother's boyfriend, and her mother got angry. Not long after, her mother accused a colored boy of raping Penny."

"Yes, we heard about that." Rachel said.

"A colored raping a white girl around these parts is very serious. I took her mother at her word and brought the boy in for a chat. I probably shouldn't have done it because word got around town. Once I talked to the boy and then to Penny, it was clear that if there was any hanky-panky going on it, Penny was likely the one who started it."

"The body that turned up in Alabama has been identified as Reche Tines," I said.

"What? In Alabama? That's a head-scratcher. Penn wouldn't have had anything to do with that."

"She's the common denominator in both cases. Both bodies were found in the water with whip marks on their back."

"Whip marks? That don't make sense. As far as I know, she was pretty sweet on that boy."

We left him to ponder the news before Rachel spoke. "Mrs. Maddox said to ask you about the funeral home."

Giddings was still scratching his head about the whip marks. "That goes back a few years. Back then, she was going by Penn. I had no idea she was working there. Old man Nash, the funeral director, had a massive heart attack and died. I suppose that's when I saw her there. She was helping the son with the services. It was when the son took over the business that some issues surfaced."

"Legal issues?" I asked.

"Are you familiar will pre-paid funeral accounts?" I looked at Rachel and said, not really. "Folks often prepay their expenses in advance. The money is supposed to be held in trust. A couple of months after the son took over the business, the state regulators came in and found that there was $40,000 missing. The son initially said that his father must have done something. When the regulators looked into it further, they found that the money had been withdrawn from the account after the old man died. The matter got settled. The son found the missing money."

"The regulators were satisfied?"

"Satisfied is likely too big of a word for it. They levied a fine and agreed to drop the matter. I believe the son took the money and then repaid it when he got caught. As for where he got the money to repay it, this brings us to the Mississippi Bureau of Investigations, who'd been running an investigation into organized crime and how a group of funeral directors had been selling body parts without the family's consent. Nash was on their list of suspects. So far, there's been one arrest in Hattiesburg. I wouldn't have put it past Bradley Nash. I've always thought he was a bit of a schemer."

"Mrs. Maddox also said something to me about how he was caught doing something with one of the bodies?"

Giddings started to chuckle. "I shouldn't laugh, but with everything we've seen, that story takes the cake. A woman named Juanita Cross wanted to speak to Nash about arrangements for her late husband's funeral. He was a man of color who died suddenly in a car accident. The door to the funeral parlor was open, and she went looking for Nash. She found him in the basement in a room where they keep the bodies. She claims she saw Bradley, naked as a jaybird on top of her husband's body. I'll leave the rest to your imagination. But whatever image springs to mind is likely pretty close to what she described. Of course, he denied it and threatened to sue. For me, there was never any doubt about her story, but it was her word against his. This town is probably no different than others. You seen that shampoo commercial where you tell two friends, and they tell two friends?"

I nodded.

"That was the final straw. Bradley Nash closed the business and sold the property. It's a municipal parking lot now."

"Do you think Penn might still be mixed up with this guy?"

"I lost track of her. This is getting on a few years now."

We thanked Sheriff Giddings for his time and got up to leave. As we did, he said, "Don't you want to know about the fire?"

We both nodded and sat down again.

"This all happened around a few months from each other. Penn's mother was still living on the family farm. She had put the run to the boyfriend. The medical examiner said she must have fallen and hit her head, leaving oil in a saucepan on the stove. She was a terrible alcoholic. The farm was all clapboard and went up like a tinder box."

"Did you talk to Penn about this, given how she felt about her?"

"Yes, and she had an alibi at the time of the fire. She never came out for the funeral."

***

"I think my head is about to explode," Rachel said once we got back to the car. "That was a lot to take in."

"Remind me never to question your intuition again."

"About what?"

"You said at the diner that you couldn't see a physically fit woman doing this all by herself."

"Do you think that she hooked up with the perv in the funeral home?"

"Yep. Do you remember when Dirk broke up a fight at the bar between Penn Maddox and a guy? His name was Bradley."

"Shit, I had forgotten about that. Maybe we should ask Weber to check on addresses for Bradley Nash."

"Pull into that gas station. While I fill up, you can use the payphone."

***

"We hit pay dirt," Rachel said once she got back into the car. "Weber said there's a current driver's license issued to a Bradley Nash. He lives in a small town near Wilmer called Tanner Williams. I have an address, 944 Tollgate Hill, Road. Weber said he'd call the sheriff in Wilmer and have him meet us there.

Chapter 58

Gabriel

It was after 7 PM by the time we found the address in Wilmer. By that time, the sun had already set. The moon was almost full, giving us enough light to see the house. We heard the crack of thunder as we got out of the car. A cruiser from Harrison County, and two others from Mobile County, were parked in front of the place. I spied Deputy Weber talking to Sheriff Harker. As we walked over, I looked up at the house. It looked pre-Civil War and had not weathered well. The two-story wooden farmhouse was set back amongst mature trees and was very secluded. An outbuilding leaned at a twenty-five-degree angle.

"Too late," Weber said as we walked up. Weber turned to Harker and added, "This is Rachel Henderson - she runs the Detective Agency."

"Find anything inside?" Rachel asked Weber, nodding to Harker.

"Three-bedroom, one bath, old fashioned eat-in kitchen. Kind of a handyman special," said Weber, as if he was describing a piece of real estate.

"I meant did you find any more bodies, any sign that they'd been here recently?" asked Rachel, hands on her hips.

Sheriff Harker jumped in. "No more bodies, but we did find something you should see." He used his flashlight to lead us down the dirt trail to the house.

"Judging by these tire marks," I said, "I'd say a compact car. With all the rain we've been having, it was here recently."

"There are dirty dishes in the kitchen. They left in a hurry and weren't intending on coming back," said Harker.

"A good forensics team should be able to tell you what kind of car made these tracks," added Weber.

"Good idea," I said. Looking at Weber, I asked, "Did you get a previous address when you did the license search?"

He checked his notebook, "An address in Vicksburg."

"The owners live in Pascagoula," said Harker. "A man named Bradley Nash rented it for a year beginning last summer. As far as they know, he was on his own. He paid cash in advance and listed his occupation as construction. He claimed he'd fix the place up, but there's not much sign of that. I asked for a description, and I got Caucasian, dark hair, broad-shouldered, maybe late twenties."

***

When we got to the back of the house, the grass had been allowed to grow and was high enough to wet my pants to the knees. Harker gestured to something near the back of the lot with his flashlight. The rain came all of a sudden, followed by a flash of lightning that illuminated a thick, weathered log standing straight up about six feet from a wooden base. An old two by four was nailed across the top, making it into a crude crucifix. At the base of the crucifix, there was a pair of rusty shackles. Rain dripped down my face as I looked on in horror, realizing it had been used as a whipping post.

No one said anything for a couple of minutes.

"We've got a team on their way," said Harkin using gloves to put the shackles in an evidence bag. "There's some blood on the base and on these shackles. We'll do all the tests, but my guess is that we found where Reche Tines was tortured."

"How old is this?" asked Rachel, nodding to the whipping post.

"Hard to say," replied Harker. "You still find this type of thing on some of the older farms around here. This dump might have been here a long time ago, but it's too small to have been a farm. It's just a piece of history now. As for the post, my guess is that Nash built this."

"What kind of a sick mind would do this?" asked Rachel, clearly upset at finding the post.

"Bradley Nash," I said, "Based on what we heard about the funeral home, I'd say big-time sicko."

***

As we walked through the house, I looked at Rachel, who had grown quiet. I could see she was upset about finding the whipping post. I put my arm around her, "Thank goodness society has moved forward, and this brutality isn't a thing anymore."

"Slaves were treated no better than pigs," said Weber. "They'd encourage them to have children and then rip the family apart, selling the kids to other plantations. Sometimes the plantation owners would rape the girls to breed them and then sell the babies. If the slaves didn't work hard enough or made mistakes, they'd get whipped. If they were caught trying to run away, they'd whip them until their back was a bloody mass of open flesh. They'd gather all of their slaves around the whipping post as a lesson to others."

"*Roots* again?" I asked him.

"Yep."

"Let's spread out and look for anything that might give us a clue about where they went."

Rachel took the kitchen, Weber took the front room, and I went up to the second floor. I found nothing in the bathroom, no toothpaste, or razors, or prescription of anti-crazy medication. One of the bedrooms was empty, and a second contained a mattress on the floor. The third, which I guessed was the room they shared, had a mattress bowed in the middle and an old wooden dresser. I quickly went through the drawers and found nothing. They had cleaned everything out. I went to the closet and found a bunch of empty wire hangers. I started looking for hiding spots, someplace they forgot.

"Not much in the front room other than an ugly couch." Weber came into the bedroom. "I looked in the cushions and found some travel brochures. I suggest we alert the Mobile airport."

"Good idea. Find anything?" I looked at Rachel, who had followed him.

"They weren't great housekeepers. There are a few beers in the fridge, some eggs, and luncheon meat. In the freezer, I found some Swanson TV dinners and a bottle of vodka."

Chapter 59

March 6th, 1985
Gulfport, Mississippi

Jacqueline was putting Jelly Bean down for his mid-day nap. She thought about Gabriel, who had left early with Rachel and wasn't expected home until late. Lunch with Rachel had gone well, and they'd had fun talking about Gabriel's bad habits. She came away with mixed feelings about the relationship between Gabriel and Rachel. Rachel appeared to have strong feelings for Don, yet her conversation seemed always to come back to 'Gabriel said this,' or 'Gabriel did that.'

Jacqueline went into the bathroom and looked at herself in the mirror. She complimented herself for regaining her pre-Benjamin figure. Her complexion showed no sign of hitting the ripe old age of twenty-seven. One might expect a wrinkle or two, having almost been buried alive twice. Rachel had said that Gabriel loved her so much that he was scared of losing her. That, according to Rachel, was the root of why he'd been acting the way he had.

It hadn't occurred to Jacqueline that Gabriel was frightened of losing his family. "Maybe I need to be more like Rachel, wear tighter clothes, fix my hair differently, be more fun-loving." She rarely saw her friend Chevon, now that she was married. Other than her, she didn't have any friends.

As if on cue, the doorbell rang. She raced to the door, hoping to answer it before Benjamin woke up. When she opened the door, a woman was holding a bunch of flyers. "Yes, can I help you?"

"You must be Jacqueline, so nice to meet you."

The woman was wearing jeans and a beige tank top. Jacqueline saw that she had a tattoo of an alligator on her arm. "Yes, I'm Jacqueline Ross. Are you delivering something?" Jacqueline let her eyes go to the flyers the woman was holding.

"I believe I spoke to you the other night when I called for Gabriel. I'm sorry if I intruded. My name's Wendy."

"Oh, yes, I remember, Wendy." Jacqueline extended her hand and said, "Won't you come in? I was just about to make tea."

"That would be very nice. I've been delivering these flyers all over the place, and I told Gabriel I'd drop some off for him."

"Let's go to the kitchen. I just put my two-year-old down for his nap. Believe me, you don't want him to wake him."

"A two-year-old…Wow, you and your husband don't look old enough to have kids."

"That's nice of you to say. Most days, I'm so exhausted chasing after him, I'm dead on my feet by the time Gabriel gets home." Jacqueline invited Wendy to have a seat as she went ahead and made tea. "Would you rather have coffee?"

"No, I love tea. That would be lovely," said Wendy sitting down. Looking around the room, "You have a beautiful home. You must be very happy."

"We are," Jacqueline said with a moment of hesitation. "Just before you rang the bell, I was telling myself that I should get out there more, meet people, be part of the community."

"And then I showed up, like magic."

Jacqueline laughed, "I like your tattoo. I've never had the guts to get one."

"I was young. Wanted to be noticed."

"And you had a pet alligator?"

"No, nothing like that. It's just something my daddy and I used to say when he went off to work. I'd say 'see you later, alligator,' and then he'd say 'in a while crocodile."

Jacqueline sat down and put a plate of cookies on the table. She started to giggle, "I hope you don't mind baby cookies. It's all I have. Gabriel and I have gotten used to them."

Wendy tried one. "Pretty good, a little different taste."

"Mom makes them from leftover baby food. I think these are sweet potatoes."

Wendy started to laugh.

Jacqueline smiled and poured the tea. Wendy was slim and looked around the same age as her. Pretty, but in a tough kind of way. She wore her blonde hair tied back into a ponytail with large hoop earrings. "I detect a bit of an accent. Whereabouts did you grow up, Wendy?"

"Up north. Small town, Mississippi. You?"

"Chicago, born and bred. My parents moved down here when they retired. So, I guess I'm a Mississippian. What's on your flyers?" Jacqueline pointed to the stack on the table.

"I don't know how much Gabriel shared with you - he's looking for a woman who I've seen at my bar. She's currently a blonde, but I suspect she's really a brunette. We think she goes by the name of Penn Maddox. She comes in to pick up men. Apparently, she likes this certain kind of drink. I convinced the boss to offer a two for one sale. Maybe it'll draw her in."

"Sounds like a good idea," Jacqueline said, looking at the flyers. They were a little graphic, showing a drawing of a topless woman holding a drink in both hands. "Leave me as many as you can. I'm off tomorrow, and I can hand them out at the grocery store."

"Great, maybe I can treat you for lunch at the Blind Tiger."

"It's a date," Jacqueline said, smiling. Just then, she heard Benjamin crying in his bedroom. "I'd better go get the little terror."

"Maybe I should go."

"No, don't be silly. He needs to meet people. I just have to change his diaper."

While Jacqueline left to tend to him, Wendy got up and wandered around the kitchen. Looking in the cupboards, she found boxes and boxes of Jell-O and Lucky Charms. Opening the fridge, she found it stocked with food, unlike her fridge. There was a stool that she figured Gabriel used to reach things. She let her hand travel lightly over their possessions, like the toaster and a knife block containing the huge cleaver. She moved on into the master bedroom and looked in the closet. She laughed at Gabriel's short little ties. He was fond of clip-ons. She was leaving the bedroom when Jacqueline emerged from the baby's room. "I was just coming to look for you, see if you needed help. Look at this cutie," she said, rustling Benjamin's hair. Benjamin gave her the lip and started to cry.

"Don't worry about him. He just never seen you before."

Chapter 60

March 7th, 1985
Talladega, Alabama

Mayor Baxter

Dear Diary

I mentioned to Wolf that Charlie might be coming around at breakfast but would need a little push. I laid it out for him, and he said he knew the right people to approach.

Things are tightening up at the machine shop. Guards were checking all the discarded metal and watching everyone closely. There's been no sign of Santiago since he was taken away.

***

After dinner, I walked back to my cell and discovered Charlie with a black eye. He was agitated and anxious to talk. He told me he was playing roundball in the yard when a couple of black guys started hassling him about playing a black man's sport.

"At first, I thought they were joking, but then one pushed me up against the fence and said I'd called him a 'nigger.' Which I didn't. Anyway, the other guy ran at

me and took a swing. The guards saw it all and didn't do a fucking thing."

"Shit, are you going to complain?"

"Yeah, right. If I do, I'll get another fucking beating tomorrow. I'll just avoid the basketball court."

I was tempted to tell him that he was going to get a shit-kicking one way or another.

Chapter 61

March 8th, 1985
Gulfport, Mississippi

Don

"If I were you, I'd quit standing in front of that window," I said to Jethro.

He yawned and gave me a shaky smile. He hadn't slept well. "Just seeing if I recognize anyone out there." He'd been pointing out every white person he saw walking down the street.

The radio was playing the Animals' *House of the Rising Sun*. I pointed to the card table. "Your bet."

"Fuck, I don't know, man. I wish Weber would call. What's taking so long? We'd better figure out this shit before next Saturday. I have a big date with Adele." The shit he was referring to was Bubba. After his threat, we'd decided to hunker down in the apartment, waiting for Lange to be arrested. "What happens if they look for the tapes and they're not there?" Jethro had asked a version of this same question three or four times already.

"Calm down. Why would Dietz move the cassettes? Connie said she'd put them back exactly as she found them. If that does happen, we'll get a warrant for his car, house,

safe deposit box... I don't see him getting rid of them –
they're his insurance."

Jethro sat down and picked up his cards, shaking his
head. "Give me two," he said, discarding a couple of cards.
We heard a door slam somewhere outside the apartment -
in the hallway, and we both looked at the gun on the table.
"You've already drawn two cards. It's betting time. It'll cost
you another ten cents if you want to call, or you can fold."
Jethro fanned his cards again - a look of despair on his face.
I knew he had nothing. He had one good hand all game.
And on that hand, I had a better one. I looked down at the
tally sheet. So far, he owed me big time. At least $6. I was
sure that was $6 more than he had.

Finally, he threw in his cards. "I'm out. I guess I just
don't have it tonight." The song ended, and the station
broke in for an important news bulletin. We both listened
in anticipation.

"*This just into our newsroom. Harrison County Sheriff's
Department has issued arrest warrants for two individu-
als in connection with a body recently retrieved from Bayou Bernard. The body was identified as being that of Dirk
Sparrow. The African American man was last seen this past
January. Wanted on murder charges are Penn Maddox and
Bradley Nash. Their last known address is Tanner Williams
in Alabama. We spoke to Deputy Sheriff Weber about the
developments. "We've put out an APB. That stands for All*

Points Bulletin," he said officiously. "We're also looking at the same pair for another body that was recently found near Wilmer, Alabama. We'll get 'em. It's just a matter of time."

Jethro and I shared a look as Weber continued, "*The woman is described as twenty-seven years old, approximately 5 foot 4 inches tall, somewhat attractive with blonde hair. Bradley Nash is also twenty-seven, 6 foot 2 inches tall, and broad shoulders with long brown hair. The pair are considered to be ultra dangerous. If anyone has information concerning this matter, they should not approach them under any circumstance. Please call the Sheriff's Department.*"

"Maybe that's why we haven't heard about the subpoena. Weber's been busy chasing down a somewhat attractive blonde." Jethro got up and went back to the window.

"Well, that's good news," I said. "Rachel was working on that case. She must have come up with enough evidence for a warrant. I'm going to give her a shout." I was about to pick up the phone when it rang. I picked up the phone and waited a moment.

"Is this Agent Kooper?"

"Who wants to know?"

"This is Agent Cross of the MBI. The Special Director has asked me to call you. She wanted me to pass on that she spoke to an assistant district attorney earlier today." He paused for a moment before continuing in an unemotional, almost robotic voice. "Well done...hurray, you came through on that one... nice job...we're all happy for you."

I heard Cross's partner Smiley shouting in the background. "Let's see if there's a conviction. Probably going to fuck that up too."

"Okay, Cross, message delivered. Anything else?"

"She said to tell you not to get upset about the pink slip you got in the mail. The matter is under review." I slammed the phone down and noticed that Jethro was back at the window.

"Do you remember Joe-Bob from the militia camp?"

"Not really," I said, going to the window.

"You see that sign for *Fleming Real Estate*. The dude with the ball cap, smoking a cigarette."

From six flights up, all I could make out was that it was a white male. "How can you be sure?"

"He was looking up at this window. I think it's him." I had no doubt people were watching the apartment. Bubba more or less said they were coming. As far as they knew, I was alone. I thought about how they'd do it. My best guess was at night when they thought I'd be asleep. *They'd send a couple of people. First, they'd have to pick the lock. Once that was done, they'd fan out, guns at the ready. One would take the bedroom, while the other would check out the living room and kitchen. My guess is that the one in the bedroom would empty their clip into the body sleeping in my bed. Once the shooting ended, I'd come out of my nest in the closet, guns a-blazing. Then when the second guy came running, he'd run right into Jethro coming out of the can, where he'd been sleeping in the tub.*

"Well, what do you think?" Jethro broke into my daydream.

"Might be. I don't think he'd be able to see this high up, but just in case, you should assume it's him and come away from the window."

I tried Rachel both at the office and her apartment and got her voicemail. I left a message congratulating her on the arrest warrant and asking her to call me back.

"How long have you and Rachel been seeing each other?"

"It's been off and on. I guess we must be coming up to one year."

"Would you ever get hitched?"

I shrugged my shoulders. "I'm not sure I'm husband material." Jethro came back and sat at the card table. "What's for supper? And don't say pizza." We'd had it three days in a row, and I was worried that they might pick up on the pattern if someone was watching. "How about Chinese?"

***

Deputy Weber called about a half-hour later and said that the judge was still considering the search warrant's validity. The issue involved the reason for the warrant. For the tapes to be admitted as evidence, we couldn't very well argue we'd already broken in and listened to them before getting the warrant. "The judge has listened to the tapes and wants to sign the warrant. He just doesn't want to have the warrant challenged."

During dinner, Rachel called and wanted to come over, but I told her it wasn't safe. She filled me in on what they'd found in Alabama.

***

We spent the evening listening to music and reading Jethro's huge supply of Playboy magazines. By 10 PM, I decided to hit the closet early.

***

It was 4:30 the next morning when I heard the phone ring. I knew it was Bubba Lange. All he said was kaboom.

Chapter 62

March 8th, 1985
Talladega, Alabama

Mayor Baxter

My Dear Diary

Today was a frustrating day. The Warden sent word some reporters from a local news station were going to be visiting the prison and wanted to interview him and then do a short interview with me.

They were planning a weekly series about famous people who have found themselves behind bars. I remember Elvis Presley spent time in jail. Then, of course, there's Johnny Cash, but he was more of a convict who became famous later. Ty Cobb, the famous ballplayer, got into an altercation at a butcher shop where he pulled a gun on a clerk and got railroaded into jail.

I don't mind the idea of being featured in the piece. Once word gets out that I'm starring in the feature, audiences will go nuts. They'll probably get the highest ratings they've ever had. The warden came to see me and asked if I was all set. The crew would be setting up in the guards' meeting room.

"I was hoping for a new suit," I told him. "Maybe something in a light spring-like color. Also, it would be nice to

have a good pair of shoes. Maybe a pair of black brogues. These crappy sandals are just going to give people the wrong impression."

He said sure and that it was a great idea. He asked me what sizes I wore.

***

A darkie named Charles Evers introduced himself and told me where to sit. I asked him to fetch me a Diet Coke, and he just smiled. The man was dressed casually in a sports shirt and a pair of khakis.

"The warden was supposed to get me a suit of clothes and some shoes."

"Why?"

"I have a reputation to uphold. I don't want my constituents to see me dressed like this."

Evers started laughing. "You're a funny man, Mr. Mayor. Do you see any cameras?"

"No, I don't."

"That's on account of this being a radio interview. I do a weekly feature called "Let's talk," which is syndicated throughout the Southern states. If this goes well, you'll have a huge audience."

"You? You're interviewing me?"

"Ya'll gonna do just fine," he grinned.

***

"This is Charles Evers, and this is "Let's Talk." Another installment of famous, or should we say infamous, people who find themselves behind bars. I have with me the former Mayor of Biloxi, Mr. John Baxter, who has recently been sentenced to 20 years in prison. Mayor Baxter, Let's talk."

"I would like to say before we begin, my sentencing and my conviction are under appeal. That Mexican judge made serious errors."

"That's good to know. You mentioned Judge Ramirez and that he is of Mexican heritage - what did you mean by that?"

"Just that he likely doesn't have the proper credentials, him being from Mehico."

"I can assure you he does. Let's move on to another topic. You've been convicted of some very serious crimes against the citizens of Biloxi. Do you take responsibility for the things that you've done?"

"No, as I've said, everything is being appealed. The only thing I'm guilty of is the terrific economic performance and development of the city. Probably the fastest growth of any American city. This was all my work."

"Since you're handing out praise to yourself, do you also have praise for your business partner, Frank Reznikov?"

"Reznikov? I hardly know him."

"Is that right? At your trial, it was brought up that Federal Authorities had tapped your phone and that over two months, there were 38 phone conversations between the two of you."

"I don't know anything about that. Calls at City Hall go through a switchboard. It could have been anyone."

"They actually traced the calls to your extension."

"I may have dialed his number by mistake. I guess his number must be similar to Dominos. The phone company is constantly getting their wires crossed."

"That's a lot of pizzas, Mr. Mayor."

"I often work late on constituent issues. Did you know I won the last election by a landslide?"

"That's not true. You did squeak out a win, but there have been allegations that your Russian friend, Mr. Reznikov, might have influenced the election. There were quite a few voting irregularities."

"If there was any funny stuff going on, I can assure you that it was by my opponent."

"Let's shift gears again and talk about Biloxi. It has recently come under national scrutiny for a series of bombings that killed 168 people. Most of those killed were African-Americans. You've been pretty silent on one of the worst cases of domestic terrorism this country has ever seen."

"I, of course, was not mayor when that happened. That was the work of a rogue MBI agent. He was disgruntled about not getting a promotion. Everybody knows it. Believe me."

"That is a theory some are promoting, but upon closer examination, it appears that this agent was a patsy, and the bombings were the work of a white supremacist group wanting to start a race war."

"I don't know anything about that. I'd be surprised if that were true."

"I thought that you'd know all about it, given your membership in the Aryan Brotherhood."

"Covfefe."

Chapter 63

March 9th, 1985
Gulfport, Mississippi

Don

I was about to tell Bubba to get stuffed when I heard an explosion so loud I thought it shook the building. My bedroom window lit up like a golden ball. I dropped the phone and looked down at the parking lot. My truck was engulfed in flames. Then a second explosion - likely the fuel tank. I watched as the flames spread to a sedan that was parked beside the truck.

"What the fuck?" Jethro ran into the room.

"Call 911," I shouted. "They just blew up my truck."

I grabbed my revolver and ran out the door dressed in nothing but my boxers and a t-shirt. I was halfway down the hall when it occurred to me that the bomb might have been meant to flush me out. I heard the fire alarm go off. When I got to the stairwell, I saw Mr. Shamir, the building super, running down the stairs. He was about to open the metal door to the parking lot when I yelled, "Stop! Don't open that door." He looked back, giving me a look of concern before opening the door. I heard a shotgun blast a moment later. I made it to the bottom of the stairs and opened the stairwell door a crack. I heard a couple of more shots and someone yell, "Hurry up and get in." Then the sound of a truck peeling off down the street.

I opened the door fully. Mr. Shamir lay in a pool of blood, the back half of his head missing.

***

"So let's go over this again," said Deputy Weber. Jethro was at the window again – watching the fire department trying to control the blaze.

I shook my head. "This is the third time, Weber."

"Listen, Don, I know it's late, but this a murder investigation now. The big enchilada, as they say in the business. I've got a mental checklist to go through. Number one on that list is to make sure I have the story straight."

"Okay," I said. "It was 4:30. It was Bubba Lange. I know that because he phones every morning at the exact same time. He wants me to know it's him. The night before last, he called and said he had more bombs and that he was coming for me. Ever since, Jethro and I have been hunkered down here waiting for you to get that warrant and arrest him."

"What specifically did he say this time?"

"All he said was kaboom."

"Kaboom?"

"Yeah, like boom," jumped in Jethro, using his hand to signal an explosion.

"He didn't say anything else?" Weber was likely writing 'kaboom' in his little notebook.

"I don't know because that's when I heard the real explosion. It was loud. I dropped the phone and ran to the window. I could see my truck was on fire. Then a moment later, there was a second explosion."

"So, he had an RDD? That's a remote detonation device. I've spent some time with our bomb squad," Weber said officiously. "You dropped the phone…you didn't hang up or say anything?"

"No, I was consumed with what was happening in the parking lot. I yelled at Jethro to call 911."

"When you picked up the phone," he said, pointing to Jethro, "was the caller still there?"

"I don't know. When I got to the phone, I pressed the plunger a couple of times because there was no dial tone."

"Tell me about the gunshot."

"Has anyone spoken to Mrs. Sharma?" I asked, wanting this nightmare to end. The image of seeing Sharma with half his head blown off was imprinted on my mind.

"I sent a deputy," Weber said quickly. I repeated what had happened to Mr. Sharma. "You said it sounded like a shotgun blast, but then you said you heard a couple of more shots. Was it more shotgun blasts, or would you say handgun?"

"I took a deep breath. "I'd say the second and third shots came from a handgun. Maybe from the guy who drove the truck."

"Likely a second shooter. Did you see the truck?"

"No. Because when I went to open the door, they fired."

"This person who yelled, 'Hurry up and get in,' Did you recognize the voice?"

"No."

"I need you guys to come with me to the station to make a statement. Grab what you need for a couple of days. When we're done, we'll find someplace safe."

Chapter 64

Mayor Baxter

Dear Diary,

I've been hanging out with Schultz and found out that he was initially sentenced to an eight-year stint for interstate bank robbery in Alabama. Once behind bars, he added a deuce by being charged with initiating a riot in the cafeteria. He beat up a colored who he claimed was butting in line.

I asked if he had a book of drawings for his tattoos, and he said he could do one better. He proceeded to strip down to show me all of his twenty-two inks, including the ones of winged swastikas, looking strangely like bumblebees, coming out of his ass. I opted for a chest-sized German eagle over a Nazi crest, and we agreed we would start work on it over the next week.

***

At lunch, I sat beside Schultz, "I know we're supposed to be looking out for each other, but the warden wants to see me this afternoon."

"What does he want?"

"Probably to fuck with me some more." I told him about the Diet Coke and the cigars.

"He likes to remind you that he's the warden, and you're a convict."

***

This time Jamie was sitting at her desk wearing a low-cut top and tight pants. She smiled at me and told me that Warden Harrigan was waiting. When I stood in the doorway, Harrigan was looking at a file on his desk. Once he saw me, he waved me in and pointed to the chair. "Good afternoon Mr. Mayor. I was just noting in your file that you helped us with that Santiago character. I appreciate your assistance. Santiago was one nasty piece of work. Most of those island beaners are."

"Glad to be of help." I waited for the Diet Coke gag.

"We have over a hundred of them. They came over when Castro figured he could save money by letting his criminals and nut cases immigrate to the US. We have ourselves your rapists, your murderers, and your thieves. Thanks to you, I was able to send Santiago to a different institution."

"Did he confess?"

"No, but he didn't deny it either. I suspect all the other beaners working the machine shop have knives. He said the one we discovered in his cubby wasn't one of theirs. He said it was inferior like a gringo made it." Harrigan paused for a moment, awaiting my reaction. "I'm going to have all of the beaners banned from the machine shop. We need lots of help with the toilets."

"Just as well."

Harrigan smiled, "You know it's funny, this is just your second month, and you have had two issues involving shivs. Your initial cellmate, whom I sent to another prison, was also implicated in the stabbing of an Italian man in the showers. In that case," he picked up the file, "It says you helped by telling us that your roommate had made threats about the man. Interesting, two months, two incidents." He let that hang in the air like a bad smell.

"I see you're hanging around with the Brotherhood. I believe I told you that joining a gang was a bad idea."

"You did. I'm not a member, although I've made a few friends. Nothing wrong with making friends."

Harrigan stared at me for a few moments before closing the file. "In this case, our interests are aligned. For now, I want to thank you and leave you with a warning. If the beaners happen to find out it was you who fingered Santiago, I don't think even the Brotherhood can save you."

I stared at him, wondering if that was a threat.

"That's all for now...Luger."

***

Robbie got beaten up again - same two guys. They told him the reason this time was because the guy who hit him yesterday had bruised his hand. I looked at him sitting there on his bunk - his nose bandaged like Nicholson in Chinatown. His lip looked like he had been stung by a bee. I felt a wave of sadness come over me. Not for him, but for me. If I couldn't convince him to do what Wolf wanted, he'd be coming after me. I decided he'd get a special surprise tomorrow.

Chapter 65

March 10th, 1985
Gulfport, Mississippi

Don

Weber came up to us as we sat in the waiting area after having given our statements. "Got some good news. The ADA took another run at the judge. This time she amended the search warrant. She added the additional detail of what happened to your truck and your confidence that it was the same person who helped organize the Hiller Park bombings. She also attached an affidavit from Connie Franklin that claims she overheard her boss talking on the phone about how things were in place for the 21st at Hiller Park. The judge said that Connie's statement was credible and sufficient justification to sign a search warrant. With luck, we're going to execute it this afternoon."

"That's something," I said. It was a bittersweet moment with all that had happened, not just because of Sharma but also the hundred and sixty-eight others who had lost their lives.

"Thank you, God!" Jethro spoke up. "I was getting pretty tired of sleeping in the bathtub."

"Until we have the evidence and, more importantly, people behind bars, you might still be at risk. As I said,

I have someplace safe for you. It should only be another day or so."

Deputy Weber's idea of someplace safe was his apartment. We went from two guys sharing my one-bedroom to three guys sharing his.

***

I looked around the small apartment. It was a little nicer than mine. There was a couch and a recliner, which Jethro had already called. Dinner was leftover pizza that had been in the fridge for some time. Weber had little else other than Captain Crunch and pickles.

It was 7 pm before Weber showed up. Jethro was engrossed in the basketball game on television. I was thinking about Sharma and hoping that one day I'd be able to say justice was done. "Hey, quite the place, huh?" When no one answered him, he said, "I got news."

He pulled out his notebook. "The search warrant was served at sixteen hundred hours - that's 4 pm. Dietz was there and flew into a rage once he saw me. I didn't tell the deputies about the cassettes, just to look for anything incriminating. They tore the office apart. We let Dietz call his lawyer – some suit named Merrill. Not much Dietz could do but sit there and watch. Of course, we found the tapes exactly where Connie said they'd be. He went full psycho - said he'd have my badge - Sheriff Pardy is his golfing buddy, blah, blah, blah. Then he tried to sell me on the idea that the tapes weren't his. That someone had planted them. I felt like asking why his voice was on the tapes, but I didn't want to let on that we'd already heard everything. He was beaking off about Sheriff Pardy and how I was in a heap of trouble when the man himself walked in as expected with the arrest warrant. That shut him up. He's locked up in a holding cell, doing his best impression of a mute."

We got up and gave Weber a high five. "That's great work, Weber. What about Bubba?" I asked.

Weber sighed and shook his head. "We have a warrant out for him and a couple of others. He's not at his restaurant or his house. I have an APB. That stands for …"

"We know, Weber," interrupted Jethro.

"We'll get him," Weber reassured me, reading the frustration on my face. "We have people watching for him."

"Someone warned him."

"Maybe, I tried to keep it quiet."

"I bet he doesn't even know what's on those cassettes. But he might be figuring if Dietz has been arrested, you probably have something incriminating." I looked at my watch; at 7:30, it was well past sunset. From Gulfport harbor, you could get to just about anywhere. "Let's go for a drive. I have an idea."

Chapter 66

Don

"So, what's the plan?" Weber asked once we were in his cruiser.

"Head to the piers in Port Christian. I used to help Bubba on the oyster boats. I'm betting he's heading out to sea."

"Makes sense," said Weber. "He must know we're after him. He probably knows about the APB and that we're watching his house."

"By now, all of the boats should be back in port," I said. "Bubba named his boats after confederate generals, but I remember the Thomas Jefferson was his favorite and the fastest."

"Worth a try. Should I radio for backup?"

"Let's wait and see if he's there," I answered.

"What do we do when we get there?" Jethro was sitting in the back seat, leaning forward.

"We're lucky Lange doesn't know Jethro's helping me," I said. "If he did, he'd never would have let Dietz hire him."

I turned to Jethro. "You mosey down to the boat and see what's up. Meanwhile, Weber and I will circle around back."

"What do I tell him if he wants to know what I'm doing there?"

"Tell him you wanted to thank him for helping get you the job and that someone at the restaurant said you could find him on his boat," suggested Weber.

"What's the plan if he's not stupid enough to believe that?"

For a moment, no one answered. Jethro added, "Shit, as soon as I say that, he's gonna haul off and shoot me."

"No, he won't," I said. "Because once he sees me, he'll forget all about you."

***

A crescent moon offered little light as Deputy Weber parked beside a deserted warehouse. I remembered the building from being locked in it for a day while Bubba's brother organized the park bombing. Jethro reluctantly made his way down the outside of one side of the warehouse while Weber and I took the other side. I thumbed the safety off my .38 and held it to my side. It was a long shot that Lange would be here, but I wasn't taking any chances.

Halfway down the side of the warehouse, Weber stopped abruptly, putting a finger to his lips. He started making weird hand gestures as if we were marines. Finally, he whispered. "There's someone back there. Let's spread out." I moved to flank him, trying to make as little noise as possible. As we got closer to the dockside warehouse entrance, there was more light from a spotlight on the pier. I heard Jethro's voice.

"Bubba? Is that you?"

"Jethro? What the fuck are you doing here?" There was a hint of suspicion in Bubba's voice.

"I wanted to thank you for getting me the gig at the Tivoli."

"That so? So you came down here to thank me?" Jethro was right. Bubba wasn't buying it. I edged closer. I was about twenty yards away. Bubba had been loading stuff on the boat when Jethro showed up.

"They told me at the restaurant you'd be here. How was the catch?"

"You come out here all alone? Where's your car?"

"I parked it back there." He gestured with his thumb to the front of the warehouse. If Bubba was to look, he might wonder why Jethro was driving a sheriff's cruiser.

"You're lying, Jethro." Lange pulled a gun from the back of his waistband and pointed it at Jethro. "Now, who's with you...and best not to lie to me."

"No one. I'm not lying." Jethro was losing it. He was likely wondering when the cavalry was going to arrive. I inched my way up behind Bubba. Jethro finally saw me, and I saw his eyes go big. So did Bubba. I was ten yards away when he turned, keeping the gun pointed at Jethro. Bubba's eyes narrowed in recognition, and his lip curled at the sight of my gun.

"Drop it, or I'll put a bullet in the kid." He gave me a weird smile. There's nothing creepier than a person with emotions that don't match the situation. They consistently look happy when others are in pain. It was like something was broken inside them – as if they got an inner boost of pleasure when they saw others' sadness. Bubba was just plain creepy. I could fire first, but so could he. It was my turn to hope for the cavalry.

"Stalemate, I'd say. If you shoot Jethro, I'm not going to miss from this range. I think you don't want to die just yet. You might have heard that Dietz has been arrested. We have your voice on tape planning the bombings. You're done, Bubba, so put the gun down."

Judging by his wrinkled brow, I didn't think Bubba had heard about Dietz and the cassette recordings. He recovered quickly. "You like what I did to your truck?" Again, the creepy smile.

"It was getting old anyway. I was going to trade it in. Killing the super was pretty nasty, though, was that you?" Bubba shrugged his shoulders as if to say, "Search me."

"Where you headed?" I asked.

He ignored the question. "How about we both lay down our guns and settle this like men. Or at least one man vs. a pussy. That all right with you, Kittyburg?"

I gave him a shrug back and nodded. "You first, ass-hole." I had fought Bubba's brother once and won because I fought dirty. Sometimes you have to, with scumbags. Bubba was bigger than his brother and twice my size. Maybe over-confidence was why he put his gun down first.

"You stay out of this, Jethro, you hear. This is between us," Bubba growled.

I reluctantly put my gun down, waiting for Deputy We-ber to jump in and tell him to freeze. I circled and faked a couple of moves, did a couple of stretches, then some rope a dope – wasting time, waiting for that cavalry.

"Quit stalling." Bubba inched closer, his fists clenched. The first blow surprised me, coming from his right leg and landing on my hip. I wasn't the only dirty fighter. I saw out of the corner of my eye that Jethro had inched his way closer to the guns, which were on the ground. Bubba fol-lowed the kick with a right fist that glanced off my shoul-der but still hurt like hell. I was rubbing my shoulder when he took a run at me, knocking me backward into the hull of his boat. While going down, I hit him with a couple of body blows that barely registered. We started wrestling on the pier. He kneed me in the stomach, and I thought I was going to throw up that pizza.

We rolled around. I tried to free up a hand while simultaneously holding Bubba back. For a moment, I thought that this might be it. He was just too strong. Seeing my own death gave me the strength to pull my hand free. I went for his eyes. He screamed and tried to push my hands away, but I kept gauging until I felt something gooey. I followed up with a knee of my own to his nuts. This sent him howling, and he rolled onto his knees. I don't like kicking a man when he's down, but I had 168 reasons. I kicked him in the ribs. "That was for Mr. Sharma." Then, I kicked him a second time. I'd still be kicking him if Weber hadn't pulled me back.

"Okay. That's enough." Weber took the handcuffs off his belt.

I looked at him, still trying to catch my breath. "Why didn't you break it up earlier?"

"Jethro and I had a little bet going. With the odds, you'll be happy to know that I just turned my 25 cents into $25."

Part 3

Chapter 67

March 12th, 1985
Gulfport, Mississippi

Gabriel

It's been a few days since we found the vacant house in Tanner Williams. Not much had happened with the case. While Rachel and I went on a road trip to bring candy to the grandmother, Wendy had left a panicky message on the office voicemail.

"Gabriel, Rachel, where are you guys?" Her voice was cracking with excitement. "She's here. Right here. I think the promotion worked. Her hair is dark brown! Oh, Gabriel, where are you? Call me as soon as you get this message. If she leaves, I'm going to follow her."

After I picked up the message, I called Wendy, and she said that she had lost her in the lunch crowd. She seemed upset that we had missed an opportunity. Wendy wanted to know where we had gone, and I told her we were revisiting Penn's grandmother because I hadn't brought her any candy and that we hadn't learned any-thing new.

***

A dental exam done on the body found in the bayou proved that the dead man was Dirk Sparrow. A funeral was held at the New Life Family Church in Biloxi. Rachel, Dep-uty Weber, Jacqueline, and I attended to pay our respects. Glenna, of course, was there with the boys. While Jacque-line and Rachel whispered how hideously inappropriate Glenna's yellow lace gown was, I scanned the crowd looking for psychos. I felt a little like Abrams. In the absence of any other explanation, Penn must be a psycho. Wendy showed up and hung out with Jacqueline, her new buddy.

As for Glenna Sparrow, she paid me for finding her hus-band, but she no longer had any interest in what had hap-pened to him. Deputy Weber opened up a murder inves-tigation, and we compared notes, but I was starting to feel the trail was growing cold. There was a picture of Bradley Nash in the papers with a statement that he was wanted for questioning. The news about the whipping post got out, and for a while, radio talk shows hosted numerous programs dedicated to an aspect of Southern history most people had long since forgotten.

I tried my best to get on with my life and to get busy with other cases. I packaged up all my notes, hand-written scrawls and put them in an envelope to give to Weber.

Ben called to tell me that the District Attorney had taken another run at Baxter, offering a new deal and relocation to Hawaii, but he'd turned them down. Two days later, the *Herald* ran a story about Frank Reznikov being acquitted.

Chapter 68

Mayor Baxter

Dear Diary,

Remind me never to play rummy with Klink. The man cheats. We were sitting in the commons area - a spot with tables bolted to the floor where cons can play cards and watch television. I threw my cards in and called him a loser. Klink is a little weasel of a man who looks after the money. I'm supposed to be helping him, but I think he thinks I'm stupid. I told him that if you took a poll of the inmates about which of us had the highest IQ, I'd win that poll by more than anybody's ever won a poll.

At first, he wouldn't tell me why he was in prison. He said it was bad form to ask cons about their crimes. He finally relented and said he'd stolen some candy. When I said, "They send you to prison for that?" He replied that while stealing the candy, he killed a couple of niggers. Funny that he thought the stealing was what got him sent here.

My attention was drawn to the television and a late-breaking news item. I couldn't hear what was being said over the noise, but there was a picture of a dark-haired man named

Nash. He and his companion, a woman named Penn Mad-dox, were wanted in connection with two murders.

Penn Maddox! That's the name of the kid. The name awakened memories I'd long since forgotten. Well before I became somebody, I met a woman through Reznikov. I can't even remember her name. It was at a party at Corbin Master's mansion. I was young and foolish - we all were. I hooked up with the woman. Years later, the slut started calling, telling me about her poor bastard daughter Penelope wanting money. I told her she was mistaken, but when she continued to call, I'd told her she was a slut and to fuck off. At the time, I was just getting started in politics. I was part of Frank's master plan, so when she threatened to sue for paternity and go to the press, I told Frank about it. I never heard from her again.

And now the little bastard is in trouble. Not much Daddy can do for you in here.

***

When I got back to my cell, I found Robbie lying on his bunk, face against the wall crying. It took a long time before I was able to get him to open up about what happened.

It was an assault in the showers. He was washing and then suddenly realized he was alone - everyone else had left. Everyone, except for the two black guys who had beaten him up. He started to towel off when he noticed they'd blocked the exits. "I told them I'd tell the guards this time. They said they wouldn't hit me as long as I played ball. If I refused, then they would fuck me up forever." Charlie put his head in his hands, "They forced me. First, one held me down and put a shiv to my throat. Then when the one finished, the other guy did it. He really hurt me. I begged him to stop. I didn't think it was ever going to end."

I was stuck for words. What are you supposed to say at moments like this? Lots of things bounced around in my mind. Should I ask if it was all that bad? Or if maybe, he might have liked it a little? Would it have been as bad if he knew he was making a little extra money? Finally, I couldn't decide what to say, so I said nothing and just sat beside him.

After looking at my watch and seeing that lights out would be in thirty minutes, I said, "Don't worry, Charlie, let's go see a friend of mine. We're going to take care of this. Those guys won't bother you anymore."

Chapter 69

Penn Maddox

From my rusted-out Corolla, I had a clear view of the Agency. I was debating whether I should keep the game going and go in and flirt with Gabriel. Maybe I'd learn what, if any, progress he'd made. The sight of Gabriel and Jacqueline at the funeral made me angry. Their perfect little fucking family. I thought back to exploring their sweet little home, how easy it would have been to use that cleaver had we not been interrupted by a phone call from a friend of Jacqueline's in New Orleans.

The perfect little marriage. Who knows - in another life, maybe, Gabriel would be coming home to me. Me and little baby Charlie. That's what I'd call him. Charlie Maddox. I wonder if anyone will ever know that Charles Manson is a distant relative. He was born in Cincinnati, Ohio, the illegitimate son of 16-year-old Kathleen Maddox, my granny's second cousin. You got to hand it to Charlie. He was great at getting people to do his bidding.

Lately, Bradley's answer to everything seems to be to get high. He's falling into a dope rut - out most nights selling meth and doing God knows what. During the day, all he wants to do is sleep.

When Gabriel told me about the body in Alabama, I knew it was time to get out. Now we're in some shithole motel in Ocean Springs. I found a gun while we were clearing out of the house in Tanner Williams. Bradley was just stupid enough to shoot himself. Guns are so impersonal. Most people who died by gunshot die too quickly.

I looked at my watch and thought about work. I've been having a hard time keeping it together myself. It was getting too hard to smile at all of the stupid people. Bradley and I talked about Monroe, which was about 75 miles from Vicksburg in Louisiana. He knew a guy who knew a guy who lived that way. It was time to get out. Start somewhere else.

My thoughts were interrupted when a woman got out of a cab and walked into the Agency. She looked familiar. My heart skipped a beat. It was the way she moved - like someone who was crippled as a child and had learned to walk by bending only one leg.

Chapter 70

March 13th, 1985
Talladega, Alabama

Mayor Baxter

Dear Diary,

You know it's funny. Here I am, bearing my inner thoughts in this journal. I'm usually someone who doesn't like to read. I always insisted that reports be verbally submitted or summarized with one of those post-it things. After breakfast today, a guard came up to me and told me that the warden wanted to see me.

When I got there, he was wearing his usual brown suit, his hair having not grown a speck since I met him over a month ago. I asked about Jamie's empty chair as I walked into his office and took my usual seat.

"She's at the doctor's, so it's just us. Want something, maybe a cold drink?"

I knew enough to say no. He paused for a moment, looking disappointed he couldn't play his little game. "I guess something bad happened to your cellmate. I understand he might have been playing around with a couple of Crips in the shower."

"He told me. He said there were no guards. No one there to stop it from happening."

"Cut the crap, Baxter, or should I say, Luger? I know everything that goes on here. I believe I warned you about gangs." He looked sad. As if he gave a rat's ass about me. "Maybe it's all for the best. I could use someone on the inside. Someone who could provide me with intelligence on what's going on here."

I finally clued in to his game. "Why would I do that?"

"Because you don't want me as an enemy. Remember our last conversation?"

He was threatening to tell the Cubans that I had fingered Santiago. I have no problem being a rat. I like rats - just as long as it benefits me. "What do I get in return for being your stoolie?"

"Maybe a promotion to shop steward in the tech shop. It'll double your hourly rate."

"You mean a whole twenty cents?" He nodded, and I asked him what kinds of things he'd want to know.

"I hear the Beaners aren't happy."

"I don't think the idea of a field trip back to Cuba is sitting well with them."

"I don't imagine it is. The question I need answered is, what are the little turds planning to do about it?"

I told him I'd ask around. As I was leaving, I said, "If we're going to be meeting like this, then I suggest we be a little more subtle. People are starting to wonder if we have a thing."

Chapter 71

March 13th, 1985
Gulfport, Mississippi

Gabriel

I was thinking about springing for lunch again when a young black woman opened the Agency door. After a brief conversation with Rachel, she walked into my office. I noticed she had an unusual walk as she came into the office.

"My name's Nia Tines."

"Nia Tines, as in Reche Tines?"

"I don't have an appointment, but I was hoping we could talk. I'm his sister."

I asked her to sit down. She had determined eyes, like a cat about to pounce on a bird. She said no to coffee, so I sat down at my desk and pulled out a notepad. "I'm sorry for your loss, Nia." I figured her for early twenties. She had a clear coffee-colored complexion and wore an unbuttoned denim shirt over a dark t-shirt and blue jeans. Her hair was hidden under a plain black ball cap.

"Thank you. I was following up with Sherriff Harker, and he said they were no longer working the case. He told me I should speak to you because you were looking into it."

I nodded and explained about Dirk Sparrow and that there was a distinct similarity in how he and her brother had died. "But I'm no longer working the case. The client, the woman who hired us to find her husband, is no longer pursuing the matter."

"That's kind of cold." I wasn't about to defend Glenna, so I nodded. Nia sat there for a moment, taking it all in. "So, what happens now?

I didn't have the heart to tell her the truth. "Tell me about your brother?"

"Reche was a rock. My rock. He was always there for me. He was a good brother."

"Were you surprised when he enlisted?"

"No, he was always talking about the Air Force. If we'd see a white streak in the sky, he'd be able to tell you whether it was an F-16. I think he had a bit of a hero complex. He wanted to be like those war heroes in the movies." She smiled and then looked away, overwhelmed by the memory. She turned back to face me; the steely-eyed determination was back.

"And when he got out, he moved in with you?"

She nodded, "I live in Moss Point now. My younger sister does too. Dad died a few years ago, but Mom is still there. I'd written to Reche about Moss Point. When he got discharged, he just showed up at my door."

"Do you remember a girl named Penn Maddox?"

The name jarred her. Harker mustn't have filled her in. "Of course, we were all pretty close. Well, we were until her mother tried to get Reche arrested." Nia shook her head as if trying to dispel an evil spirit. "Her mother wasn't a nice person. Reche would never have done what she said."

"When was the last time you saw Penn?"

"She went by Penny back then. I haven't seen her since we left Utica. I was angry, and I took it out on her. Reche said it was her mother and not her. But I knew her better than he did. She was severely messed up. If she couldn't manipulate you into getting what she wanted, then she'd find a way to hurt you."

"Was your brother planning to lay down roots in Moss Point?"

"He got a good job at Northrup because of his Air Force experience, so I guess so. He said he met a girl and seemed happy."

"Tell me about this girl."

"I never met her," she said dismissively. "He said he ran into her at a bar. He must have liked her because he started spending more and more time at her place."

"Did he talk about her?"

"I remember he said she was a white girl and that she was beautiful. That's why I thought the Klan was involved. Come to think of it, he was kind of tight-lipped about her, except for this one time. It wasn't long before he disappeared."

"Tell me about it."

Nia took a deep breath, "One night, Reche came home pretty agitated. He had smoked some weed with this girl and her roommate. That was the first I had heard that the girl had a roommate. He told me the roommate seemed nice enough. But on this night, the girl was getting a little frisky, and the roommate was sitting right there watching everything. My brother said it was weird. He wanted to go to the bedroom, but the girl was turned on by having an audience. Reche said the whole thing made him uncomfortable."

"Nia, do you think this girl could have been Penny Maddox?"

She went to say something then stopped. She finally got the words out, "It would be a pretty big coincidence. Them meeting up in a bar in the middle of nowhere."

"What if it wasn't a coincidence? What if the reason she and this roommate moved to Tanner Williams was because she wanted to be close by?"

"Then why wouldn't she call me?"

"I don't know. But do you think it could have been her?"

"No."

"Why not?"

"Because Reche said her name was Wendy."

I sat there, stunned. "Did Penny have a tattoo?"

"No." She paused for a moment before adding, "We talked about it once. We were going to cut classes and visit a tattoo parlor in Vicksburg. I chickened out. My dad would have been angry. He once told me that if I ever got one, he'd cut it out."

I nodded, feeling a sense of relief. But then Nia continued. "If she ever got one, she said she'd get an alligator tattoo."

I grabbed the phone, not waiting for Nia to finish. I dialed home. After about five agonizing rings, Jacqueline answered, out of breath.

"Jacqueline, have you heard from Wendy today?" I blurted out quickly.

"No, we might do something later this afternoon when Benjamin gets up from his nap. What's the matter? You sound upset."

I took a long breath. "Listen, I'm pretty sure she's this Penn Maddox we've been looking for."

"What? She's the one who told you about her. She's been helping you,"

That was true. But when I rewound the reel, I remembered something. "When I first met her, I asked if she had a customer named Penn Maddox. I gave her the name. She later tried to tell me that it was likely a made-up name. Remember, she called the house and said she thought that Penn was a brunette. As for helping me, killers quite often try to insert themselves into an investigation. Come to think of it, that's probably how she knew to leave the house in Alabama."

"God, Gabriel. She's been to our house. She held Benjamin." Jacqueline was slowly climbing Mount Hysterical.

"It's okay. We're safe - I'm going to call Weber and see what he suggests. In the meantime, lock the doors. If she turns up, don't let her in."

Chapter 72

Penn Maddox

I watched my old friend go into the Agency. I always thought the girl was a fool. Nia never clued in that our friendship was only a means to an end. Reche had been the prize. When her brother was accused of rape, Nia's true colors came out. Rather than being supportive, she blamed me for what my mother had done.

When I'd reconnected with Reche, I'd known he was living with Nia. I'd been adamant with him that he needed to be careful around his family if he wanted to be with me. It was because of my mother that they'd had to move. I told him that there was no more Penelope, no more Penny, no more Penn. They were all dead. There was just Wendy.

So why was Nia visiting Gabriel? Were they in there talking about me? Did they know what happened?

Gabriel

Weber arrived at the Agency in record time. As he walked into my office, he saw Nia. A look of uncertainty flashed across his face, "Didn't you tell me that Penn Maddox was a white girl?"

"Deputy Weber, this is Nia Tines. She's the sister of Reche Tines, whose body was recovered in Alabama. She and Penn Maddox were close in high school. I believe we now know what happened to him." Gabriel and Nia took turns telling the story of what had happened when Reche got out of the army.

"So, this roommate just sat there and watched while your brother and this girl had sex?" he asked, a tone of skepticism in his voice.

"That's what he told me."

"Go on, what happened next?" Weber said, leaning forward.

"He didn't go into graphic details. That's pretty much all he said."

"And how long between this happening and his disappearance?" I asked.

"I'd say a couple of weeks. At first, I wasn't concerned because Reche was in the habit of staying out all night and not coming home. After he didn't come home for two days, I got worried and called his work. I spoke to someone there who said my brother hadn't shown up for work. I got worried and called my mom. Ever since that business in Utica, she hasn't had much use for the police. She felt there were two sets of laws, one for white people and one for blacks. Besides, I didn't know who this "Wendy" was or where she lived."

Weber turned to Gabriel. "How can you be sure that the girl from the bar is the same one doing the 'you know what' with this woman's brother?"

I told him what Nia had said about the tattoo. "I'm 100% sure."

***

Penn Maddox

I watched as the deputy sheriff's cruiser drove up, and a man who looked like he was made of boxes got out. He had a boxy head on a boxy body. "Fuck! This is all your fault, Bradley," I said to myself. Now, what am I supposed to do? Did Reche tell Nia that he'd hooked up with Penny? I bet he did. He must have. Why would she be here? And now they've called the cops. Fuck! I felt panic build up like a sparkplug in my belly. I started to hyperventilate and caught a glimpse of my face in the side mirror. I look like shit. What the fuck do I do now?

Then I thought of something my mama told me, '*When you corner a polecat, they rarely make a run for it. Be like the polecat and fight*'.

***

Gabriel

Rachel came into the office, "Sorry to interrupt, you'll never guess who's on the phone."

I heard Wendy's panicky voice when I picked up the extension. "Gabriel? I need help."

"I'm here, Wendy."

"I'm sorry." Her voice quivered. "I should have told you the truth. I was scared he said if I told, he would kill me."

"Who said that?"

"Bradley. I should have seen it coming; it's all my fault. He gets so jealous."

"Where are you, Wendy?"

"I'm calling from a safe place. I can't go to work. He'll find me there."

"I'll come get you, Wendy. Just tell me where you are."

"I'm downtown at the lighthouse. The payphone across the street." I looked at Weber and quickly scratched a note on a piece of paper. *Phonebooth across from the lighthouse.* He looked at what I had written and turned the paper sideways. I shook my head, "Where's Bradley?"

"Last I saw him," she whimpered. "He was at the *Good Night Motel* in Ocean Springs, room eleven. Please be careful, Gabriel. He's taken something, and he has a gun."

Once I hung up, Weber said, "Phoneboob across from the whorehouse?"

Chapter 73

Gabriel

Weber called the Jackson County Sheriff Department and told his counterpart about the fugitive. "Be careful. We have information that the suspect, Bradley Nash, is armed and extremely dangerous. He is a suspect in at least two murders."

When he got off the phone, Deputy Weber and I took the cruiser to pick up Wendy. Rachel said she and Nia would meet us at the Harrison County Sheriff's office. Based on the way he was driving, I thought Weber was a little excited. I asked him what he thought about Nia's story. He answered in his usual, I've-seen-it-all attitude. "In this job, you see more than your share of sexually motivated crimes."

"It's a pretty big leap from what she described to torture and murder. I think this has to be all Nash."

"I wish I was going to pick him up. I haven't blown anyone away since Hiller Park. I could use the practice." Weber made a shooting motion with an imaginary gun.

"A crazy who's hopped up on meth with a gun? I hope they call out their rapid response team."

***

We spotted Penn / Wendy waiting for us across from the lighthouse. She'd been crying as Weber put her in the back seat. Penn resumed her hysterical crying when she got in, screaming sobs only interrupted by her need to draw breath. She threw herself down onto the back seat. I looked over at Weber, neither of us knowing what to say. Weber put the cruiser in gear and began driving to the police station. Wendy eventually stopped wailing and sat up, still sniffling. She put her hand on my shoulder - a simple gesture of friendship.

"It's going to be okay, Wendy. Deputy Weber is going to drive us to the police station, where you can give your statement. The Sheriff's Department in Jackson County will pick up Bradley. Thanks for your help. It'll all be over soon." I looked back and saw that her red eyes were looking out the window. It struck me how different she looked. When I'd seen her in the bar, she was cocky, funny, confident. Now she looked miserable. "You have a bruise on your cheek."

"Bradley. It was my fault. I provoked him."

Chapter 74

March 13th, 1985
Ocean Springs, Mississippi

The *Good Night Motel* was a run-down dump on the outskirts of Ocean Springs. The Pakistani owner had long given up on making it a viable business and was just trying to unload it. It had been allowed to wither away from neglect. There were a few cars in the parking lot when Deputies Jeff Michaels and Susan Gibbons arrived.

Gibbons went to the office to see what she could find out. She came out five minutes later, "The room is rented week by week by a Mr. and Mrs. Bradley. They drive a 1972 Toyota. Since it's not here, he has no idea who might be in the room, if anyone. He described the woman as pretty hot and said he doesn't remember Mr. Bradley. I asked him to call and have them come to the office, but the owner cut off the rooms' service. The deputy from Harrison said the man was armed and dangerous. We should call for the emergency response team."

"Nah, I've met Deputy Weber. He's a bit of an oddball. Let's just knock and talk to the guy."

They went to number eleven, and Susan Gibbons knocked. They stood on either side of the door, with their guns down by their side. When the first knock wasn't answered, she tried again. "Open up, phone company - I'm here to hook up your service." They heard some rustling coming from inside the room and nodded to each other.

"Hold on, hold on," came a groggy man's voice from inside the room. They readied, knowing the next few moments would be critical. The door opened, and a man dressed in an open terry cloth robe over white jockey shorts looked out. When he didn't see anyone, he scratched his head and went back in, shutting the door behind him. Deputy Michaels kept the door from closing all the way and followed him in. He pointed his gun at the back of the man's head.

"Deputy Sheriff," he yelled. "Put your hands up and kneel on the floor." Deputy Gibbons followed them into the room, keeping her weapon on the man.

"Hey, yo' said yo' were fum th' phone compenny." Bradley whined.

"We lied." Michaels grabbed his handcuffs. "Now, I said, put your hands up."

Bradley turned suddenly, pulling a gun from his robe.

"Gun," yelled Gibbons. She didn't hesitate and fired twice.

***

Gabriel

The interview room at The Harrison County Sheriff's Department was small. Wendy was sitting on one side of the table while Weber sat across from her. He'd pulled some strings and gotten permission for me to sit in as an observer. The deputy had a tape recorder and said "testing, testing 1 2 3, testing 123," a bunch of times to make sure he had the right volume. Finally, he asked Wendy if he could get her something to drink.

"Sure," she said, looking at me, "How about a slippery nipple?"

Weber looked back and forth at Wendy and me. He laughed uncertainly. "I was thinking of a glass of water."

When Wendy shook her head, Weber pressed the record button and put the microphone between them. He deepened his voice and spoke up, "This is Deputy Sheriff Weber of the Harrison County Sheriff's Department. This is Wednesday, March 13th, 1985. With me is a woman who has been identified to me simply as Wendy. She is here voluntarily to make a statement regarding the murders of Reche Tines and Dirk Sparrow. Also sitting in is Gabriel Ross, known to this woman and a consultant on this matter. Miss., I am going to ask you some routine questions first. Please state your full name and date of birth."

Wendy sat back in her chair and took her time before speaking, "I was born Penelope Pearl Maddox on August 5th, 1958."

"Where did you grow up, and what are your parents' names?"

Wendy's eyes started to mist over. Weber handed her a handkerchief. "I was born in a farmhouse in Utica, Mississippi. My daddy's name was Braxton. My mother's name's not important."

Weber looked like he was going to insist. "Let's leave that for now," I said. "I know why she doesn't want to speak the name." Wendy turned and thanked me with her eyes.

"Can I call you Penn?" Weber asked. She gave him a 'whatever' look.

"My name's Penny." She went from teary-eyed to bored.

"What is your current address and occupation, Penny?"

"I live in room eleven at the *Good Night Motel* in Ocean Springs. I do this and that."

Weber looked frustrated again by her answer. "When did you first meet Bradley Nash?"

"When I was twelve. My daddy was killed in a robbery. Bradley's father owned a funeral home in Vicksburg. That was when I first met him. He was the assistant funeral director."

"Describe your relationship with Bradley."

"A few years after my dad died, I needed a job, and Bradley's father gave me one. Shortly after, Bradley and I started fucking."

Weber flashed a quick look at me.

"What? Don't like that word?" She then leaned forward and picked up the microphone and said, "fuck, fuck, fuck." Weber reached forward and struggled with her before taking the mike away.

"You're saying that this Bradley Nash raped you."

She gave us a wise-guy look. "Sure, whatever you say, chief."

When things settled down, Weber said, "Tell us about Reche Tines."

"I fucked Reche back when I was in high school. I met him through his younger sister, Nia, who was in my class. My mother disapproved because he was a nigger. She made up a story and told the sheriff he was forcing himself on me. She did that because her boyfriend liked fucking me better than her."

"Were you having sex with this Reche Tines and with your mother's boyfriend at the same time?" Weber asked.

"Not together. Reche got arrested, but charges were dropped when they got around to talking to me." She started chuckling but stopped abruptly when she saw no one else was laughing. "Word got around about Reche anyway. People can be such assholes – they were getting threatening calls. One morning they found a noose strung from the oak tree in their front yard. Reche's family moved to get away from it."

She paused for a moment and looked over at me as if looking for validation. I kept my expression neutral, and she continued. "When Reche turned eighteen, he enlisted in the Air Force. We stayed in touch by letter. His family is now living in Moss Point. While he was in the Air Force, I lived with Bradley, who can be a sweet guy when he's not stoned. The problem is he was selling drugs and was using way too much. When he gets stoned, he can get violent." She pointed to the bruise on her face. "It's like he's a different person." I saw a glimmer of the abused Penelope, and for the first time, I thought she might have more than one personality.

She sat up and spoke into the microphone. "Because his family lived in Moss Point, I convinced Bradley to rent a place in Wilmer. That's where we were living when Reche got out of the Air Force."

She stopped at that point and sat back. She turned to me. "We're about to get to the juicy part - I could use a drink."

"Sure," I said, "Water?"

"How about some Baileys with a little Sambuca and a touch of Grenadine?"

I smiled and excused myself. When I left the room, I found Rachel and Nia pacing the floor like tigers in a cage.

"That's her," Nia said right away. They'd been watching and listening through the two-way glass.

While we talked about the interview, a Jackson County Deputy came up and asked if I could give Deputy Weber a message. "We raided the *Good Night* motel in Oceans Springs. A man later identified as Bradley Nash pulled a gun and was shot. He died on the way to the hospital."

I nodded and wondered if that was what Penn had wanted. She'd known his state of mind and that he had a gun. Like a movie director, had she put the whole thing in motion? The deputy talked to me a bit more before I went to the water cooler and filled a paper cone.

Chapter 75

March 13th, 1985
Talladega, Alabama

Mayor Baxter

Dear Diary,

I decided to keep my conversation with the warden to myself for now. When Schultz asked about it, I sluffed it off, saying Harrigan wanted to know what had happened to my cellmate in the showers. "I told him I hadn't heard about it."

The conversation with the warden stuck in my mind over the next few days. I could use the connection to manipulate Harrigan, feeding him whatever I wanted. The situation was no different than on the outside. All the warden wanted was order. He knew that the drugs, gambling, and prostitution were necessary as long as it was controlled. I thought about what he'd said about the Cubans. Were they planning something? He'd be happy to see them all sent back to that shithole country of theirs. I suggested to Schultz that Reagan would be wise to build a big wall to keep them out. Schultz gave me a funny look and said, "There's already a wall; it's called an ocean."

I tried to make friends with a couple of the beaners, but their American was pretty bad. I asked them if they were anxious to be going home. They just told me to mind my own business.

Chapter 76

Gabriel

Penn drank the water and then crushed the paper cup and threw it at Weber. The tough punk act was back. She put her feet up on the table. For a moment, I thought Weber was going to take a swing at her.

"And then what happened?" I asked, trying to break the spell.

She turned to me and said, "When Reche got out of the service, he got a job at Northrup. I knew the bar where they liked to go after work. It was nothing to bump into him. From there, you probably know the rest of the story."

"Actually, we don't," said Weber. "Were you intimate with him?"

"Intimate? That's a funny word. Almost as bad as initiator," she said, looking at me. "You mean, were we fucking? Oops, I said it again. Maybe I should come up with another word so that you don't get offended, Chief. Let's say we were doing the horizontal polka. Is that better?"

"How about you call it intercourse?" suggested Weber.

"Sure, thing, Chief. Yeah, we were having intercourse. At first, I didn't know how Bradley would be with it. So Reche and I snuck around and did it in the car. Ever have sex in a car, deputy? Have you ever had sex at all?" I could see Weber's face go red. She was getting to him, and she knew it.

"Just go on." Weber ignored her questions.

"Later Bradley and I talked, and he admitted he had this thing about black men and said he would be into watching."

"Like a voyeur?" asked Weber.

"Voyeur. Where the fuck do you get these words? He gets off watching his girl having 'intercourse' with a black man. So, Reche would come over, we'd all smoke some weed, and then I'd get a little frisky. At first, Reche was uncomfortable, you know, with Bradley being there. But I told him it was a turn-on and that we should just go with it. I figured I could get Reche to do just about anything. So, we started doing it in front of Bradley."

Weber looked over at me, an uncomfortable look on his face. *Something told me it was going to get worse, a lot worse.*

"I need to say something," said Penn putting her feet back on the floor and sitting up straight, "I have feelings for Bradley. We've been together for a long time. It wasn't all beautiful and sweet like your marriage, Gabriel, but I didn't want him to be hurt. Later simply watching wasn't enough. Bradley wanted a three-way."

"What do you mean by that?" Asked Weber.

"One, two, three people having sex together." Penn started laughing at Weber and turned again to me for validation.

"I think what the deputy wants to know is whether the two men were having intercourse together."

"You're jumping ahead. In answer to your question. Not at first. For a while, it was a tag team, if you know what I mean. I was cool with it. It's just fun, and as I said, I didn't want to leave Bradley behind. Oops! A pun! The breaking point for Reche was when Bradley tried to do stuff with him. Have you ever had sex with another man, Chief?"

Weber ignored the question. "How did Reche respond?"

"He told Bradley to get the fuck away from him. Called him a homo."

I took a glance at my watch. I wanted to get to what had happened with Dirk, and Weber was looking increasingly uncomfortable. He'd loosen his collar and was sweating. I took charge of the interview. "How did Bradley react to being called a homo?"

"Not well. Bradley has a few issues - one is black men. You should look into what happened at the funeral home."

"I heard something about that," I said.

Penn looked at Weber. "Some nigger lady came to the funeral home to ask a question about her late husband. She burst into a room in the basement and found Bradley, naked and shoving his dick in the dead guy's mouth."

"That's disgusting." Weber made a face. "How could you stay with a man like that?"

"I thought it was funny. Look, maybe I thought I could change him, help him. Anyway, getting back to the story, the night of the blowup was the last time I saw Reche."

"What do you think happened to him?" I already knew where this was going.

"I don't know, but I read in the papers that he drowned in the lake."

"Did you see Bradley the day after the argument?" I asked.

"I was working late. I'm sure I saw him that night, but I don't remember."

"Reche was whipped and drowned in the lake," said Weber jumping in, his tone accusing.

"I wouldn't know anything about that, but I already told you that Bradley has a temper. Maybe he got offended when Reche called him a fag,"

"When we were at the house in Wilmer, we found a whipping post in the backyard," I said, watching her closely.

"I know Bradley put up some kind of crucifix back there. Figured he was religious."

There it was - the play. She's hanging all this on Bradley, the homo, the voyeur, the drug dealer, the guy with a bad temper who had a problem with blacks. "Tell us about Dirk Sparrow."

She took a deep breath as if she was bored, not with killing people but with the questions. "I met him in a bar. It was a setup. I had been missing Reche, and Dirk was handsome. Bradley and I staged a little fight, and Dirk came to the rescue. I liked him a lot. He's married to some bitch. When I asked him over for a drink, he was more than willing."

"Did you have intercourse with him?" asked Weber.

"The night he drove me home, we got in the backseat, and I gave him head. He liked it. We made arrangements to meet again. Then I introduced him to Bradley. In his case, he didn't mind a little bisexual action, but then he just stopped calling me."

"How did that make you feel, Penn?" I asked.

"I was upset. He was fun."

"How was Bradley with him leaving, seeing how well they were getting along?" I asked, looking over at Weber.

"He was angry. He wanted Dirk to help sell drugs out of his garage. Dirk said, thanks, but no thanks."

There it was, the missing piece. In addition to everything else, Bradley was now the spurned businessman. "So, the day he disappeared, did you meet with him?"

"I'm sure I did. He stayed at the house with us for a spell. At least he did until he decided to leave and go back to his wife. I have no idea what happened to him after that. I even called the station and spoke to some guy. He said Dirk was on vacation."

There was just the slightest grain of truth to Penn's story to make you want to believe it. I looked at Weber to see if he had more questions. He just shrugged.

"Okay, then, am I free to go?"

"Are you in a hurry to go somewhere?" asked Weber.

"I voluntarily came here to make a statement. I've answered your questions, so unless you're charging me with something, then I want to go home."

"Back to the motel? Back to Bradley?" I asked.

She stared at me but didn't answer. There was no way I wanted this psycho on the street. She hadn't directly threatened my family, but even the reference to them bothered me. I looked over at Weber and shook my head.

"We'd like you to stick around until we interview Bradley Nash. Get his side of the story," Weber said.

"That's bullshit. I know my rights. If you're not going to charge me, then you can't keep me here."

"I saw you assault Deputy Weber," I said. "With that cup."

She looked at me with a sarcastic grin. "More bullshit."

"Because you're an out-of-state resident, we need to check with Sherriff Harker up in Mobile county. That's where Reche Tines was found," said Weber.

***

We left a screaming and cursing Penn Maddox in the interview room. When we got out to the hall, Weber said, "Jesus, that was some story from her. I liked your paper cup angle, but that's not going to fly."

"We need a little more time. I sent Rachel and Nia and one of the deputies on an errand."

"What's that?"

"When the deputy from Jackson County got back, he said that Bradley Nash was dead. He was killed in a shoot-out when they tried to arrest him. That's why she gave us his location and made sure we knew he was armed. She wanted him dead so he couldn't contradict her story. He told the medic that it was all her idea on the way to the hospital. He told him to have us check under the wheel well in the Toyota. We need to stall long enough for them to get to the car, figure out how to open the trunk, and find out what's in there."

"Oh, shit. I'll go speak to Sheriff Pardy and maybe link in Harker." Our attention was drawn to the two-way mirror. Penn had thrown a chair at it. They watched as the woman went into a complete meltdown. Weber went to the window and pressed a button, enabling sound. "Miss., you calm down now."

This just enraged her more, and she threw herself at the mirror, "You piece of shit. You fucking nigger-loving fool. Come in here again, and I'll fucking rip that smile off your face." Weber turned off the speaker and looked at me.

"That's number four," I counted on my fingers. "We have the fun-loving Wendy from the bar, the poor innocent abused Penelope, the tough little punk Penny, and now the totally off her gourde Penn."

Weber gave me a frightened look and told me to watch her.

Chapter 77

March 13th, 1985
Talladega, Alabama

Mayor Baxter

Dear Diary,

I, John Baxter, AKA Luger, was the star of today's Brotherhood meeting. I was unanimously inducted into the Brotherhood. When I showed off my German eagle, I got a standing ovation. Wolf said I was the best new member in years. He asked me if I would help Klink with the club finances because who better to ask than an embezzler?

After the oath, Wolf said we had a couple of pieces of business to cover. "One is a new prospect who Luger is recommending for membership. Robbie Bintwater assures me that he is pure of blood and has read and agrees with our constitution. He brings new skills, which I can attest to myself. Skills that will bring in much-needed revenue. Luger, you are responsible for your recruit, who we will call Raider. In another month, Raider, assuming we all agree, you will be able to show off your tattoo just as Luger did."

There was a round of applause from everyone, and then Wolf continued, "The second piece of business is about these Cubans. You might have heard that good old Uncle Sam wants to deport them all back to Cuba. I understand the beaners are pretty upset about it. For the time being, I'm told they have stopped talking about what happened to Santiago. So, the pressure's off. You no longer have to buddy up."

Chapter 78

March 13th, 1985
Gulfport, Mississippi

Gabriel

I went outside to clear my head. I don't usually smoke, but I bummed one off a deputy. One day, when the truth comes out, she'll be diagnosed as crazy as a loon. How could she not be? Her mother was evil and abusive; her father was murdered. Then her mother had the boy she loved arrested, and she ended up with a pervert who liked having sex with corpses. I should have suspected something earlier. Had I been too trusting? Too willing to believe a pretty girl? Weber had said it best - it was quite the story.

One of the deputies came out and told me that I had a phone call. I pitched the smoke and went in to pick up the extension. It was Rachel.

"Gabriel, we found the car. It was parked in a lot down near the lighthouse. A deputy used a thing-a-ma-jiggy to open the door, and there was a trunk release. He's bringing what we found back to the station. There was a bullwhip as well as a bottle of ketamine. They're going to check everything for prints."

***

Two hours later, when Weber and I went back to the interview room, Penn was in a straitjacket, chained to a chair. When we walked in, she gave us a smug look.

"When my lawyer hears about this, you're going to be royally fucked."

"Save the act," I said, sitting down, "Are you Penelope, Penny, Wendy, or Penn? It's all over. We talked to Bradley. He gave us permission to search his car. We found it where you left it by the lighthouse. In the trunk, we found the whip you used and the bottle of Ketamine, all with your prints."

"Nice try. You're lying. I've never been fingerprinted."

"Do you member that paper cup you threw at Weber?"

Part 4

Chapter 79

April 15th, 1985
Gulfport, Mississippi

Gabriel

I was sitting in my office reading the *Herald* when I spied an update on the Penn Maddox trial. A lawyer with the unusual name of Sechfinger was representing her. Penn pled not guilty, and the judge ruled that she be kept at the Ocean's Behavioral Psychiatric Hospital pending an assessment.

There was still something nagging at me. I called the hospital and asked if Penn was up for a visitor. They checked with a doctor, and he called me back an hour later.

"Mr. Ross," said Dr. Ainsley, "I've read about your exploits in the *Herald*. I understand that you have requested a visit with Miss Maddox. Do you mind me asking why?"

Actually, I was hoping to speak to Wendy, not Penn, Penny, or Penelope. "This has been a difficult case for all involved. I have no desire to upset her, but I grew fond of Wendy during the investigation. I wanted her to know that she wasn't alone."

"I just finished meeting with her. She's a very disturbed young lady. I suppose your visit might be therapeutic. I asked her, and she would like to see you. She is heavily medicated, and I can't guarantee that the person you meet with, you'd recognize as Wendy."

"Doctor, I know you probably can't speak to her specific case, but at the police station when we were interviewing her, her personality was changing."

"A person with Dissociative Identity Disorder may have multiple distinct personalities. What's more, in some of the more severe cases, the individual might not even remember acting like one of the other personalities."

"How common is that?"

"More prevalent than you would think, especially with women. Most cases are mild and go undiagnosed. Sometimes the condition might be attributed to mood shifts or situations where they believe they are expected to act differently. Studies estimate that in a city like Biloxi with a population of 50,000, there might be a half dozen."

"Someone like Wendy, who has had a very tragic childhood, would they be more prone to this?"

"Absolutely - the brain can only stand so much. In people who have suffered childhood trauma, it's like the mind creates its own defense system, or at least tries to find the right way to deal with the stress they're facing."

"Are the shifts in their personality triggered by anything specific? The reason I ask is that I'd like to visit Wendy and not Penn Maddox."

"Again, I can't guarantee how she will respond. I've seen several triggers in these types of patients. It could be remembering something, seeing a particular object like a teddy bear, maybe hearing a song. Stress is kind of a wild card. If you bring up a stressful situation, the mind will try to adjust. Some people believe that with time, one's dominant personality, in this case, Penn, takes over."

***

When I walked into Wendy's room with a bouquet of flowers, she was sitting staring at the wall. There was no television, no windows, or pictures on the walls. The psychiatric ward had once been called an asylum, yet this was no asylum, not by the word's true meaning. It should be a place of refuge from the storms of the mind. If she had suffered kidney failure, the room would be colorfully decorated but not here.

A tray was attached to her chair, similar to the one I put on Benjamin's high chair. Her wrists were tethered. Ainsley had prescribed some medication to relax her and help her control her psychosis. When I walked into her view, she gave me a tentative smile. "Hi, Wendy. Do you have slippery nipples?"

"Hey." She smiled at me. "I'm kind of short of Bailey's, but I have some yummy apple juice here." I laughed and said I was happy she agreed to my visit. "How are Jacqueline and Benjamin?" Her brown eyes looked lifeless.

"They're great - wanted me to say hi." I lied. Jacqueline was still standing on Mount Hysteria that Wendy had been in her house. "How are you feeling?"

"Pretty good. I've been batting my eyes at a couple of cute orderlies."

"Really?" It struck me that this was similar to what her grandmother had said.

She smiled, "How's the case coming? Have you found the girl?"

I didn't know if she was playing me or if somehow the personalities were so distinct, she might not know. I ducked the question. "I wanted to thank you for all your help with the case, Wendy." Using her name more might reinforce the personality I wanted to talk to.

"You owe me $50 bucks."

"You're right, you called me. Wendy, maybe you could help me figure something out. Would you be willing to try?"

Her eyes closed for a moment, and I worried that I was losing her. She opened them a few moments later and gave me an expectant look.

"That girl we were looking for."

She smiled and said, "I wrote it on your hand, remember?"

"I remember, Wendy. I think she might have hurt the two men whose bodies we found. But I don't know why."

I watched her lifeless eyes. They didn't move. Suddenly her forehead creased as if she was having a migraine. Her eyes were closed tightly, like a child trying to ward off a night terror. This went on for a minute before she relaxed again into the same lifeless daze.

"Are you okay Wendy, do you need me to get someone?" I put my hand on her shoulder as she had done to me a few weeks ago.

She slowly turned her head towards me. Her eyes bulged, a scowl across her face. "Get your fucking hand off me." I recoiled, immediately taken aback by her transformation. Even her voice had changed. "What the fuck do you want?" She pulled against the straps of the chair, trying to get at me.

"I want to know about Reche Tines and Dirk Sparrow. What happened to them?"

Her eyes were ablaze with defiance. "Bradley killed them."

I knew I was throwing caution to the wind in challenging her. "I don't believe you. Bradley said it was you. Your prints are on everything."

"You think you're so smart. You tell me."

I debated the issue in my head. Lately, going with my gut hasn't been working out so well. "Alright, Penn. Just between you and me. I know your story. You've had a tough life. I'm not surprised that you're carrying some baggage. Everyone who ever meant anything to you left you. Then you meet Bradley, who is a whole new level of sicko. I think Reche, after leaving you once before, was going to leave again. Not because of you but because of Bradley. You wanted to hurt him, maybe get him to change his mind."

"Dirk Sparrow wanted to go back to his family. I think when they went to leave, something snapped in you. I don't think you were equipped to accept their rejection. You and Bradley whipped them like runaway slaves, and then you killed them."

We sat in silence. I wanted her to say something. To either validate my theory or say I was full of hooey. After five minutes, I figured I must have hit pretty close to the mark. All she said when I stood up to leave was, "Good story, you should be a writer."

Chapter 80

April 15th, 1985
Gulfport, Mississippi

Gabriel

I was telling Rachel about my meeting with Wendy when the Agency door opened. In walked a woman who looked vaguely familiar. I noticed a Jaguar arrogantly double-parked in front of the office. The car went with the outfit, expensive pantsuit, pearls, and a diamond on her finger the size of a crab apple.

"My name's Madge Sechfinger. You're Gabriel Ross." I already knew who I was. I was wondering where I'd heard that name when she clarified, "I used to be Madge Baxter."

She asked to see me in my office. I offered to get her a coffee, but she waved me off. Once she was settled in a chair, she spoke. "My late husband told me about you and your friend Ben O'Shea. He credits you for ruining his life."

"Well, I'm sorry." News of what had happened at Talledega prison had been reported extensively in the *Herald*. I was about to explain that I had just been doing my job when she interrupted me.

"I'm not upset or anything. I don't think he had any redeeming qualities. I'm here to give you something." She reached into her handbag and pulled out a book. "A guard got in touch with me after they searched John's cell and found this."

I took the book and flipped through it quickly. It was filled with pages and pages of handwritten notes. "Have you read it?" I asked without taking my eyes from the diary.

"Of course, at least the pages that were legible. My new husband is a lawyer. You might have heard of him - his name is Larry Sechfinger. He was John's lawyer for a while before John fired him. Larry told me to burn the diary, but I thought you and Mr. O'Shea should at least be given a chance to read it."

"Does this diary explain what happened?"

"No, but the same guard gave me this." She pulled a few pages of typed paper from her purse. "It's his statement to the Bureau of Prisons. It's quite revealing."

"You sure I can't get you a coffee?" I took the folded-up piece of paper. It was signed by a guard named Robert Pender.

"I only drink espresso. I'll leave you now. I'm having lunch with someone you know."

I doubted that. We didn't travel in the same circles. "Who might that be?"

"Glenna Sparrow."

***

I shook off the evil thoughts I had about Glenna and went to get Rachel. We filled our coffee cups and went into the office, and began reading former Mayor John Baxter's diary.

***

Nothing was surprising to me in the diary. What little I'd known of Mayor Baxter had come from Ben's experiences as a detective with Biloxi PD. Ben had thought Baxter was a crook right from the beginning. The man was a narcissist, a liar, and a selfish bastard. He only got elected because he knew the right people - money men like Frank Reznikov. There had been rumors about Baxter and the Russian mob and their influence, but nothing could ever be proven. Or, like Hollis Huntley, they found themselves flying in the air.

I opened up the extra pages Mrs. Sechfinger had given me.

April 2nd, 1985
Talladega Federal Penitentiary

<u>Statement given by Robert Pender, Guard employed at the Talladega Federal Penitentiary</u>

This statement is my recollection of the events of March 29th, 1985, at the Talladega Federal Prison. While I can swear to first-hand knowledge of my conversations with Mayor Baxter, there are parts where I could only attest to what I heard, for example, when Mayor Baxter spoke on the phone. I believe what happened was the result of something the warden said to the Cuban leader.

The mayor told me he was an undercover agent working for the warden. He was charged with getting information on what the Cubans were planning. On the day the hostages were taken, the guards were assaulted by about 20 Cubans carrying homemade knives. They took our weapons and marched us together with a couple of women office workers and Mayor Baxter into a room in Cell Block A.

We were made to sit on the ground while a Cuban threatened us. We were told that they were in control of the whole cell block. I was sitting right beside the mayor, and we spoke at length. The room was roughly twelve by twelve, with a couple of tables and some folding chairs stacked upfront. Two windows looked out over the corridor to the cells. The Cubans were in and out of the room carrying mattresses to cover the windows. The one giving orders was a hard-looking man with dark hair and a scar on his left cheek. He spoke to us in broken English.

"My name is Miguel Garcia," he said. "Mis amigos, you are our hostages until your government meets our demands. If they do not, then," he said in an easy come, easy go tone, "we will have to shoot you."

The mayor raised his hand. Garcia looked at him and spat on the floor. "Are you asking to be killed first?"

'No, no...I have an orange jumpsuit." He pointed to his clothes. "That means I'm like you. I'm not supposed to be here."

"And yet, you are here."

"Listen, no one cares about me. Please, pretty please, let me go?"

Garcia said something to the other Cubans, and they all started laughing. The mayor laughed along with them and said, "I know about these things. I am Mayor Baxter from Biloxi. Releasing me would be a sign of good faith. Believe me, it would go a long way in getting them to negotiate. I'm known for putting deals together, beautiful deals..."

"Shut up. You are an important gringo? Do you like Cubans?"

Baxter stammered. "I like Cubans just fine. You know, like chicky-chicky-boom?"

"You are a funny man, Mr. Mayor. If you say another word… I will shoot you. Comprender?" Garcia turned his back on Baxter and spoke to the other Cubans. I caught the word 'estupido.'

Baxter asked me if I understood Cuban.

"I told him the language was Spanish and that he'd just been called an asshole."

After a few minutes, Baxter whispered under his breath. "Do you think you could rush them, maybe get your gun back?" I thought the idea was ridiculous, and I asked him why we would do that. He nodded to the two women. "How long before they decide to have some fun. Most of these spics are rapists. Everyone knows that."

We were interrupted by the sound of a phone ringing. Garcia went over the phone on the wall and picked it up. "Yeah … My name is Miguel Garcia, and I am in charge.… No, shut up," he said angrily. "No, you shut up," he shouted before slamming down the phone. "Estupido!"

"That went well," Baxter whispered. A couple of other hostages also started whispering, which stopped suddenly when Garcia turned and glared at us.

A couple of minutes later, the phone rang again. Garcia waited until the seventh ring before answering. "I have hostages, and I have guns. I will shoot a hostage if you do not give me what I want."

Garcia listened for a while before replying. "Eight guards and two women, and an estupido like you, named Baxter." Garcia didn't say anything for a minute, then told the voice on the line to go fuck himself. He said something in Cuban to the armed prisoners, and they started checking their weapons.

He went to Baxter and hunched down to his level. "The warden, he don't like you. He say, I should ..." he held the gun up to Baxter's forehead. The moment seemed to last an eternity before Garcia added, "I was going to kill you as a sign that I mean business, but now I cannot do this, as they will think I do this for them. Next time the phone rings, I will let you talk to them, Mr. Big Deal."

Ten minutes later, we heard a gunshot. There was movement out in the hallway and then a volley of gunshots. Baxter tensed and said that the police were storming the cell block. The Cubans returned fire. While the Cubans were distracted, Baxter crawled to the back of the room near the women and knelt behind two metal chairs.

The gunfire ended quickly, and Garcia spoke to his men, slapping a couple on the back. The phone rang again, and Garcia ignored it this time. When it stopped ringing, Baxter raised his hand from the back of the room. It took a moment for Garcia to see him hiding behind the chairs. "Oh, Mayor Baxter, you hide with the women."

"I need to go ... you know," he looked around him... "I might even have... you know, a bit."

Garcia rolled his eyes and nodded to one of the men. "Take him, but if he does anything, shoot it off."

When Baxter returned from the washroom, Garcia was swearing at the phone again. Garcia handed him the phone. "You speak...gringo to gringo."

Baxter took the receiver and said smoothly, "Hello, this is Mayor Baxter."

The call went on for a while before Baxter hung up. He explained to Garcia that the Bureau of Prisons and the FBI were on their way. He stated that the warden had also said they should lay down their weapons and that he and the warden could negotiate a deal, a beautiful deal.

Garcia didn't like what Baxter had said and stuck his gun under his chin.

The phone rang again, and Garcia told the warden to go to hell. He handed the phone to Baxter, who spoke to the warden again for a few minutes. From what I could hear, Baxter told the warden that the Cubans wanted the American Government to end their extradition.

Baxter told Garcia the warden didn't have the authority to end extradition and wanted to know if they could do anything locally in exchange for hostages. Baxter whispered something to Garcia for a couple of minutes, and then he told the warden they wanted a dozen authentic Cuban pizzas with mustard for sauce and chorizos and plantains. Along with lots of cold Diet Cokes.

Baxter said the warden wanted him to be released in return for the food. I later heard that the warden had asked for the women to be released, not Baxter, but I could only hear what Baxter said to Garcia. There was a lot of back and forth before they agreed that one of the women would be released. She was nine months pregnant, and I don't think Garcia wanted to deal with that. According to Baxter, the warden was getting angry that Baxter couldn't get them to agree.

The warden called back ten minutes later to say that the FBI had just pulled into the parking lot. I heard Baxter on the phone. It sounded like he was saying, "No, I'm not going to do that. You have to promise to honor their requests." Then in a lower voice, "Just tell them that you will." The warden must have said something else then, and the phone got passed to Garcia.

What happened next happened very quickly. Garcia was listening to the warden when I saw his eyes go wild and his jaw clench. Something had made him angry. Garcia turned and glared at Baxter, who had inched his way to the front door, and said one word, "Santiago."

Baxter made a run for the hallway. He hadn't gone ten feet before the Cubans killed him.

Epilogue

Gabriel

By the time the news of the arrests of Dietz, Bubba Lange, Steve Schaffer, and Reverend MacGloyn were reported in the *Herald,* Don Kittyburg had already been fired. His former boss, MBI Director of Special Operations Joyce Coogan, called numerous times to tell him that the matter was under review pending the trials' outcome. I heard from Rachel that Don had told Coogan to take the job and shove it 'cause he ain't working there no more.

In a similar move, both Adele and Connie quit on the spot once their boss was arrested. Connie applied for an accounting job at the bottling plant that Jacqueline had suggested for me. Adele started seeing Jethro, who was very happy. The two of them entered a statewide air-guitar competition.

Rachel and Don made up, broke up, and then made up again. One of their arguments had to do with the Agency and me. She's still sitting on the fence about running the business, but moving away didn't feel right. Her brother's legal battles are ongoing. He stubbornly refused to give up the fight, although he and his partner moved to the suburbs, hoping for more enlightened neighbors.

I shared Baxter's diary with Ben. His reaction after reading it was a shrug as if to say, 'I told you he was a fucktard'. Ben gave the diary to Samantha Fitzgerald of the State Attorney's office, in case she wanted to show it to the family of Hector Lopez.

Penn Maddox was found not guilty by reason of insanity. Her official diagnosis was that she had a dissociative personality disorder. I'm not sure what that means. Jacqueline and I discussed why she'd done what she did. She had a much simpler explanation and twirled her index finger around her temple.

Jacqueline and I talked everything through. It was touch and go for a while. She wasn't happy about Wendy having been in our home. I reminded her that she was the one that had let her in. The argument is still going on.

Benjamin learned how to deal with the vegetables in his Jell-O. Now big green blobs are flying at his mother.

I never saw Glenna Sparrow again, which made me happy. However, I did pick up a little statue of a boy with a twelve-inch boner at a local yard sale. I figure it couldn't hurt.

The end

Thank you for supporting the cause, and I hope you enjoyed the story.

Joe

www.ingramcontent.com/pod-product-compliance
Lightning Source LLC
Chambersburg PA
CBHW030629020726
47493CB00006B/1635